AF059436

Max
A Novel

By
Katherine Cecil Thurston

Max
A Novel
by Katherine Cecil Thurston

Copyright © 2024

All Rights reserved.

No part of this publication may be reproduced, stored in a retrieval system, or transmitted in any form or by any means, electronic, mechanical, photocopying or Otherwise, without the written permission of the publisher.
The author/editor asserts the moral right to be identified as the author/editor of this work.

ISBN: 978-93-61429-94-1

Published by

DOUBLE 9 BOOKS
2/13-B, Ansari Road
Daryaganj, New Delhi – 110002
info@double9books.com
www.double9books.com
Tel. 011-40042856

This book is under public domain

ABOUT THE AUTHOR

Irish author Katherine Cecil Thurston, who lived from 18 April 1874 to 5 September 1911, is well known for her two political thrillers. At Wood's Gift on Blackrock Road, the family home, she had a private education. Five weeks after her father passed away, on February 16, 1901, she wed the author Ernest Temple Thurston (1879-1933). On the basis of his infidelity and desertion, they divorced in 1910 after separating in 1907. American and British readers like Katherine Thurston's books. Her most well-known piece was a political suspense novel called John Chilcote, M.P. (also known as The Masquerader), which was released in 1904 and spent two years on the New York Times bestseller list. Her illicit love stories The Fly on the Wheel, published in 1908, was hailed as a "lost gem of Irish fiction" in 2022. An epileptic, Thurston's career was cut short at the age of 37 when she was found dead in her hotel room in Cork. The official enquiry gave the cause of death as asphyxia as result of a seizure. The story of her final years and her relations with Bulkeley Gavin are the subject of a published thesis by C. M. Copeland.

CONTENTS

PART I
CHAPTER I 7

CHAPTER II 18

CHAPTER III 28

CHAPTER IV 35

CHAPTER V 39

CHAPTER VI 46

CHAPTER VII 51

CHAPTER VIII 58

CHAPTER IX 65

CHAPTER X 74

CHAPTER XI 84

PART II
CHAPTER XII 91

CHAPTER XIII 98

CHAPTER XIV 104

CHAPTER XV 113

CHAPTER XVI 116

CHAPTER XVII 120

CHAPTER XVIII 126

CHAPTER XIX 129

CHAPTER XX 137

CHAPTER XXI 141

PART III

CHAPTER XXII 148

CHAPTER XXIII 153

CHAPTER XXIV 159

CHAPTER XXV 164

CHAPTER XXVI 167

CHAPTER XXVII 170

CHAPTER XXVIII 175

CHAPTER XXIX 181

CHAPTER XXX 186

CHAPTER XXXI 190

CHAPTER XXXII 194

CHAPTER XXXIII 198

CHAPTER XXXIV 202

CHAPTER XXXV 206

PART IV

CHAPTER XXXVI 210

CHAPTER XXXVII 213

CHAPTER XXXVIII 218

CHAPTER XXXIX 220

CHAPTER XL 226

CHAPTER XLI 236

PART I

CHAPTER I

A NIGHT journey is essentially a thing of possibilities. To those who count it as mere transit, mere linking of experiences, it is, of course, a commonplace; but to the imaginative, who by gift divine see a picture in every cloud, a story behind every shadow, it suggests romance—romance in the very making.

Such a vessel of inspiration was the powerful north express as it thundered over the sleeping plains of Germany and France on its night journey from Cologne to Paris. A thing of possibilities indeed, with its varying human freight—stolid Teutons, hard-headed Scandinavians, Slavs whom expediency or caprice had forced to descend upon Paris across the sea of ice. It was the month of January, and an unlikely and unlovely night for long and arduous travel. There were few pleasure-passengers on the express, and if one could have looked through the carriage windows, blurred with damp mist, one would have seen upon almost every face the look—resigned or resolute—of those who fare forth by necessity rather than by choice. In the sleeping-cars all the berths were occupied, but here and them throughout the length of the train an occasional traveller slept on the seat of his carriage, wrapped in coats and rugs, while in the dining-saloon a couple of sleepy waiters lurched to and fro in attendance upon a party of three men whose energy precluded the thought of wasting even the night hours and who were playing cards at one of the small tables. Up and down the whole overheated, swaying train there was the suggestion of mystery, of contrast and effect, and the twinkling eyes of the electric lamps seemed to wink from behind their drawn hoods as though they, worldly wise and watchful, saw the individuality—the inevitable story—behind the drowsy units who sat or lay or lounged unguarded beneath them.

In one carriage, the fifth or sixth from the thundering engine, these lights winked and even laughed one to the other each time the train lurched over the points, and the dark, shrouding hoods quivered, allowing a glimpse at the occupant of the compartment.

It was the figure of a boy upon which the twinkling lamp-eyes flickered—a boy who had as yet scarce passed the barrier of manhood, for the skin of the face was clean and smooth, and the limbs, seen vaguely under a rough overcoat, had the freedom and supple grace that belongs to early youth.

He was sleeping, this solitary traveller—one hand under his head, the other instinctively guarding something that lay deep and snug in the pocket of his overcoat. His attitude was relaxed, but not entirely abandoned to the solace of repose; even in his sleep a something of self-consciousness seemed to cling to him—a need for caution that lay near to the surface of his drowsing senses—for once or twice he started, once or twice his straight, dark eyebrows twitched into a frown, once or twice his fingers tightened nervously upon their treasure. He was subconsciously aware that, deserted though the compartment was, it yet exhaled an alien suggestion, embodied in the rugs, the coats, the hand-baggage of the card-playing travellers, which was heaped upon the seat opposite.

But, despite this physical uneasiness, he was dreaming as the train tore along through the damp, peaceful country—dreaming with that odd confusion of time and scene that follows upon keen excitement, stress of feeling or stress of circumstance.

As he dreamed, he was standing again in the outer court of a house in Petersburg—a house to which he was debtor for one night's shelter; it was early morning and deadly cold. The whole picture was sharp as a cut crystal—the triple court-yard, the stone pavement, the gray well, and frozen pile of firewood. He saw, recognized, lost it, and knew himself to be skimming down the Nevskiy Prospekt and across the Winter Palace Square, where the great angel towers upon its rose-granite monument. Forward, forward he was carried, along the bank of the frozen Neva and over the Troitskiy bridge, the powdered snow stinging his face like pinpoints as it flew up from the nails in his little horse's shoes. Then followed a magnifying of the picture—massed buildings rising from the snow—buildings gold and turquoise-domed, that, even as they materialized, lost splendor and merged into the unpretentious frontage of the Finland station.

The scroll of the dream unwound; the dreamer moved, easing his position, shaking back a lock of dark hair that had fallen across his forehead. He was no longer rocking to the power of the north express; he was standing on the platform at the end of a little train that puffed out of the Finland station—a primitive, miniature train, white with frost and powdered with the ashes of its wood fuel. The vision came and passed a sketch, not a picture—a suggestion of straight tracks, wide snow plains, and the blue, misty blur of fir woods. Then a shifting, a juggling of effects! Åbo, the Finnish port, painted itself upon his imagination, and he was embarked upon the lonely sledge-drive, to the harbor. He started in his sleep, shivered and sighed at that remembered drive. The train passed over new points, the hoods of the lamps swayed, the lights blinked and winked, and his mind swung onward in response to the physical jar.

Åbo was obliterated. He was on board a ship—a ship ploughing her way through the ice-fields as she neared Stockholm; salt sea air flicked his nostrils, he heard the broken ice tearing the keel like a million files, he was sensible of the crucial sensation—the tremendous quiver—as the vessel slipped from her bondage into the cradle of the sea, a sentient thing welcoming her own element!

The heart of the dreamer leaped to that strange sensation. He drew a long, sharp breath, and sat up, suddenly awake. It was over and done with—the coldness, the rigor, the region of ice bonds! The fingers of the future beckoned to him; the promises of the future lapped his ears as the waves had lapped the ship's sides.

He looked about him, at first excitedly, then confusedly, then a little shamedfacedly, for we are always involuntarily shamed at being tricked by our emotions into a false conception. Drawing his hand from his coat-pocket, he stretched himself with an assumption of ease, as though he saw and recognized the twinkle in the electric lamps and spontaneously rose to its demands.

The train was flying forward at unabated speed. Outside, the raw January air was clinging in a film to the carriage window; inside, the dim light and overheated air made an artificial atmosphere, enervating or stimulating according to the traveller's gifts. To this solitary voyager stimulation was obviously the effect produced, for, try as he might to cheat the inquisitive lamps, interest in every detail of his surroundings was portrayed in his face, in the poise of his head, the quickness of his glance as he gazed round the compartment, verifying the impression that he was alone.

"STANDING AGAIN IN THE OUTER COURT OF A HOUSE IN PETERSBURG"

Yes, he was absolutely alone! Everything was as it had been when he settled himself to sleep on the departure of the three strangers. There, on the opposite seat, were their rugs, their fur-lined coats, their illustrated papers—all the impedimenta of prosperous travellers; and there, on the rack above them, was his own modest hand-bag without initials or label—a common little bag that might have belonged to some poor Russian clerk or held the possessions of some needy Polish student. The owner's glance scanned and appraised it, then by suggestion fell to the plain rough overcoat that covered him from his neck to the tops of his high boots, and whose replica was to be seen any day in the meaner streets of Petersburg or Moscow. Like the bag, it was a little strange, a little incongruous in its comfortable surroundings—a little savoring of mystery.

The traveller's pulses quickened, his being lifted to the moment, for in his soul was the spark of adventure, in his eyes the adventurous look—fearless, observant, questioning. In composition, in expression and essence, this boy was that free and fascinating creature, the born adventurer—high of courage, prodigal of emotion, capturer of the world's loot.

The spirit within him shone out in the moment of solitude; he passed his hands down the front, of his coat, revelling in its coarse texture; he rose to his feet, turned to the sheet of gray, misted glass, and, letting down the window, leaned out into the night.

The scene was vague and ghostly, but to eyes accustomed to northern whiteness it was full of suggestion, full of secrecy; to nostrils accustomed to keen, rarefied air there was something poignant and delicious in the scent of turned earth, the savor of vegetation. He could see little or nothing as the train rocked and the landscape tore past, but the atmosphere spoke to him as it speaks to blind men, penetrating his consciousness. Here were open spaces, tracts of country fructifying for the spring to come. A land of promise—of growth—of fulfilment!

He closed his eyes, living in the suggestion, and his spirit sped forward with the onrush of the train. Somewhere beyond the darkness lay the land of his desires! Somewhere behind the veil shone the lights of Paris! With a quick, exulting excitement he laughed; but even as the laugh was caught and scattered to the winds by the thunder of the engine, his bearing changed, the excitement dropped from him, a mask of immobility fell upon his face, and he wheeled round from the window. The card-playing travellers had opened the door of the carriage.

From his shadowy corner the boy eyed them; and they, alert from their game, slightly dazed by the darkness of the carriage, peered back at him, frankly curious. When they had left the compartment he had been a huddled figure demanding no attention; now he was awake and an individual, and human nature prompted interest.

Each in turn looked at him, and at each new glance his coldness of demeanor deepened; until, as the eldest of the party came down the carriage and appropriated the seat beside him, he turned away, pulling up the window with resentful haste.

"Don't do that!" said the third man, pausing in the doorway and speaking in French easily and pleasantly. "Don't do that—if you want the air!"

The boy started and looked round.

"I thank you! But I do not need the air!"

The man smiled acquiescence, but as he stepped into the carriage he took a sharp look at the boy's clothes—the common Russian clothes—and a slightly questioning, slightly satirical expression crossed his face. He was a man who knew his world the globe over, and in his bearing lurked the toleration, the kindly scepticism that such knowledge breeds.

"As you please!" he said, settling himself comfortably in the corner by the door, while the elder of his companions—a tall, spare American—crossed his long legs and lighted a thin black cigar, and the younger—a spruce young Englishman wearing an eye-glass and a small mustache—wrapped himself in his rugs, took a clean pocket-handkerchief from his dressing-case, and opened a large bundle of illustrated papers—French, German, and English.

For a space the train rocked on. No one attempted to speak, and the Russian boy continued to stand by the window, pretending to look through the blurred panes, in reality wondering how he could with least commotion pass down the carriage to his own vacated place.

At last the man with the long cigar broke the silence in a slow, cool voice that betrayed his nationality.

"We're well on time, Blake," he remarked, drawing out his watch.

The youth by the window shot an involuntary, fleeting glance at the two younger men, to see which would answer to the name; and the student of human nature noted the fact that he understood English.

"Oh, it's a good service!" he acquiesced, the tolerant look—half sceptical, half humorous—- passing again over his face.

"I don't know! I think we could do with another few kilometres to the hour." The thin man studied his flat gold watch with the loving interest of one to whom time is a sacred thing.

At this point the youngest of the three raised his head.

"Marvellous sight you have, McCutcheon! Wish I could see by this light!"

McCutcheon leaned forward, replacing his watch. "What! Can't you see your picture-books? Let's have the blinkers off!" He rose, his long, spidery figure stretching up like a grotesque shadow, but as his arm went out to the nearest of the shrouded lamps he was compelled to draw back against the seat of the carriage, and an exclamation of surprise escaped him.

Without warning or apology the Russian boy had turned from the window, and stepping down the carriage, had tumbled into his former seat, hunching himself up with his face to the cushions and his back to his fellow-travellers.

It was a sudden and an uncivil proceeding. The man called Blake smiled; the Englishman shrugged his shoulders; the American, with a movement of quiet determination, drew back the lamp hoods.

In the flood of light the carriage lost its air of mystery, and Blake, who had a fancy for the mysterious, dropped back into his corner and took out his cigar-case with a little feeling of regret. In traversing the world's pathways, beaten or wild, he always made a point of seeing the story behind the circumstance; and, had he realized it, a common instinct bound him in a triangular link to the peering, winking lamps, and to the Russian boy lying unsociably wrapped in his heavy coat. All three had an eye for an adventure.

But the lights were up, and the curtain down—it was a theatre between the acts; and presently the calculating voice of McCutcheon broke forth again, as he relapsed into his original attitude, coiling up his long limbs and nursing his cigar to a glow.

"I can't get over that 'four jacks,'" he said. "To think I could have been funked into seeing Billy at fifty!"

Blake laughed. "'Twas the eye-glass did it, Mac! A man shouldn't be allowed to play poker with an eye-glass; it's taking an undue advantage."

McCutcheon smiled his dry smile and shot a quizzical glance at the neat young Englishman, who had become absorbed in one of his papers.

"Solid face, Blake!" he agreed. "Nothing so fine as an eye-glass for sheer bluff. What would Billy be without one? Well, perhaps we won't say. But with it you have no use for doubt—he's a diplomat all the time."

The young man named Billy showed no irritation. With the composure which he wore as a garment, he went on with his occupation.

For a time McCutcheon bore this aloofness, then he opened a new attack. "What are you reading, my son? Makes a man sort of want his breakfast to see that hungry look in your eyes. Share the provender, won't you?"

Billy looked up sedately.

"You fellows think my life's a game," he said. "But I tell you it takes some doing to keep in touch with things."

Blake laughed chaffingly. "And the illustrated weekly papers are an excellent substitute for Blue-books?"

Billy remained undisturbed. "It's all very well to scoff, but one may get a side-light anywhere. In diplomacy nothing's too insignificant to notice."

Again Blake laughed. "The principle on which it offers you a living?"

"Oh, come," said Billy, "that's rather rough! You know very well what I mean. 'Tisn't always in the serious reports you get the color of a fact, just as the gossip of a dinner-table is often more enlightening than a cabinet council."

"Apropos?"

"I was thinking of this Petersburg affair."

"What? The everlasting Duma business?" McCutcheon drew in a long breath of smoke.

Billy looked superior, as befitted a man who dealt in subtler matters than mere politics. "Not at all," he said. "The disappearance of the Princess Davorska."

Here Blake made a murmur of impatience. "Oh, Billy, don't!" he said. "It's so frightfully banal."

McCutcheon took his cigar from his mouth. "The woman who disappeared on the eve of her marriage?"

"Yes," broke in Blake, "disappeared on the eve of her marriage to elope with some poet or painter, and set society by the ears. Thoroughly modern and banal!"

The young diplomat glanced up once more.

"I don't think there's any suggestion of a lover."

"Fact is more potent than suggestion, Billy. Of course there is a lover. Princesses don't disappear alone."

"You're a Socialist, Ned." Billy's eyes returned to his paper. "Like all good Socialists, crammed to the neck with class bigotry. Nobody is such an individualist as the man who advocates equality!"

Blake smiled. "That seems to sound all right," he said; "but it doesn't remove the lover."

The good-humored scepticism at last forced a way to Billy's susceptibilities.

"Look here," he said, crossly, "if hearing's not believing, perhaps seeing is! Look at these pictures; they're not particularly modern or banal."

He held out his paper, but Blake shook his head.

"No! No, Billy, not for me. If it was some little Rumanian gypsy who had run away from her tribe I'd take her to my heart and welcome. But a Princess Davorska—no!"

At this point McCutcheon stretched out his long arm and took the paper from Billy's hand. "Let's have a squint!" he said. "Lover or no lover, she must be a bit wide awake." And, curling himself up again, he began to read from the paper, in a monotonous murmuring voice: "'*The Princess, as well as being a woman of artistic accomplishments, is an ardent sportswoman, having in her early girlhood hunted and shot with keen zest on her father's estates. The above picture shows her at the age of seventeen, carrying a gun.*' By the Lord, she is wide awake!" he added, by way of comment. "She is wide awake carrying that gun, but I'd lay my money on the second picture. Say, Billy, she looks a queen in her court finery!"

But here real disgust crossed Blake's face. "Oh, that'll do, Mac! Give us peace about the woman. I'm sick to death of all such nonsense. We're due in a couple of hours. I think I'll try for forty winks." He threw away his cigar and tucked his rug about him.

McCutcheon glanced at him, and, seeing that he was in earnest, handed the paper back to Billy.

"Thanks, Mac!" Blake murmured. "Sorry if I was a bear! Don't switch off the light, it won't bother me." He nodded, smiled, drew his rug closer about his knees, and settled himself to sleep with the ease of the accustomed traveller.

For close upon an hour complete silence reigned in the heated carriage. Blake slept silently and peacefully; Billy went methodically through his papers, dropping them one by one at his feet as he finished with them; McCutcheon smoked, gazing into space with the blank expression of the strenuous man who has learned to utilize his momentary respites; while, stretched along the cushions of the carriage, his face hidden, his eyes wide open and attentive, lay the young Russian, his fingers tentatively caressing the treasure in the pocket of his coat.

But at last the spell was broken. The diplomatic Englishman dropped his last paper, and McCutcheon stretched himself and looked once more at his watch.

"Paris in an hour, Billy! Didn't those loafers in the dining-car promise us coffee somewhat about this time?"

Billy looked up, unruffled of mind and body as in the first moment of the journey. "I believe they did," he said. "Tell you what! You jog their memories, while I go and wash. What about calling Ned?"

At sound of his own name, Blake's eyes opened. His waking was characteristic of him. It was no slow recovery of the senses; he was asleep and then awake—fully, easily awake, with a complete consciousness of his position—a complete, assured grasp of time and place.

"We're getting on, eh?" he said. "I suppose you're going to tub before those fat Belgians in the sleeping-car, Billy? If you are, keep a second place for me, like a good boy. There's nothing more fiendishly triumphant than taking a bath in the basin while the rest of the train is rattling the door-handle. Don't forget! Second place!" Then he turned to the American. "What about the coffee, Mac? I expect those poor devils of waiters have slept your order off."

"I was just about to negotiate that coffee transaction." McCutcheon stood up. "You come too, my son! A little exercise will give you an appetite." He paused to stretch his long, lean body, and incidentally his glance fell upon their travelling companion, and he indicated the recumbent figure with a jerk of the head.

"Say, Ned, ought we to wake our unsociable friend?" Blake cast one quick glance at the huddled form, then he answered, tersely: "Let him alone! He's not asleep—and, anyway, he understands English."

At which McCutcheon made a comprehending grimace, and the two left the carriage.

For many minutes the young Russian did not move; then, when positive certainty of his solitude had grown into his mind, he lifted himself on one elbow and looked cautiously about him.

A change had passed over his face in the last hour—an interesting change. The smooth cheek that the night air had cooled to paleness was now flushed, and there was a spark of anger in the bright eyes. Unquestionably this boy had a temper and a spirit of his own, and both had been aroused. There was a certain arrogance, a certain contempt in his glance now as it swept the inoffensive coats and rugs of the departed travellers, a certain antagonism as he sat up, tossed back the lock of hair that had again fallen across his forehead, and turned his eyes to the heap of papers lying upon the carriage floor.

For long he gazed upon these papers, as though they exercised a magnetic influence, and at last, with a swift impulse, extremely characteristic, he stretched out his arm and drew forth the lowest of the heap.

He regained his former position with a quick, lithe movement of the body, and in an instant he was poring over the paper, the pages turning with incredible speed under the eagerness of his touch. At last he reached the page he sought, the page that had offered ground for discussion to the three voyagers an hour earlier.

His eyes flashed, his fingers tightened, his dark head was bent lower over the paper. Two pictures confronted him. The first was of a woman in

Russian court dress, who wore her jewels and her splendor of apparel with an air of pride and careless supremacy that had in it something magnificent, something semi-barbaric. The boy looked at this curious and arresting picture, but only for a moment; by some affinity, some subtle attraction, his eyes turned instantly to the second portrait—the girl carrying the gun—and as if in answer to some secret sympathy, some silent comprehension, the frown upon his brows relaxed and his lips parted.

It was still the woman of the jewels and the splendid apparel, but it was a woman infinitely free, infinitely unhampered. The plain, serviceable clothes fitted the slight figure as though they had been long worn and loved; the hair was closely coiled, so that the young face looked out upon the world frank and unadorned as a boy's. Here, as in the first picture, the eyes looked forth with a curious, proud directness; but beneath the directness was a glint of humor, a flash of daring absent in the other face; the mouth smiled, seeming to anticipate life's secrets, the ungloved hand held the gun with a touch peculiarly caressing, peculiarly firm.

The traveller looked, looked again, and then, with a deliberation odd in so slight a circumstance, folded the paper, rose, and stepped to the window of the carriage.

The night mist beat in, still raw and cold, but somewhere behind the darkness was the stirring, the vague presage of the day to come. He leaned out, fingers close about the paper, lips and nostrils breathing in the suggestive, vaporous air. For a moment he stood, steadying himself to the motion of the train, palpitating to his secret thoughts; then, with a little theatricality all for his own edification, he opened his fingers and, freeing the paper, watched it swirl away, hang for a second like a moth against the lighted window, and vanish into the night.

CHAPTER II

'JOURNEYS end in lovers' meeting.' The phrase conjures a picture. The court-yard of some inn, glowing ripe in the tints of the setting sun—open doors—an ancient coach disgorging its passengers! This—or, perhaps, some quay alive with sound and movement—cries of command in varying tongues—crowded gangways—rigging massed against the sky—all the paraphernalia of romance and travel. But the real journey—the journey of adventure itself—is frequently another matter: often gray, often loverless, often demanding from the secret soul of the adventurer spirit and inspiration, lest the blood turn cold in sick dismay, and the brain cloud under its weight of nostalgia.

Paris in the dawn of a wet day is a sorry sight; the Gare du Nord in the hours of early morning is a place of infinite gloom. As the north express thundered into its recesses, waking strange and hollow echoes, the long sweep of the platform brought a shudder to more than one tired mind. A string of sleepy porters—gray silhouettes against a gray background—was the only sign of life. Colors there were none, lovers there were none, Parisian joy of living there was not one vestige.

Paris! The murmur crept through the train, stirring the weariest to mechanical action. Paris! Heads were thrust through the windows, wraps and hand-bags passed out to the shadowy, mysterious porters who received them in a silence born of the godless hour and the penetrating, chilling dampness of the atmosphere.

In the carriage fifth or sixth from the engine the three fellow-travellers greeted the arrival in the orthodox way. The tall American stretched his long limbs and groaned wearily as he got his belongings together, while the dapper young Englishman thrust his head out of the window and withdrew it as rapidly.

"Beastly morning!" he announced. "Paris on a wet day is like a woman with draggled skirts."

"Get rid of our belongings first, Billy, make epigrams after!" The man called Blake pushed him quietly aside and, stepping to the window, dropped a leather bag into the hands of a porter.

Of the three, his manner was the most indifferent, his temper the most unruffled; and of the three, he alone remembered the fourth occupant of the carriage, for, being relieved of his bag, he turned with his hand still upon the window, and his eyes sought the youthful figure drawn with lonely isolation into its corner.

"Do you want a porter?" he asked.

The question was unexpected. The boy started and sat straighter in his seat. For one moment he seemed to sway between two impulses, then, with a new determination, he looked straight at his questioner with his clear eyes.

"No," he said, speaking slowly and with a grave deliberation, "I do not need a porter. I have no luggage—but this." He rose, as if to prove the truth of his declaration, and lifted his valise from the rack.

It was a simple movement, simple as the question and answer that had preceded it, but it held interest for Blake. He could not have analyzed the impression, but something in the boy's air touched him, something in the young figure so plainly clad, so aloof, stood out with sharp appeal in the grayness and unreality of the dawn. A feeling that was neither curiosity nor pity, and yet savored of both, urged him to further speech. As his two companions, anxious to be free of the train, passed out into the corridor, he glanced once more at the slight figure, at the high Russian boots, the long overcoat, the fur cap drawn down over the dark hair.

"Look here! you aren't alone in Paris?" he asked in the easy, impersonal way that spoke his nationality. "You have people—friends to meet you?"

For an instant the look that had possessed the boy's face during the journey—the look of suspicion akin to fear—leaped up, but on the moment it was conquered. The well-poised head was thrown back, and again the eyes met Blake's in a deliberate gaze.

"Why do you ask, monsieur?"

The words were clipped, the tone proud and a little cold.

Another man might have hesitated to reply truthfully, but Blake was an Irishman and used to self-expression.

"I ask," he said, simply, "because you are so young."

A new expression—a new daring—swept the boy's mobile face. A spirit of raillery gleamed in his eyes, and he smiled for the first time.

"How old, monsieur?"

The question, the smile touched Blake anew. He laughed involuntarily with a sudden sense of friendliness.

"Sixteen?—seventeen?"

The boy, still smiling, shook his head.

"Guess again, monsieur."

Blake's interest flashed out. Here, in the gray station, in this damp hour of dawn, he had touched something magnetic—some force that drew and held him. A quality intangible and indescribable seemed to emanate from this unknown boy, some strange radiance of vitality that flooded his surroundings as with sunshine.

"Eighteen, then!" He laughed once more, with a curious sense of pleasure.

But from the corridor outside a slow voice was borne back on the damp, close air, forbidding further parley.

"Blake! I say, Blake! For the Lord's sake, get a move on!"

The spell was broken, the moment of companionship passed. Blake drifted toward the carriage door, the boy following.

Outside in the corridor they were sucked into the stream of departing passengers—that odd medley of men and women, unadorned, jaded, careless, that a night train disgorges. Slowly, step by step, the procession made its way, each unit that composed it glancing involuntarily into the empty carriages that he passed—the carriages that, in their dimmed light, their airlessness, their *débris* of papers, seemed to be a reflection of his own exhausted condition; then a gust of chilly air told of the outer world, and one by one the travellers slid through the narrow doorway, each instinctively pausing to brace himself against the biting cold before stepping down upon the platform.

At last it was Blake's turn. He, too, paused; then he, too, took the final plunge, shivered, glanced at where McCutcheon and the Englishman were talking to their porters, then turned to watch the Russian boy swing himself lithely down from the high step of the train.

All about him was the consciousness of the awakening crowd, conveyed by the jostling of elbows, the deepening hum of voices.

"Look here!" he said again, in response to his original impulse. "You have somebody to meet you?"

The boy glanced up, a secret emotion burning in his eyes. "No, monsieur."

"You are quite alone?"

"Yes, monsieur."

"And why are you here—to play or to work?"

The question was unwarrantable, but an Irishman can dispense with warranty in a manner unknown to other men. It had ever been Blake's way to ask what he desired to know.

This time no offence showed itself in the boy's face.

"In part to work, in part to play, monsieur," he answered, gravely; "in part to learn life."

The reply was strange to Blake's ears—strange in its grave sincerity, stranger still in its quiet fearlessness.

"But you are such a child!" he cried, impulsively. "You—"

Imperceptibly the slight figure stiffened, the proud look flashed again into the eyes.

"Many thanks, monsieur, but I am older than you think—and very independent. I have the honor monsieur, to wish you good-bye."

The tone was absolutely courteous, but it was final. He bowed with easy foreign grace, raised his fur cap, and, turning, swung down the platform and out of sight.

Blake stood watching him—watching until the high head, the straight shoulders, the lithe, swinging body were but a memory; then he turned with a start, as a hand was laid upon his shoulder, and the pleasant, prosaic voice of the young Englishman assailed his ears.

"My dear chap, what in the world are you doing? Not day-dreaming with the mercury at thirty?"

"Foolish—but I was!" Blake answered, calmly. "I was watching that young Russian stalk away into the unknown, and I was wondering—"

"What?"

He smiled a little cynically. "I was wondering, Billy, what type of individual and what particular process fate will choose to let him break himself upon."

The most splendid moment of an adventure is not always the moment of fulfilment, not even the moment of conception, but the moment of first accomplishment, when the adventurer deliberately sets his face toward the new road, knowing that his boats are burned.

Nothing could have been less inspiring than the dreary Gare du Nord, nothing less inviting than the glimpse of Paris to be caught through its open doorways; but had the whole world laughed him a welcome, the young

Russian's step could not have been more elastic, his courage higher, his heart more ready to pulse to the quick march of his thoughts, as he strode down the gray platform and out into the open.

In the open he paused to study his surroundings. As yet the full tale of passengers had not emerged, and only an occasional wayfarer, devoid of baggage as himself, had fared forth into the gloom. Outside, the artificial light of the station ceased to do battle with nature, and only an occasional street lamp gave challenge to the gloomy dawn. The damp mist that all night had enshrouded Paris still clung about the streets like ragged graveclothes, and at the edge of the pavement half a dozen *fiacres* were ranged in a melancholy line, the wretched horses dozing as they stood, the drivers huddled into their fur capes and numbed by the clinging cold. Everywhere was darkness and chill and the listless misery of a winter dawn, when vitality is at its lowest ebb and the passions of man are sunk in lethargy.

Only a creature infinitely young could have held firm in face of such dejection, only eyes as alert and wakeful as those of this wayfaring boy could possibly have looked undaunted at the shabby streets with their flaunting travesty of joy exhibited in the dripping awnings of the deserted *cafés*, that offered *Bière, Billard*, and yet again *Bière* to an impassive world.

But the eyes were wakeful, the soul of the adventurer was infinitely young. He looked at it all with a certain steadfastness that seemed to say, "Yes, I see you! You are hideous, slatternly, unfriendly; but through all the disguise I recognize you. Through the mask I trace the features—subtle, alluring, fascinating. You are Paris! Paris!"

The idea quickened action as a draught of wine might quicken thought; his hand involuntarily tightened upon his valise, his body braced itself afresh, and, as if resigning himself finally to chance, that deity loved of all true adventurers, he stepped from the pavement into the greasy roadway.

Seeing him move, a loafer, crouching in the shadow of the station, slunk reluctantly into the open and offered to procure him a *fiacre*; but the boy's shake of the head was determined, and, crossing the road, he turned to the left, gazing up with eager interest at the many hotels that rub shoulders in that uninteresting region.

One after the other he reviewed and rejected them, moving onward with the excitement that is born of absolute uncertainty. Onward he went, without pause, until the pavement was intersected by a side-street, and peering up through the misty light he read the legend, "rue de Dunkerque."

Rue de Dunkerque! It conveyed nothing to his mind. But was he not seeking the unknown? Again his head went up, again his shoulders stiffened, and, smiling to himself at some secret thought, he swung round the corner and plunged into the unexplored.

Half way down the rue de Dunkerque stands the Hôtel Railleux. It is a tall and narrow house, somewhat dirty and entirely undistinguished; there is nothing to recommend it save perhaps an air of privacy, a certain insignificance that wedges it between the surrounding buildings in a manner tempting to one anxious to avoid his fellows.

This quality it was that caught the boy's attention. He paused and studied the Hôtel Railleux with an attention that he had denied to the large and common hostelries that front the station. He looked at it long and meditatively, then very slowly and thoughtfully he walked to the end of the street. At the end of the street he turned, his mind made up, and, hurrying back, went straight into the hall of the hotel as though thirsting to pledge himself irrevocably to his decision.

It is impossible for the sensible individual to see romance in this entry into a third-rate Parisian hotel—to see daring or to see danger—but the boy's heart was beating fast as the glass door swung behind him, and his tongue was dry as he stepped into the little office on the right of the poor hall.

Here in the office the story of the streets was repeated. A dingy gas-jet shed a faint light, as though reluctantly awake; behind a small partition, half counter, half desk, a wan and sleepy—looking man was cowering over a stove. As the boy entered he looked up uncertainly, then he rose and smiled, for your Parisian is exhausted indeed when he fails to conjure up a smile.

"Good-day, monsieur!"

The words were a travesty in view of the miserable dawn, but the boy took heart. There was greeting in the tone. He moistened his lips, which felt dry as his tongue in his momentary nervousness, then he stepped closer to the counter.

"Good-day, monsieur! I require a bedroom."

"A bedroom? But certainly, monsieur!" The shrewd though tired eyes of the man passed over his visitor's clothes and the valise in his hand. "We can give you a most excellent room at"—he raised his eyebrows in tactful hesitation—"at five francs?"

The boy's eyes opened in genuine, instant surprise. "For so little?" he exclaimed. Then, covered with confusion, he reddened furiously and stammered, "For—for so much, I mean?"

The man in the office was all smooth, politeness, anxious to cover a foreigner's slip of speech. 'But certainly, no! If five francs was more than monsieur cared to pay, then for three francs there was a most charming, a most agreeable room on the fifth floor. True, it did not look upon the street, but then perhaps monsieur preferred quiet. If monsieur would give himself the trouble of mounting—'

Monsieur, still confused by his own mistake, and nervously anxious to insist upon his position, repeated again that five francs was out of the question, and that, without giving himself the trouble of mounting, he would then and there decide upon the agreeable and quiet room at three francs.

'But certainly! It was understood!' The guardian of the office, now fully awake and aroused to interest in this princely transaction, disappeared from behind the counter into the back regions of the hotel, and could be heard calling "Jean! Jean!" in a high, insistent tone.

After some moments of silence he returned, followed by a large and amiable individual in a dirty blue blouse, who had apparently but lately arisen from sleep.

'Now if monsieur would intrust his baggage to the valet—'

The guardian of the office took a key from a nail in the wall. Jean stepped forward, pleased and self-conscious, and took the valise from the boy's hand. Then all three smiled and bowed.

It was one of those foolish little comedies—utterly unnecessary, curiously pleasant—that occur twenty times a day in Parisian life. Involuntarily the adventurer's heart warmed to the pallid clerk and to the dirty hotel porter. He had arrived here without luggage, shabby, unrecommended, yet no princely compatriot of his own could have been made more sensible of welcome. He stepped out of the office and followed his guide, conscious that, if only for an instant, Paris had lifted her mask and smiled—the radiant, anticipated smile.

There is no such unnecessary luxury as a lift in the Hôtel Railleux. At the back of the hall the spiral staircase begins its steep ascent, mounting to unimagined heights.

Jean, breathing audibly, led the way, pausing at every landing to assure monsieur that the ascent was nothing—a mere nothing, and that before another thought could pass through monsieur's mind the fifth floor would be reached. The boy followed, climbing and ever climbing, until the meagre hand-rail appeared to lengthen into dream-like coils, and the threadbare, drab-hued carpet, with its vivid red border, to assume the proportions of some confusing scroll.

But at length the end was reached, and Jean, beaming and triumphant, announced their goal.

'This way! If monsieur would have the goodness to take two steps in this direction!' He dived into a long, dark corridor, illuminated by a single flickering gas-jet, twin brother to that which lighted the office below; and, still eager, still breathing loudly, he ushered the guest toward what in his humble soul he believed to be the luxurious, the impressive bedroom supplied by the Hôtel Railleux at three francs a night.

The boy looked about him as he passed down the dim corridor. Apparently he and Jean alone were awake in this gloomy maze of closed doors and sleeping passages. One sign of humanity—and one alone—came to his senses with a suggestion of sordid drama. On the floor, at the closed door of one of the rooms, stood a battered black tray on which reposed an empty champagne bottle and two soiled glasses.

Life! His quick imagination conjured a picture—conjured and shrank from it. He turned away with a sense of sharp disgust and almost ran down the corridor to where Jean was fitting a key into the door of his prospective bedroom.

"The room, monsieur!" Jean's voice was full of pride. He had lived for ten years in the Hôtel Railleux, working as six men and six women together would not have worked in the fashionable quarter, and he had never been shaken in his belief that Paris held no more inviting hostelry.

The boy obediently stepped forward into the tiny apartment, in which a big wooden bedstead loomed out of all proportion. His movements were hasty, as though he desired to escape from some impression; his voice, when he spoke, was vague.

"Very nice! Very nice!" he said. "And—and what is the view?"

"The view? Oh, but monsieur will like the view!" Jean stepped to the window, drew back the heavy cretonne curtains, and threw open the long window, admitting a breath of chilling cold. "The court-yard! See, monsieur! The court-yard!"

The boy came forward into the biting air and gazed down into the well-like depths of gloom, at the bottom of which could be discerned a small flagged court, ornamented by a couple of dwarfed and frost-bitten trees in painted tubs.

Jean, watchful of the visitor's face, broke forth anew with inexhaustible tact.

'It was a fine view—monsieur would admit that! But, naturally, it was not the street! Now No. 107, across the corridor—at five francs—?'

Monsieur was aroused. "No! No! certainly not. The view was of no consequence. The bed looked all right."

'The bed!' Here Jean spoke with deep feeling. 'There was no better bed in Paris. Had he not himself put clean sheets on it that day?' He turned from the window, and with the hand of an expert displayed the beauties of the sparse blankets, the cotton sheets, and the mountainous double mattress.

'But monsieur was anxious to retire? Doubtless monsieur would sleep until *déjeuner*? A most excellent *déjeuner* was served in the *salle-à-manger* on the second floor.'

The words flowed forth in a stream—agreeable, monotonous, reminiscent of the far-away province that had long ago bred this good creature. Suddenly the exhaustion of the long journey, the sleep so long denied rose about the traveller like a misty vapor. He longed for solitude; he pined for rest.

"I am satisfied with everything," he said, abruptly. "Leave me. I have not been in bed for two nights."

A flood of sympathy overspread Jean's face: he threw up his hands. "Poor boy! Poor boy! What a terrible thing!" With a touch as light as a woman's his work-worn fingers smoothed the pillow invitingly, and, tiptoeing to the door, he disappeared in tactful and silent comprehension of the situation.

Vaguely the boy was conscious of his departure. A great lassitude was falling upon him, making him value the isolation of his three-franc room with a deep gratitude, turning his gaze toward the unpromising bed with an indescribable longing. Mechanically, as the door closed, he threw off his heavy overcoat, kicked off his high boots, discarded his coat and trousers, and, without waiting to search in his bag for another garment, stepped into bed and curled himself up in the flannel shirt he had worn all day.

The bed was uncomfortable with that extraordinary discomfort of the old-fashioned French bed, that feels as though it were padded with cotton wool of indescribable heaviness. The sheets were coarse, the multitudinous clothes were weighty without being warm, but no prince on his bed of roses ever rested with more luxury of repose than did this young adventurer as, drawing the blankets to his chin, he stretched his limbs with the slow, delicious enjoyment born of long travel.

Jean had drawn the cretonne curtains, but through their chinks streaks of bluish, shadowy light presaged the coming day. From his lair the boy looked out at these ghostly fingers of the morning, then his eyes travelled round the dark room until at last they rested upon his clothes lying, as he had thrown them, on the floor. He looked at them—the boots, the coat and trousers, the heavy overcoat—and suddenly some imperative thought banished sleep from his eyes. He sat up in bed; he shivered as the cold air nipped his shoulder; then, unhesitatingly, he slipped from between the sheets and slid out upon the floor.

The room was small; the clothes lay within an arm's length. He shivered again, stooped, and, picking up the overcoat, dived his hand into the deep pocket, and drew forth the packet that he had guarded so tenaciously in the train.

For a moment he stood looking at it in the blue light of the dawn—a thick brown packet, seven or eight inches long, tied with string and sealed. Once or twice he looked at it, seemingly lost in reflection; once or twice he turned it about in his hand as if to make certain it was intact; then, with a deep sigh indicative of satisfaction, he stepped back into bed, slipped the packet under his pillow and, with his fingers faithfully enlaced in the string, fell asleep.

CHAPTER III

IT was eleven o'clock when the boy woke. All the excitement of the past days had culminated in the great exhaustion of the night before.

He had slept as a child might sleep—dreamlessly, happily, unthinkingly. In that silent hour Nature had drawn him into her wide embrace, lulling him with a mother's gentleness; and now, in the moment of waking, it seemed that again the same beneficent agency was dispensing love and favor, for he opened his eyes upon a changed world. A magician's wand had been waved over the city during his hours of sleep; the mist and oppression of the night had disappeared with the darkness. Paris was under the dominion of the frost.

Instinctively, even before his eyelids lifted, the northern soul within him apprised him of this change. He inhaled the crisp coldness of the air with a vague familiarity; he opened his eyes slowly and stared about the unknown room in an instant of hesitating doubt; then, with a great leap of the spirit, he recognized his position. Last night—the days and nights that had preceded it—flooded his consciousness, and in a moment he was out of bed and pulling back the drab-hued curtains that hid the window.

Having freed the daylight, he leaned out, peering greedily down into the well-like court, where even the stunted trees in their painted tubs were coated white with rime; then, with another impulse, as quickly conceived, as quickly executed, he drew back into the room, fired with the desire to be out and about in this newly created world.

By day, the details of the room stood out with a prominence that had been denied them in the dim candle-light of the night before, and he realized now, what had escaped him then, that there was neither dressing-table, wardrobe, nor chest of drawers, that the entire space of the small apartment was filled by the clumsy bed, a folding wash-stand, and two ponderous arm-chairs covered in shabby red velvet. These, with a dingy gold-framed mirror hanging above the tiny corner fireplace, and a gilt clock under a glass shade, formed the comforts purchasable for three francs.

He studied it all solemnly and attentively, not omitting the gray wall-paper of melancholy design, and content that he had acquitted himself dutifully toward his surroundings, he unpacked his valise, and proceeded to dress for the day's happenings.

The contents of the valise were not imposing—a change of linen, a soft felt hat, a pair of shoes, and a well-worn blue serge suit. The boy looked at each article as he drew it forth with a quaint attentiveness quite disproportionate to either its appearance or its value. But the process seemed to please him, and he lingered over it, ceasing almost reluctantly to appraise his belongings, and beginning to dress.

This morning he discarded the high Russian boots and the fur cap of yesterday, and arrayed himself instead, and with much precision, in the serge suit. Worn as this suit was, it evidently retained a pristine value in its owner's eyes, for no sooner had he fastened the last button of the coat than he looked instinctively for the mirror in which to study the effect.

The mirror unfortunately was high and, crane his neck as he might, he could see nothing beyond the waves of his short, dark hair and his eager, questioning eyes. But the effect must be observed, and, with an anxiety in seeming contrast to his nature, he pulled one of the massive velvet chairs to the fireplace and, mounting upon it, surveyed himself at every angle with deep intentness. At last, satisfied, he jumped to the ground, and taking the brown-paper packet from the hiding-place where it had reposed all night, bestowed it again in the pocket of his overcoat and, picking up the felt hat, left the room.

The corridor, despite the advent of the day, was still dark, save where an occasional door stood ajar and a shaft of sun from the outer world shot across the drab carpet; but Jean had been over the floor with his broom while the hotel slept, and the battered tray with its suggestion of sordid festivity had been removed. Even here the electric air of the morning had made entry, and, yielding to its seduction, the boy gave rein to his eagerness as he hurried forward to the head of the stairs and laid his hand upon the meagre banister.

From the hall below the white light of the day ascended with subtle invitation, while outside the world hummed with possibilities. He began the descent, light as a Mercury, his feet scarcely touching the steps that last night had offered so toilsome a progress, and on the third floor he encountered Jean, bearing another tray laden with plates and covered dishes.

At sight of the young face, the good creature's smile broke forth irresistibly.

'Ah, but monsieur had slept!' The little eyes ran over the face and figure of the guest with visible pleasure.

The boy laughed—the full, light-hearted laugh that belongs to the beginning of things.

"Yes, I have slept; and now, you may believe, I have an appetite!"

Jean echoed the laugh with a spontaneity that held no disrespect. He lingered, drawn, as the Irishman in the train had been drawn, by something original, something vital, in the youthful personality.

'His faith! But monsieur had the spirit as well as the appetite!'

"Ah, the spirit!" For a fleeting second the boy's eyes looked away beyond Jean—untidy, attentive, comprehending—beyond the neutral-tinted walls and the shabby carpet of the Hôtel Railleux, seeing in vision the things that were to come. Then, with his swift impulsiveness, he flung his dream from him. What mattered the future? What mattered the past? He was here in the present—in the moment; and the moment, great or small, demanded living.

"Never mind the spirit, Jean! Let us consider the flesh! Where is the *salle-à-manger*?"

'The *salle-à-manger* was on the second floor.'

'The second floor? But of course! Had not Jean mentioned that fact last night?' With a nod and a smile, he was away down the intervening steps and at the door of the eating-room before Jean could balance his tray for his renewed ascent.

The room that the boy entered was in keeping with the rest of the house—old-fashioned and in ill-repair. The floor was devoid of covering, the ceiling low, the only furniture a dozen small tables meagrely set out for *déjeuner*. On the moment of his entry eleven of these tables were unoccupied, but at the twelfth an eager young waiter attended upon a stout provincial Frenchwoman who was partaking heartily of a pungently smelling stew.

On the opening of the door the waiter glanced round in strained anticipation, and the lady of the stew looked up and bowed a greeting to the new-comer.

It struck the boy as curious—this welcome from a total stranger, but it woke anew the pleasant warmth, the agreeable sense of friendliness. With the tingling sensation of doing a daring deed, he glanced round the empty room, scanned the two long windows on which the cold, bright sun played laughingly, and through which the rattle and hum of the rue de Dunkerque penetrated like an exhilarating accompaniment, then, he walked straight to the table of the lady, smiled and, in his own turn, bowed.

'Would madame permit him to sit at her table? It was sad to be alone upon so fine a morning.'

A woman of any other nationality might have looked at him askance; but madame was French. She was fifty years of age, she was fat, she was ugly — but she was French. The sense of a pleasant encounter — the appreciation of romance was in her blood. She smiled at the debonair boy with as agreeable a self-consciousness as though she had been a young girl.

'But certainly, if monsieur desired. The pleasure was for her.'

Again an interchange of bows and smiles, sympathetically repeated by the interested young waiter. Then the boy, laying his hat and coat aside, seated himself at the table and entered upon the business of the hour, while madame became tactfully absorbed in her odoriferous stew.

'What did monsieur desire?' The waiter stood anxiously attentive, his head inclining gravely to one side, his dirty napkin swinging from his left hand.

The boy glanced up.

'What could the Hôtel Railleux offer?'

The waiter met his eye steadfastly. 'Anything that monsieur cared to order.'

The boy encountered the steadfast look, and a little gleam of humor shot into his eyes.

'Well, then, to begin with, should they say *Sole Waleska*?'

The waiter's glance wavered, he threw the weight of his body from one foot to the other. Involuntarily madame looked up.

The boy buried himself behind an expression of profound seriousness.

"Yes! *Sole Waleska*! Or, perhaps, *Coulibiac à la Russe!*"

The waiter's mouth opened in a desperate resolve to meet the worst. Madame's eyes discreetly sought her plate.

The boy threw back his head and laughed aloud at his own small jest. "Bring me two eggs *en cocotte*," he substituted, and laughed again in sheer pleasure at the waiter's sudden smile, his sudden restoration to dignity, as he hurried away to put a seal upon an order that permitted the hotel to retain its self-respect.

Again madame looked up. 'Monsieur was fond of his little pleasantry! This waiter was a good boy, but slow. They did not keep a sufficiency of servants at the Hôtel Railleux. But doubtless monsieur had noticed that?'

The boy met her inquisitive glance with disarming frankness, but his words when he answered gave little information.

'No. He had not as yet had time to notice anything.'

'But of course! Monsieur was a new arrival? He had come—when was it—?' Madame appeared to search her memory.

'Yesterday.'

'But of course. Yesterday! And what a day it had been! What weather for a long journey! It had been a long journey, had it not?'

The boy looked vague. 'Oh, it had been of a sufficient length!'

Madame toyed with the remnants of her stew. 'It had, perhaps, been a journey from England? Monsieur was not French, although he had so charming a fluency in the language?' Her eyes, her whole provincial, inquisitive face begged for information, but the boy was firm.

'We are each of the country God has given us!' he informed her. Then he added with convincing certainty that madame was without doubt *Parisienne*.

Madame bridled at the soothing little falsehood.

'Alas! nothing so interesting. She was of the provinces.'

'Provincial! Impossible!'

At once the ice was broken; at once they were on the footing of friends, and madame's soul poured forth its secret vanities.

'Monsieur was too kind. No, she was provincial—though, of a truth, Paris was so well known to her that she might almost claim to be *Parisienne*.'

The boy's interest was undiminished. 'Might he venture to ask if it was pleasure alone that had brought madame to the capital—or had business—?' He left the sentence discreetly unfinished.

Madame pushed her empty plate away and took a toothpick from the table.

'How observant was monsieur!' She eyed the bright young face with growing approval. 'Yes, business, alas, was the pivot of her visit! This terrible business—exacting so much, giving so little in return!' She heaved a weighty sigh, then her fat face melted into smiles. 'But after all, what would you?' She shrugged her ample shoulders, and the toothpick came into full play.

'What would you, indeed?' The boy began to feel a little disconcerted under her glance of slow approval, and a swift sense of relief passed through him as the door opened and the waiter reappeared, carrying the two eggs.

'What would you, indeed? One must live!' Madame, disregarding the waiter, continued to study the boyish face—the curious dark-gray eyes, in which the morning sun was discovering little flecks of gold. 'And every year conditions were becoming harder, as monsieur doubtless knew.'

Monsieur nodded his head sagely, and began to eat his eggs with keen zest.

Madame looked slowly round at the waiter and ordered coffee, then her glance returned to the boy.

'How good, how refreshing it was to see him eat! How easy to comprehend that he was young!' She sighed again, this time more softly. 'Youth was a marvellous thing—and Paris was the city of the young! Was monsieur making a long stay at the Hôtel Railleux?'

The waiter again appeared and placed the coffee upon the table. Monsieur, suddenly and unaccountably uneasy, finished his eggs hastily and pushed his plate aside.

'Did monsieur desire coffee?' Madame leaned forward. 'If so, it would be but the matter of a moment to procure a second cup; and, as her coffee-pot was quite full—' She raised the lid coquettishly, and again her eyes lingered upon the short dark hair and the straight brows above the gray eyes.

The waiter with ready tact departed in search of the second cup; madame replaced the lid of the coffee-pot.

'Now that they were alone, would it be an unpardonable liberty to ask how old monsieur really was?'

Monsieur blushed.

'How old would madame suppose?'

Madame laughed. 'Oh, it was difficult to say! One might imagine from those bright eyes that monsieur had nineteen years; but, again, it was impossible to suppose that a razor had ever touched that soft cheek.' There was another little laugh, lower this time and more subtle in tone; and madame, with a movement wonderfully swift considering her years and her proportions, leaned across the table and touched the boy's face.

The effect was instant. A tide of color rushed into his cheeks, he rose with an alacrity that was comic.

'He—he was much older than madame supposed!'

Madame laughed delightedly. 'How charming! How ingenuous! He positively must sit down again. It was assured that they would become friends! Where was that waiter? Where was that second coffee-cup?'

But monsieur remained standing.

Madame's eyes, now alive with interest, literally danced to her thoughts.

'Come! Come! They must not allow the coffee to become cold!'

But monsieur picked up his hat and coat.

'What! He was not going? Oh, it was impossible! He could not be so unkind!' Her face expressed dismay.

But her only answer was a stiff little bow, and a second later the door had closed and the boy was running down the stairs of the hotel as though some enemy were in hot pursuit.

CHAPTER IV

THE mind of the boy was very full as he passed out of the hotel, so full that he scarcely noticed the whip of cold air that stung his face or the white mantle that lay upon the streets, wrapping in a silver sheath all that was sordid, all that was dirty and unpicturesque in that corner of Paris. The human note had been touched in that moment in the salle-à-manger, and his ears still tingled to its sound. Alarm, disgust, and a strange exultant satisfaction warred within him in a manner to be comprehended by his own soul alone.

As he stepped out into the rue de Dunkerque he scarcely questioned in what direction his feet should carry him. North, south, east, or west were equal on that first day. Everywhere was promise—everywhere a call. Nonchalantly and without intention he turned to the left and found himself once more in face of the Gare du Nord.

It is a good thing to rejoice in spite of the world; it is an infinitely better thing to rejoice in company with it. With solitude and freedom, the alarm, the disgust receded, and as he went forward the exultation grew, until once again his mercurial spirits lifted him as upon wings.

The majority of passers-by at this morning hour were workers—work-girls out upon their errands, business men going to or from the cafés; but here and there was to be seen an artist, consciously indifferent to appearances; here and there an artisan, unconsciously picturesque in his coarse working-clothes; here and there a well-dressed woman, sunning herself in the cold, bright air like a bird of gay plumage. It was the world in miniature, and it stirred and piqued his interest. A wish to stop one of these people, and to pour forth his longings, his hopes, his dreams, surged within him in a glow of fellowship and, smiling to himself at the pleasant wildness of the thought, he made his way through the wider spaces of the Place Lafayette and the Square Montholon into the long, busy rue Lafayette.

Here, in the rue Lafayette, the gloomy aspects of the district he had made his own dropped behind him, and a wealth of bustle and gayety greeted and fascinated him. Here the sun seemed fuller, the traffic was more dense, and the shops offered visions to please every sense. Wine shops were here, curio shops, shops all golden and tempting with cheeses and butter, and hat shops that foretold the spring in a glitter of blues and greens. He passed on, jostling the crowd good-humoredly, being jostled in the same spirit, hugging his freedom with a silent joy.

Down the rue Halévy he went and on into the Place de l'Opéra; but here he slackened his pace, and something of his *insouciance* dropped from him. The wide space filled with its cosmopolitan crowd, the opera-house itself, so aloof in its dark splendor, spoke to him of another Paris—the Paris that might be Vienna, Petersburg, London, for all it has to say of individual life. His mood changed; he paused and looked back over his shoulder in the direction from whence he had come. But the hesitation was fleeting; a quick courage followed on the doubt. The adventurer must take life in every aspect—must face all questions, all moments! He turned up the collar of his coat, as though preparing to face a chillier region, and went forward boldly as before.

One or two narrow streets brought him out upon the Place de Rivoli, where Joan of Arc sat astride her golden horse, and where great heaps of flowers were stacked at the street corners—mimosa, lilac, violets. He halted irresistibly to glance at these flowers breathing of the south, and to glance at the shining statue. Then he crossed the rue de Rivoli and, passing through the garden of the Tuileries, emerged upon the Place de la Concorde.

On the Place de la Concorde the cool, clean hand of the morning had drawn its most striking picture; here, in the great, unsheltered spaces, the frost had fallen heavily, softening and beautifying to an inconceivable degree. The suggestion of modernity that ordinarily hangs over the place was veiled, and the subtle hints of history stole forth, binding the imagination. It needed but a touch to materialize the dream as the boy crossed the white roadway, shadowed by the white statuary, and with an odd appropriateness the touch was given.

One moment his mind was a sea of shifting visions, the next it was caught and held by an inevitably thrilling sound—the sound of feet tramping to a martial tune. The touch had been given: the vague visions of tradition and history crystallized into a picture, and his heart leaped to the pulsing, steady tramp, to the clash of fife and drum ringing out upon the fine cold air.

All humanity is drawn by the sight of soldiers. There is a primitive exhilaration in the idea of marching men that will last while the nations live. Stung by the same impulse that affected every man and woman in the Place de la Concorde, the boy paused—his head up, his pulses quickened, his eyes and ears strained toward the sound.

It was a regiment of infantry marching down the Cours la Reine and defiling out upon the Place de la Concorde toward the rue de Rivoli. By a common impulse he paused, and by an equally common desire to be close to the object of interest, he ran forward to where a little crowd had gathered in the soldiers' route.

The French soldier is not individually interesting, and this body of men looked insignificant enough upon close inspection. Yet it was a regiment; it stirred the fancy; and the boy gazed with keen interest at the small figures in the ill-fitting uniforms and at the faces, many as young as his own, that denied past him in confusing numbers. On and on the regiment wound, a coiling line of dull red and bluish-gray against the frosty background, the feet tramping steadily, the fifes and drums beating out with an incessant clamor.

Then, without warning, a new interest touched the knot of watchers, a thrill passed from one member of the crowd to another, and hats were raised. The colors were being borne by: Frenchmen were saluting their flag.

The knowledge sprang to the boy's mind with the swiftness and poignancy of an inspiration. This body of men might be insignificant, but it represented the army of France—a thing of infinite tradition, of infinite romance. The blood mounted to his face, his heart beat faster, and with a strange, half-shy sense of participating in some fine moment, his hand went up to his hat.

Unconsciously he made a picture as he stood there, his dark hair stirred by the light, early air, his young face beautiful in its sudden enthusiasm; and to one pair of eyes in the little crowd it seemed better worth watching than the passing soldiers.

The owner of these eyes had been observant of him from the moment that he had run forward, drawn by the rattle of the drums; and now, as if in acceptance of an anticipated opportunity, he forced a way through the knot of people and, pausing behind the boy, addressed him in an easy, familiar voice, as one friend might address another.

"Isn't it odd," he said, "to look at those insignificant creatures, and to think that the soldiers of France have kissed the women and thrashed the men the world over?"

Had a gun been discharged close to his car the boy could not have started more violently. Fear leaped into his eyes, he wheeled round; then a sharp, nervous laugh of relief escaped him.

"How you frightened me!" he exclaimed. "Oh, how you frightened me!" Then he laughed again.

His travelling companion of the night before smiled down on him from his superior height, and the boy noted for the first time that this smile had a peculiarly attractive way of communicating itself from the clean-shaven lips to the grayish-green eyes of the stranger, banishing the slightly satirical look that marked his face in repose.

"Well?" The Irishman was still studying him.

"Well? We're all on the knees of the gods, you see! 'Twas written that we were to meet; you can't avoid me."

The flag had been carried past; the boy replaced his hat, glad of a moment in which to collect his thoughts. What must he do? The question beat in his brain. Wisdom whispered avoidance of this stranger. To-day was the first day; was it wise to bring into it anything from yesterday? No, it was not wise—reason upheld wisdom. He pulled his hat into place, his lips came together in an obstinate line, and he raised his eyes.

The sun was dancing on a silvery world, from the rue de Rivoli the fifes and drums still rattled out their march, close beside him the Irishman was looking at him with his pleasant smile.

Suddenly, as a daring horseman might give rein to a young horse, rejoicing in the risk, the boy discarded wisdom and its whispering curb; his nature leaped forth in sudden comradeship, and impulsively he held out his hand.

"Monsieur, forgive me!" he said. "The gods know best!"

He said the words in English, perfectly, easily, with that faintest of all foreign intonations—the intonation that clings to the Russian voice.

CHAPTER V

SO the step was taken, and two souls, drawn together from different countries, different races, touched in a first subtle fusion. With an ease kindled by the fine and stinging air, stimulated by the crisp summons of the flutes and the martial rattle of the drums, they bridged the thousand preliminaries that usually hedge a friendship, and arrived in a moment of intuition at that consciousness of fellowship that is the most divine of human gifts.

As though the affair had been prearranged through countless ages, they turned by one accord and forced a way through the crowd that still encompassed them. Across the Place de la Concorde they went, past the white statues, past the open space through which the soldiers were still defiling like a dark stream in a snowbound country. Each was drawn instinctively toward the Cours la Reine—the point from whence the stream was pouring, the point where the crowd of loiterers was sparsest, where the bare and frosted trees caught the sun in a million dancing facets. Reaching it, the boy looked up into the stranger's face with his fascinating look of question and interest.

"Monsieur, tell me something! How did you know me again? And why did you speak to me?"

The question was grave, with the charming gravity that was wont to cross his gayety as shadows chase each other across a sunlit pool. His lips were parted naïvely, his curious slate-gray eyes demanded the truth.

TWO SOULS, DRAWN TOGETHER, TOUCHED IN A FIRST SUBTLE FUSION

The Irishman recognized the demand, and answered it.

"Now that you put it to me," he said, thoughtfully, "I'm not sure that I can tell you. There's something about you—" His thoughtfulness deepened, and he studied the boy through narrowed eyes. "It isn't that you're odd in any way."

The boy reddened.

"It isn't that you're odd," he insisted, "but somehow you're such a slip of a boy—" His voice grew meditative and he recurred to his native trick of phrasing, as he always did when interested or moved.

"But why did you speak to me? I'm not interesting."

"Oh yes, you are!"

"How am I interesting?" There was a flash in the gray eyes that revealed new flecks of gold.

The Irishman hesitated.

"Well, I can't explain it," he said, slowly, "unless I tell you that you throw a sort of spell—and that sounds absurd. You see, I've knocked about the world a bit, east and west, but at the back of everything I'm an Irishman; I have a fondness for the curious and the poetical and the mysterious, and somehow you seemed to me last night to be mystery itself, with your silence and your intentness." He dropped his voice to the meditative key, unconsciously enjoying its soft, half-melancholy cadences, and as he spoke the boy felt some chord in his own personality vibrate to the mind that had asked for no introduction, demanded no credentials, that had decreed their friendship and materialized it.

"No," the Irishman mused on, "there's no explaining it. You were mystery itself, and you fired my imagination, because I happen to come from a country of dreams. We Irish are born dreamers; sometimes we never wake up at all, and then we're counted failures. But, I tell you what, when all's said and done, we see what other men don't see. For instance, what do you think my two friends saw in you last night?"

The boy shook his head, and there was a tremor of nervousness about his mouth.

"They saw something dangerous—something to be avoided. Yet Mac is a millionaire several times over, and Billy is distinctly a diplomatist with a future."

The boy forced a smile; he was beginning to shrink from the pleasant scrutiny, to wish that the vaporous fog of last night might dim the searching light of the morning.

"What did they see?" he asked.

The Irishman looked at him humorously. "I hardly like to tell it to you," he said, "but they marked you for an anarchist. An anarchist, for all the world! As if any anarchist alive would travel first-class in third-class clothes! You see, I'm blunt."

The boy, studying him, half in fear, half in doubt, laughed suddenly in quick relief and amusement.

"An anarchist! How droll!"

"Wasn't it? I told them so. I also told them—"

"What?"

"My own beliefs."

"And your beliefs?"

"No! No! You won't draw me! But I'll tell you this much, for I've told it before. I knew you were no common creature of intrigue; I accepted you as mystery personified."

"And now you would solve me?" In his returning confidence the boy's eyes danced.

"God forbid!" The vehemence of the reply was comic, and the Irishman himself laughed as the words escaped him. "Oh no!" he added, soberly. "Keep your mask! I don't want to tear it from you. Later on, perhaps, I'll take a peep behind; but I can accept mysteries and miracles—I was born into the Roman Catholic Church."

"And I into the Greek."

"Ah! My first peep!"

"And what do you see?"

"Do you know, I see a queer thing. I see a boy who has thought. You have thought. Don't deny it!"

"On religion?"

"On religion—and other things; you acknowledge it in one look."

The boy laughed, like a child who has been caught at some forbidden game.

"Perhaps it was your imagination."

"Perhaps! But, look here, we can't stand all day discoursing in the Cours la Reine! Where shall we wander—left or right?" He nodded first in the direction of the river, then toward the large building that faced them on the right, from the roof of which an array of small flags fluttered an invitation.

The boy's eyes followed his movement. "Pictures!" he exclaimed. "I didn't know there was an exhibition open."

"Live and learn! Come along!"

Together they stepped into the roadway, where the frosty surface was scarred by the soldiers' feet, and together they reached the doorway of the large building and read the legend, "*Soctiété Peintres et Sculpteurs Français.*"

The Irishman read the words with the faintly humorous, faintly sceptical glance that he seemed to bestow upon the world at large.

"Remember I'm throwing out no bait, but I expect 'twill be value for a couple of francs."

They entered the bare hall and, mounting a cold and rigid staircase, found themselves confronted by a turnstile.

The Irishman was in the act of laying a two-franc piece in the hand of the custodian when the boy plucked him by the sleeve and, turning, he saw the curious eyes full of a sudden anxiety.

"Monsieur, pardon me! You know Paris well?"

"I live here for five months out of the twelve."

"Then you can tell me if—if this exhibition will be well attended. I want with all my heart to see the pictures, but I—I dislike crowds—fashionable crowds." His voice was agitated; it was as if he had suddenly awakened from his pleasant dream of Bohemian comradeship to a remembrance of the Paris that lay about him.

The Irishman expressed no surprise: his only reply was to move nearer to the guardian of the turnstile.

"Monsieur," he said in French, "have the goodness to inform me how many persons have passed through the turnstile this morning?"

The man looked at him without interest, though with some surprise. 'Not many of the world were to be seen at such an hour,' he informed him. 'So far, he had admitted two gentlemen—artists, and three ladies—American.'

The Irishman waved his hand toward the turnstile.

"In with you! The world forgetting, by the world forgot!"

His ease of manner was contagious. Whatever misgivings had assailed the boy were banished with this reassurance, and his confidence flowed back as the custodian took the two-franc piece and the turnstile clicked twice, making them free of the long, bare galleries that opened in front of them.

Inured as he was to cold, he shivered as they passed into the first of these long rooms, and involuntarily buried his chin in the collar of his coat. The chill of the place was vaultlike; the cold, gray light that penetrated it held nothing of the sun's comfort, while the small, black stove set in the middle of the room was a mere travesty of warmth.

"God bless my soul!" began the Irishman, "this is art for art's sake—"

But there he stopped, for his companion, with the impetuosity of his temperament, had suddenly caught sight of a picture that interested him, and had darted across the room, leaving him to his own reflections.

The boy was standing perfectly still, entirely engrossed, when he came silently up behind him, and paused to look over his shoulder. They were alone in the vast and chilly room save for one attendant who dozed over some knitting in a corner near the door. Away into the distance stretched the other rooms, bound one to the other like links in a chain. From the third of these came the penetrating voices of the American ladies, descanting unhesitatingly upon the pictures; while in the second the two artists could be seen flitting from one canvas to another with a restless, nervous activity.

These facts came subconsciously to the Irishman, for his eyes and his thoughts were for the boy and the subject of the boy's interest—a picture curiously repulsive, yet curiously binding in its realism of conception. It was a large canvas that formed one of a group of five or six studies by a particular artist. The details of the picture scarcely held the mind, for the imagination of the beholder was instantly caught and enchained by the central figure—the figure of a great ape, painted with cruel and extraordinary truth. The animal was squatting upon the ground, devouring a luscious fruit; its small and greedy eyes were alight with gluttony; in its unbridled appetite, its hairy fingers crushed the fruit against its sharp teeth, while the juice dripped from its mouth.

The intimate, undisguised portrayal of greed shocked the susceptibilities, but it was the hideous human attributes patent in the brute that disgusted the imagination. With a terrible cunning of mind and brush the artist had laid bare a vice that civilization cloaks.

For two or three minutes the boy stood immovable, then he looked back over his shoulder, and the man behind him was surprised at the expression that had overspread his face, the sombre light that glowed in his eyes. In a moment the adventurer was lost, another being had come uppermost—a strange, unexpected being.

"What do you think of this picture?"

The Irishman did not answer for a moment, then his eyes returned to the canvas and his tongue was loosed.

"If you want to know," he said, "I think it's the most damnable thing I've ever seen. When the Gallic mind runs to morbidity there's nothing to touch it for filth."

"Why filth?"

"Why filth? My dear boy, look at this—and this!" He pointed to the other pictures, each a study of monkey life, each a travesty of some human passion.

The boy obeyed, conscientiously and slowly, then once more his eyes challenged his companion's.

"I say again, why filth?"

"Because there is enough of the beast in every man without advertising it."

"You admit that there is something of the beast in every man?"

"Naturally."

"Then why fear to see it?" The boy's face was pale, his eyes still challenged.

The other made a gesture of impatience. "It isn't a question of fear; it is a question of—well, of taste."

"Taste!" The boy tossed the word to scorn.

"What would you substitute?"

"Truth." There was a tremor in his voice, a veil seemed to fall upon his youth, arresting its carelessness, sobering its vitality.

The Irishman raised his brows. "Truth, eh?"

"Yes. It is only possible to live when we know life truly, see it and value it truly."

"There may be perverted truth."

"You say that because this truth we speak of displeases you; yet this is no more a perversion of the truth than"—he glanced round the walls—"than that, for example; yet you would approve of that."

He waved his hand toward another painting, a delicate and charming conception of a half-clothed woman, a picture in which the flesh-tints, the drapery, the lights all harmonized with exquisite art.

"You would approve of that because it pleases your eye and soothes your senses, yet you know that all womankind is not slim and graciou—that all life is not lived in boudoirs."

"Neither is man all beast."

"Ah, that is it! If we are to be students of human nature we must not be swayed in one direction or the other; and that is the difficulty—to be dispassionate. Sometimes it is—very difficult!"

It came with a charm indescribable, this sudden admission of weakness, accompanied by a deprecating, pleading glance, and the Irishman was filled with a sudden sense of having recovered something personal and precious.

"What are you?" he cried. "It's my turn to seek the truth now. What are you, you incomprehensible being?"

The boy laughed, the old careless, light-hearted laugh of the creature infinitely free.

"Do not ask! Do not ask!" he said. "A riddle is only interesting while it is unsolved."

CHAPTER VI

WITH the laugh the personal moment passed. Henceforward it was the technique of the pictures, the individualism of the artists that claimed the boy's attention, and in this new field he proved himself yet another being—a creature of quick perception and curiously mature judgment, appreciative and observant, critical and generous.

In warm and interested discussion they made the tour of the rooms, and when they emerged again into the frosty morning air and were greeted by the dazzle of the sun, each was conscious of a deeper understanding. A new expression of interest and something of respect was visible in the Irishman's face as he looked down on the puzzling, elusive being whom he had picked up from the skirts of chance as he might have filched a jewel or a coin.

"Look here, boy!" he said, "we mustn't say good-bye just yet. Come across the river, and let's find some little place where we can get a seat and a cup of coffee."

The boy's only answer was to turn obediently, as the other slipped his hand through his arm, and to allow himself to be guided back across the Cours la Reine and over the Pont Alexandre III.

The bridge looked almost as impressive as the Place de la Concorde under its white garment, and his glance ranged from the high columns, topped by the winged horses, to the thronging bronze lamps, while the sense of breath and freedom fitted with his secret thoughts.

Leaving the river behind them, they made their way onward across the Esplanade des Invalides, through the serried lines of trees, stark and formal against the January sky, to the rue Fabert. Here, in the rue Fabert, lay that note of contrast that is bound into the very atmosphere of Paris—the note that touches the imagination to so acute an interest. Here shabby, broken-down shops rubbed shoulders with fine old entries, entries that savored of other times in the hint of roomy court-yard and green garden to be caught behind their gateways; here were creameries that conjured the country to the eager senses, and laundries that exhaled a very aroma of work in the hot steam that poured through their windows and in the babble of voices that arose from the women who stood side by side, iron in hand, bending over the long, spotless tables piled with linen.

It was a touch of Parisian life, small in itself, but subtle and suggestive as the premonition of spring awakened by the twittering of the sparrows in the tall, leafless trees, and the throbbing song of a caged canary that floated down from a window above a shop. It was suggestive of that Parisian life that is as restless as the sea, as uncontrollable, as possessed of hidden currents.

Involuntarily the boy paused and glanced up at the bird in its cage—the bird that, regardless of the garden of greenstuffs pushed through its bars, was pouring forth its heart to the pale sun in a frenzy of worship.

"How strange that is!" he said. "If I were a bird and saw the great sky, knowing myself imprisoned, I should beat my life out against my cage."

The Irishman looked down upon him. "I wonder!" he said, slowly.

The quick, gray eyes flashed up to his. "You doubt it?"

"I don't know! 'On my soul, I don't know!"

"Would you not beat your life out against a cage?"

"I wonder that too! I'd like to think I would, but—"

"You imagine you would hesitate? You think you would shrink?"

"I don't know! Human nature is so damnably patient. Come along! here's the place we're looking for." He drew the boy across the road to the doorway of a little *café*, over the door of which hung the somewhat pretentious sign Maison Gustav.

The Maison Gustav was scarcely a more appetizing place than the Hôtel Railleux. One-half of its interior was partitioned off and filled with long tables, at which, earlier in the day, workmen were served with *déjeuner*, while the other and smaller portion, reserved for more fastidious guests, was fitted with a counter, ranged with fruit and cakes, and with half a dozen round marble-topped tables, provided with chairs.

This more refined portion of the *café* was empty of customers as the two entered. With the ease and decision of an *habitué*, the Irishman chose the table nearest to the counter, and presently a woman appeared from some inner region, and, approaching her customers, eyed them with that mixture of shrewd observation and polite welcome that belongs to the Frenchwoman who follows the ways of commerce.

"Good-day, messieurs!" She inclined her head to one side like a plump and speculative bird, and her hands began mechanically to smooth her black alpaca apron.

"Good-day, madame!" The Irishman rose and took off his hat with a flourish that was essentially flattering.

The bright little eyes of the *Parisienne* sparkled, and her round face relaxed into the inevitable smile.

'What could she have the pleasure of offering monsieur? It was late, but she had an excellent *ragoût*, now a little cold, perhaps, but capable in an instant—'

The stranger put up his hand. "Madame, we could not think of giving you the trouble—"

"Monsieur, a pleasure—"

"No, madame, it is past the hour of *déjeuner*. All we need is your charming hospitality and two cups of coffee."

'Coffee! But certainly! While monsieur was saying the word it would be made and served.'

Madame hurried off, and in silence the Irishman took out his cigarette-case and offered it to the boy. Bare and even cold as the *café* was, there was a certain sense of shelter in the closed glass door, in the blue film of cigarette smoke that presently began to mount upward toward the ceiling, and in the pleasant smell of coffee borne to them from unseen regions mingling with the shrill, cheerful tones of their hostess's voice.

"A wonderful place, Paris, when all's said and done!" murmured the Irishman, drawing in a long, luxurious breath of smoke. "How an English restaurant-keeper would stare you out of countenance if you demanded a modest cup of coffee when he had luncheon for you to eat! But here, bless you, they acknowledge the rights of man. If you want coffee, coffee you must have—and that with the best grace in the world, lest your self-esteem be hurt! They're like my people at home: consideration for the individual is the first thing. It means nothing, a Saxon will tell you, and probably he's quite right; but I'd sooner have a pleasant-spoken sinner any day than a disagreeable saint. Ah, here comes madame!" The last words he added in French, and the boy watched him in amused wonder as he jumped to his feet and, meeting their hostess at the kitchen door, insisted upon taking the tray from her hands.

Laughing, excited, and flattered, the little woman followed him to the table.

'It was really too much! Monsieur was too kind!'

'On the contrary! It was not meant that woman should wait upon man! Madame had accomplished her share in making this most excellent coffee!'

He sniffed at the steaming pot with the air of a connoisseur.

Madame laughed again, this time self-consciously. 'Well, her coffee had been spoken of before now! Monsieur, her husband, who was quite a *gourmet*—'

'Always declared there was no such coffee in all Paris! Was not that so?'

Madame's laugh was now a gurgle of delight. 'How clever of monsieur! Yes, it was what he said.'

'Of course it was! And now, how was this good husband? And how was life treating them both?' He put the questions with deep solicitude as he poured out the coffee, and madame, standing by the table and smoothing her apron, grew serious, and before she was aware was pouring forth the grievance that at the moment was darkening her existence—the disappointment that had befallen the Maison Gustav when her father-in-law, a market gardener near Issy, who had a nice little sum of money laid by, had married again at the age of sixty-four.

'Could monsieur conceive anything more grotesque? An old man of sixty-four marrying a young woman of twenty! Of course there would be a child!' Her shoulders went up, her hands went out in expressive gesture. 'And her little Léon would be cheated of his grandfather's money by this creature who—'

At this juncture the sound of a kettle boiling over brought the story to an abrupt end, and madame flew off, leaving her guests to a not unwelcome solitude.

As her black skirt whisked round the corner of the door the boy looked at his companion.

"You come here often," he said.

The other laughed. "I've never set foot in the place before. It's a way we Irish have of putting our fingers into other people's pies! Some call it intrusion"—he glanced quizzically at the boy—"but these good creatures understand it. They're more human than the Saxon or the—" Again a glint of humor crossed his face, as he paused on his unfinished sentence.

The boy reddened and impulsively leaned across the table.

"You have taught me something, monsieur," he said, shyly, "and I have much to learn."

The other returned the glance seriously, intently. "What is it I have taught you?"

"That in the smaller ways of life it is not possible to stand quite alone."

Max A Novel | 49

The Irishman laid down his cigarette. With native quickness of comprehension, the spirit of banter dropped from him, his mood merged into the boy's mood.

"No," he said, "we are not meant to stand quite alone, and when two of us are flung up against each other as we have been flung, by a wave of circumstance, you may take it that the gods control the currents. In our case I would say, 'Let's bow to the inevitable! Let's be friends!'" He put out his hand and took the boy's strong, slim fingers in his grasp.

"I don't want your secret," he added, with a quickening interest, "but I want to know one thing. Tell me what you are seeking here in Paris? Is it pleasure, or money, or what?"

He watched the boy's mobile face as he put his question: he saw it swept by emotion, transfigured as if by some inner light; then the hand in his trembled a little, and the gray eyes with their flecks of gold were lifted to his own, giving insight into the hidden soul.

"I want more than pleasure, monsieur—more than money," he said. "I want first life—and then fame."

CHAPTER VII

IT trembled and hung upon the air—that brief word "fame"—as it has so often hung and trembled in the streets and in the *cafés* of Paris, winged with the exuberance of youth, the faith in his mystic star that abides in the heart of the artist. In that moment of confession the individuality of the boy was submerged in his ambition; he belonged to no country, to no sex. He was inspiration made manifest—the flame fanned into being by the winds of the universe, blown as those winds listed.

The Irishman looked into his burning face, and a curious unnamable feeling thrilled him—a sense of enthusiasm, of profound sadness, of poignant envy.

"You're not only seeking the greatest thing in the world," he said, slowly, "but the cruellest. Failure may be cruel, but success is crueller still. The gods are usurers, you know; they lend to mortals, but they exact a desperate interest."

The boy's hand, still lying unconsciously in his, trembled again.

"I know that; but it does not frighten me."

"A challenge? Take care! The gods are always listening."

"I know that. I am not afraid."

"So be it, then! I'll watch the duel. But what road do you follow—music? literature? Art of some sort, of course; you are artist all over."

Again the fire leaped to the boy's eyes. He snatched his hand away in quick excitement.

"Look! I will show you!"

With the swiftness of lightning he whipped a pencil from his pocket, pushed aside his coffee-cup, and began to draw upon the marble-topped table as though his life depended upon his speed.

For ten minutes he worked feverishly, his face intensely earnest, his head bent over his task, a lock of dark hair drooping across his forehead; then he looked up, throwing himself back in his chair and gazing up at his companion with the egotistical triumph—the intense, childish satisfaction of the artist in the first flush of accomplished work.

"Look! Look, now, at this!"

The Irishman laughed sympathetically; the artist, as belonging to a race apart, was known by him and liked, but he rose and came round the table with a certain scepticism. Life had taught him that temperament and output are different things.

He leaned over the boy's chair; then suddenly he laid his hand on his shoulder and gripped it, his own face lighting up.

"Why, boy!" he cried. "This is clever—clever—clever! I'm a Dutchman, if this isn't the real thing! Why on earth didn't you tell me you could do it?"

The boy laughed in sheer delight and, bending over the table, added a lingering touch or two to his work—a rough expressive sketch of himself standing back from an easel, a palette in his left hand, a brush in his right, his hair unkempt, his whole attitude comically suggestive of an artist in a moment of delirious oblivion. It was the curt, abrupt expression of a mood, but there was cleverness, distinction, humor in every line.

"Boy, this is fine! Fine! That duel will be fought, take my word for it. But, look here, we must toast this first attempt! Madame! Madame!" He literally shouted the words, and madame came flying out.

"Madame, have you a liqueur brandy—very old? I have discovered that this is a *fête* day."

"But certainly, monsieur! A *cognac* of the finest excellence."

"Out with it, then! And bring two glasses—no, bring three glasses! You must drink a toast with us!"

Madame bustled off, laughing and excited, and again the Irishman gripped the boy's shoulder.

"You've taken me in!" he cried. "Absolutely and entirely taken me in! I thought you a slip of a boy with a head full of notions, and what do I find but that it's a little genius I've got! A genius, upon my word! And here comes the blessed liquor!"

His whole-hearted enthusiasm was like fire, it leaped from one to the other of his companions. As madame came back, gasping in her haste, he ran to meet her, and, seizing the brandy and the glasses, drew her with him to the table.

"Madame, you are a Frenchwoman—therefore an artist. Tell me what you think of this!"

In his excitement he spoke in English, but madame understood his actions if not his words. Full of curiosity she bent over the boy's shoulder, peered into the sketch, then threw up her hands in genuine admiration.

'Ah, but he was an artist, was monsieur! A true artist! It was delicious—ravishing!' She turned from one of her customers to the other. 'If monsieur would but put his name to this picture she would never again have the table washed; and in time to come, when he had made his big success—'

"Good, madame! Good! When he has made his big success he will come back here and laugh and cry over this, and say, 'God be with the youth of us!' as we say in my old country. Come, boy, put your name to it!"

"WHY, BOY, THIS IS CLEVER—CLEVER—CLEVER!"

The boy glanced up at him. His face was aglow, there were tears of emotion in his eyes.

"I can say nothing," he cried, "but that I—I have never been so happy in my life." And, bending over his sketch, he wrote across the marble-topped table a single word—the word 'Max.'

The Frenchwoman bent over his shoulder. "Max!" she murmured. "A pretty name!"

The Irishman looked as well. "Max! So that's what they call you? Max! Well, let's drink to it!" He filled the three glasses and raised his own.

"To the name of Max!" he said. "May it be known from here to the back of God's speed!" He swallowed the brandy and laid down his glass.

"To M. Max!" The Frenchwoman smiled. "A great future, monsieur!" She sipped and bowed.

Of the three, the boy alone sat motionless. His heart felt strangely full, the tears in his eyes were dangerously near to falling.

"Come, Max! Up with your glass!"

"Monsieur, I—I beg you to excuse me! My heart is very full of your kindness."

"Nonsense, boy! Drink!"

The boy laughed with a catch in his breath, then he drank a little with nervous haste, coughing as he laid his glass down. The *cognac* of the Maison Gustav was of a fiery nature.

The Irishman laughed. "Ah, another peep behind the mask! You may be an artist, young man—- you may have advanced ideas—but, for all that, you're only out of the nursery! It's for me to make a man of you, I see. Come, madame, the *addition*, if you please! We must be going."

For a moment madame was lost in calculation, then she decorously mentioned the amount of their debt.

The Irishman paid with the manner of a prince, and, slipping his arm again through the boy's, moved to the door; there he looked back.

"Good-day, madame! Many thanks for your charming hospitality! Give my respects to monsieur, your husband—and kiss the little Léon for me!"

They passed out into the rue Fabert, into the fresh and frosty air, and involuntarily the boy's arm pressed his.

"How am I to thank you?" he murmured. "It is too much—this kindness to a stranger."

The Irishman paused and looked at him. "Thanks be damned!—and stranger be damned!" he said with sudden vehemence. "Aren't we citizens of a free world? Must I know a man for years before I can call him my friend? And must every one I've known since childhood be my friend? I tell you I saw you and I liked you—that was all, and 'twas enough."

Max looked at him with a certain grave simplicity. "Forgive me!" he said.

Instantly the other's annoyance was dispelled. "Forgive! Nonsense! Tell me your plans, that's all I want."

"My plans are very easy to explain. I shall rent a studio here in Paris—and there I shall work."

"As a student?"

"No, I have had my years of study; I am older than you think." He took no notice of the other's raised eyebrows. "I want to paint a picture—a great picture. I am seeking the idea."

"Good! Good! Then we'll make that our basis—the search for the idea. The search for the great idea!"

Max thrilled. 'The search for the idea! How splendid! Where must it begin? Not in fashionable Paris! Oh, not in fashionable Paris!'

"Fashionable Paris!" The Irishman laughed in loud disdain. "Oh no! For us it must be the highways and the byways, eh?"

Max freed his arm. "Ah yes! that is what I want—that is what I want. The highways and the byways. It is necessary that I am very solitary here in Paris. Quite unknown, you understand?—quite unnoticed."

"The mystery? I understand. And now, tell me, shall it be the highways or the byways—Montmartre or the Quartier Latin?"

Max smiled decisively. "Montmartre."

"You know Montmartre?"

"No."

The Irishman laughed again. "Good!" he cried. "You're a fine adventurer! You have the right spirit! Always know your own mind, whatever else you're ignorant about! But I ought to tell you that Montmartre swarms with your needy fellow-countrymen."

The boy looked up. "My needy fellow-countrymen will not harm me— or know me."

"Good again! Then the coast is clear! I only thought to warn you."

"I appreciate the thought." For an instant the old reserve touched the voice.

"Now, Max! Now! Now!" The other turned to him, caught his arm again, and swung him out into the Esplanade des Invalides. "You're not to be doing that, you know! You're not! You're not! I see through you like a pane of glass. Sometimes you forget yourself and get natural, like you did in the *café* this time back; then, all of a sudden, some imp of suspicion shakes his tail at you and says, 'Look here, young man, put that Irishman in his place! Keep him at a respectable arm's length!' Now, isn't that gospel truth?"

The boy laughed, vanquished. "Monsieur," he said, naïvely, "I will not do it again."

"That's right! You see, I'm not interesting or picturesque enough to suspect. When all's said and done, I'm just a poor devil of an Irishman with enough imagination to prevent his doing any particular harm in this world, and enough money to prevent his doing any special good. My name is Edward Fitzgerald Blake, and I have an old barracks of a castle in County Clare. I have five aunts, seven uncles, and twenty-four first cousins, every one of whom thinks me a lost soul; but I have neither sister nor brother, wife nor child to help or hinder me. There now! I have gone to confession, and you must give me absolution and an easy penance!"

Max laughed. "Thank you, monsieur!"

"Not 'monsieur,' for goodness' sake! Plain Ned, if you don't mind."

"Ned?" The slight uncertainty, coupled with the foreign intonation, lent a charm to the name.

"That's it! But I never heard it sound half so well before. Personally, it always struck me as being rather like its owner—of no particular significance. But I must be coming down to earth again, I have an appointment with our friend McCutcheon at three o'clock." He drew out his watch. "Oh, by the powers and dominations, I have only two minutes to keep it in! How the time has raced! I say, there's an auto-taxi looming on the horizon, over by the Invalides; I must catch it if I can. Come, boy! Put your best foot foremost!"

Laughing and running like a couple of school-boys, they zigzagged through the labyrinth of formal trees, and secured the cab as it was wheeling toward the *quais*.

"Good!" exclaimed Blake. "And now, what next? Can I give you a lift?" His foot was on the step of the cab, his fingers on the handle of the door, his face, flushed from his run and from the cold, looked pleasantly young. The boy's heart went out to him in a glow of comradeship.

"No, I will remain here. But I—I want to see you soon again. May I?"

"May you? Say the word! To-morrow? To-night?" The cab was snorting impatience; Blake opened the door and stepped inside.

The boy colored. "To-night?"

"Right! To-night it shall be! To-night we'll scale the heights." He held out his hand.

Max took it smilingly. "You have not asked me where I live."

"Never thought of it! Where is it?"

"The Hôtel Railleux, in the rue de Dunkerque."

"Not a very festive locality! But sufficient for the day, eh? Well, I'll be outside the door of the Hôtel Railleux at nine o'clock."

"At nine o'clock. I shall be awaiting you."

"Right again! Good-bye! It's been a good morning."

Max smiled, a smile that seemed to have caught something of the sun's brightness, something of the promise of spring trembling in the pale sky.

"It has been a good morning. I shall never forget it."

Blake laughed. "Don't say that, boy! We'll oust it with many a better."

He released the boy's hand and gave the address to the chauffeur. There was a moment's pause, a rasp and wrench of machinery, and the willing little cab flew off toward the nearest bridge.

Max stood watching it, obsessed by a strange sensation. This morning he had been utterly alone; this morning the fair, cold face of Paris had been immobile and speculative. Now a miracle had come to pass; the coldness had been swept aside and the beauty, the warm, palpitating humanity had shone into his eyes, dazzling him—fascinating him.

CHAPTER VIII

NINE o'clock found Max waiting in the rue de Dunkerque. Paris, consummate actress that she is, was already arraying herself for the nightly appeal to her audience of pleasure-seekers. Like a dancer in her dressing-room, she but awaited the signal to step forth into the glamour of the footlights; the rouge was on her lips, the stars shone in her hair, the jewelled slippers caressed her light feet. Even here, in the colorless region of the Gare du Nord, the perfumed breath of the courtesan city crept like the fumes of wine; the insidious sense of nocturnal energy swept the brain, as the traffic jingled by and the crowds upon the footpaths thronged into the *cafés* and overflowed into the roadway.

To the boy, walking slowly up and down, with eager eyes that sought the one face among the many, the scene came as a joyous revelation that called inevitably to his youth and his vitality. He made no pretence of analyzing his sensations: he was stirred, intoxicated by the movement, the lights, the naturalness and artificiality that walked hand-in-hand in so strange a fellowship. A new excitement, unlike the excitement of the morning, was at work within him; his blood danced, his brain answered to every fleeting picture. He was in that subtlest of all moods when the mind swings out upon the human tide, comprehending its every ripple with a deep intuition that seems like a retrospective knowledge. He had never until this moment stood alone in a Paris street at night; he had never before rubbed shoulders with a Parisian night crowd; but the inspiration was there—the exaltation—that made him one with this restless throng of men and women whose antecedents were unknown to him, whose future was veiled to his gaze.

The sensation culminated when, out of the crowd, a hand was laid upon his shoulder and a familiar voice rose above the babble of sound.

"Well, and are we girded for the heights?"

It came at the right moment, it lilted absolutely with his thoughts—the soft, pleasant tones, the easy friendliness that seemed to accept all things as they came. His instant answer was to smile into the Irishman's face and to press the arm that had been slipped through his.

"It's too early for anything very characteristic, but there are always impressions to be got."

Again the boy replied by a pressure of the arm, and together he and Blake began to walk. The strange pleasure of yielding himself to this man's will filtered through Max's being again, as it had done that morning, painting the world in rosy tints. The situation was anomalous, but he ignored the anomaly. His boats were burned; the great ice-bound sea protected him from the past; he was here in Paris, in the first moments of a fascinating present, under the guardianship of this comrade whose face he had never seen until yesterday, whose very name was still unfamiliar to his ears. It was anomalous, but it held happiness; and who, equipped with youth and health, starting out upon life's road, stops to question happiness? He was the adventuring prince in the fairy-tale: every step was taken upon enchanted ground.

Nothing gave him cause for quarrel as they made their way onward. Even the Boulevard de Magenta, with its prosaic tram-lines, its large, cheap shops, its common *brasseries* and spanning railway bridge, seemed a place of promise; and as they passed on, ever mounting toward Montmartre, his brain quickened to new joy, new curiosity in every flaunting advertisement, every cobble-stone in the long steep way of the Boulevard Barbés, the rue de la Nature, and the rue de Clignancourt, until at length they emerged into the rue André de Sarte—that narrow street, quaint indeed in its dark old houses and its small, mysterious wine shops that savor of Italy or Spain.

They paused, at the corner of the rue André de Sarte, by the doorway of an old, overcrowded curio shop—the curio shop that in time to come was destined to become so familiar a landmark to them both, to stand sentinel at the gateway of so many emotions.

The lights, the shadows, the effects were all uncertain in this strange and fascinating neighborhood. High above them, white against the winter sky, glimmered the domes of the Sacré-Coeur, looking down in symbolic silence upon the restless city; to the left stretched the rue Ronsard, with its deserted market and lonely pavement; to the right, the Escalier de Sainte-Marie, picturesque as its name, wound its precipitous way apparently to the very stars, while at their feet, creeping upward to the threshold of the church, was the plantation of rocks, trees, and holly bushes that in the mysterious darkness seemed aquiver with a thousand whispered secrets. There was deep contrast here to the excitement, the vivacity of the boulevards; it seemed as if some shadow from the white domes above had given sanctuary to the spirit of the place—the familiar spirit of the time-stained houses, the stone steps worn by many feet, the dark, naked trees.

The boy's hand again pressed his companion's arm.

"What are those steps?" He pointed to the right.

"The Escalier de Sainte-Marie; they lead up to the rue Müller, and, if you desire it, to the Sacré-Coeur itself. Shall we climb?"

"But yes! Certainly!" The boy's voice was tense and eager. He hurried forward, drawing his companion with him, and side by side they began the mounting of the stone steps—those steps, flanked by the row of houses, that rise one above the other, as if emulous to attain the skies.

Up they went, their ears attentive to the conflicting sounds that drifted forth from the doorways, their nostrils assailed by the faintly pungent scent of the shrubs in the plantation. Higher and higher they climbed, sensible with each step of a greater isolation, of a rarer, clearer air. Above them, in one of the higher houses in the rue Müller, some one was playing a fiddle, and the piercing sweet sounds came through the night like a human voice, adding the poignancy, the passion and pathos of human things to the aloofness and unreality of the scene.

The boy was the first to catch this lonely music, and as though it called to him in some curious way, he suddenly freed his arm from Blake's and ran forward up the steps.

When Blake overtook him he had passed up the rue Müller, and was leaning over the wooden paling that fronts the Sacré-Coeur, his elbows resting upon it, his face between his hands, his eyes held by the glitter of Paris lying below him.

Blake came quietly up behind him. "I thought you had given me the slip."

He turned. Again the light of inspiration, the curious illumination was apparent in his face.

"This is most wonderful!" he said. "Most wonderful! It is here that I shall live. Here—here—with Paris at my feet."

Blake laughed—laughed good-humoredly at the finality, the artless arrogance of the tone.

"It may not be so easy to find a dwelling in the shadow of the Sacré-Coeur."

Max looked at him with calm, grave eyes. "I do not consider difficulties, monsieur. It is here that I shall live. My mind is made up."

"But this is not the artists' quarter. You may seek your inspiration in Montmartre, but you must have your studio across the river."

"Why must I? What compels me?"

The Irishman shrugged his shoulders. "Nothing compels you, but it is the thing to do. You can live here, certainly, if you want to—there is no law to forbid it—and you can find a studio on the Boulevard de Clichy; but the other is the thing to do."

The boy smiled his young wise smile. "Monsieur, there is only one thing to do—the thing one wants to do, the thing the heart compels. If I am to know Paris I will know her from here—study her, love her from here. This place is one of miracle. One might know life here, living in the skies. Listen! That musician knows it!" He thrust out his hand impulsively and caught Blake's in a pressure full of nervous tension, full of magnetism. "What is it he plays? Tell me! Tell me!"

His touch, his excitement fired Blake's Celtic blood, banishing his mood of criticism.

"The man is playing scraps from *Louise*—Charpentier's *Louise*."

"I have never heard *Louise*."

"What! And you a student of Paris? Why, it's Charpentier's hymn to Montmartre. Listen, now!" His voice quickened. "He's playing a bit out of the night scene. He's playing the declaration of the *Noctambule*:

"Je suis le Plaisir de Paris!
Je vais vers les Amantes—que le Désir tourmente!
Je vais, cherchant les coeurs qu'oubli a le bonheur.
Là-bas glanant le Rire, ici semant l'Envie,
Prêchant partout le droit de tous à la folie;
Je suis le Procureur de la grande Cité!
Ton humble serviteur—ou ton maître!"

He murmured the words below his breath, pausing as the music deepened with the passion of the player and the sinister song poured into the night.

Then came a break, a pause, and the music flowed forth again, but curiously altered, curiously softened in character.

Max's fingers tightened. "Ah, but listen now, my friend!"

Blake turned to him in quick appreciation. "Good! Good! You are an artist! That's Louise singing in the third act, on the day she is to be Muse of Montmartre. It is up here in the little house her lover has provided for her; it is twilight, and she is in the garden, looking down upon all this"— he waved his hand comprehensively—"it is her moment—the triumph and climax of love. Try to think what she is saying!" He paused, and they stood breathless and enchained, while the violin trembled under the hand of its master, vibrant and penetrating.

"What is it she says?" Max whispered the words.

Blake's reply was to murmur the burden of the song in the same hushed way as he had spoken the song of the *Noctambule*.

"Depuis le jour où je me suis donnée, toute fleurie semble ma destinée.
Je crois rêver sous un ciel de féerie, l'âme encore grisée de ton premier baiser!"

But, abruptly—abruptly as a light might be extinguished—the music ceased, and Max released Blake's hand.

"It is all most wonderful," he said; "but the words of that song—they do not quite please me."

"Why? Have you never sung that *'l'âme encore grisée de ton premier baiser*!'"

Then, as if half ashamed of the emotional moment, he gave a little laugh, satirical and yet sad.

"Was there never a little dancer," he added, "never a little model in all these years—and you so very ancient?"

The boy ignored the jest.

"I am not a believer in love," he said, evasively.

"Not a believer in love! Well, upon my soul, the world is getting very old! You look like a child from school, and you talk like some quaint little book I might have picked up on the *quais*. What does it all mean?"

At the perplexity of the tone Max laughed. "Very little, *mon ami*! I am no philosopher; but about this love, I have thought a little, and have gained to a conclusion. It is like this! Light love is desire of pleasure; great love is fear of being alone."

"Then you hold that man should be alone?"

"Why not?" Max shrugged his shoulders. "We come into the world alone; we go out of it alone."

"A cold philosophy!"

"A true one, I think. If more lives were based upon it we would have more achievement and less emotion."

The Irishman's enthusiasm caught sudden fire.

"And who wants less emotion? Isn't emotion the salt of life? Why, where would a poor devil of a wanderer like myself be, if he hadn't the dream in the back of his head that the right woman was waiting for him somewhere?"

Max watched him seriously.

"Then you have never loved?"

"Never loved? God save us! I have been in and out of love ever since I was seventeen. But, bless your heart, that has nothing to do with the right woman!"

Max's intent eyes flashed. "And you think the right woman will be content to take you—after all that?"

Blake came a step nearer, leaning over the parapet, his shoulder touching his companion's.

"Boy," he said, in a changed tone, "listen to me. It's a big subject, this subject of love and liking—too big for me to riddle out, perhaps. But this I know, the world was made as it is, and neither you nor I can change it; no, nor ten thousand cleverer than we! It's all a mystery, and the queerest bit of mystery in it is that a man may go down into the depths and rub shoulders with the worst, and yet keep the soul of him clean for the one woman."

"Don't you think there are men who can do without either the depths or the one woman?"

"There are abnormalities, of course."

Max waived the words. "I am serious. I ask you if you do not believe that there are certain people to whom these things you speak of are poor things—people who believe that they are sufficient unto themselves?"

The other's mouth twisted into a sarcastic smile.

"Show me the man who is sufficient unto himself!"

Swiftly—as swiftly as he had whipped the pencil from his pocket in the *café* that morning—Max stepped back, his head up, his hand resting lightly on the wooden parapet.

"Monsieur! You see him!"

Blake's expression changed to keen surprise; he turned sharply and peered into the boy's face.

"You?" he said, incredulously. "You, a slip of a boy, to ignore the softer side of life and set yourself up against Nature? Take that fairy-tale elsewhere!"

Max laughed. "Very well, my friend, wait and see!"

"And do you know how long I give you to defy the world, the flesh, and the devil? A full-blooded young animal like you!"

"How long?"

"Three months—not a day more."

"Three months!" Max laughed, and, as had happened before, his mood altered with the laugh. The moment of artistic exaltation passed; again he was the boy—the adventurer, brimming with spirits, thirsting to break a lance with life. "Three months! Very well! Wait and see! And, in the mean time, Paris is awake, is she not?"

Blake looked at the laughing face, the bright eyes, and shook his head.

"I believe you're a cluricaun, come all the way from the bogs of Clare! Come here, and take my arm again, or you'll be vanishing into that plantation!"

It is unlikely that Max understood all the other's phrases, but he understood the lenient, bantering tone that had in it a touch of something bordering upon affection, and with a gracious eagerness he stepped forward and slipped his hand through the proffered arm.

"Where are you going to take me?" All the lightness, all the arrogance had melted from his voice, his tone was almost as soft, almost as submissive as a woman's.

Blake looked down upon him. "I hardly know—after that philosophy of yours! I thought of taking you to a little Montmartre *cabaret*, where many a poet wrote his first verses and many an artist sang his first song—a dingy place, but a place with atmosphere."

Max clung to his arm, the light flashing into his eyes. "Oh, my friend, that is the place! That is the place! Let us go—let us run, lest we miss a moment!"

"Good! Then hey for the Boulevard de Clichy and the quest of the great idea!"

CHAPTER IX

THE ascent of the heights had been exciting, the descent held a sense of satisfaction. At a more sober pace, with a finer, less exuberant sense of comradeship, the two passed down the hundred-odd steps of the Escalier de Sainte-Marie, taking an occasional peep into some dark and silent corner, halting here and there to glance into the dimly lighted hallway of some mysterious house. On the upward way they had been all anticipation; now, with appetites appeased, they toyed with their sensations like diners with their dessert.

"Who are the people living in these houses?" The boy put the question in a whisper, as if fearful of disturbing the strange silence, the close secrecy that hung about them.

"The people who live here? God knows! Probably you would find a *blanchisseuse* on the ground floor, and on the fourth a poet or perhaps a musician, like our fiddler of *Louise*. This is the real Bohemia, you know—not the conscious Bohemia, but the true one, that is lawless simply because it knows no laws."

They had come to the end of the steps and were once again traversing the dim rue André de Sarte, the boy's eyes and ears awake to every impression.

"Yes," he said in slow and meditative answer. "Yes, I think I understand. It must be wonderful to be born unfettered."

"I don't know about wonderful; it's a profoundly interesting condition. You get that blending of egoism and originality—daring and scepticism—that may produce the artist or may produce the criminal."

"But you believe that the creature of temperament—of egoism and originality—may spring up in a lawful atmosphere as well as in a lawless one?" The question came softly. Max had ceased to look about him, ceased to observe the streets that grew more crowded, more brightly lighted as they made their downward way.

Blake smiled. "The tares among the wheat, eh?"

"Yes."

"Oh, of course I admit the tares among the wheat; but such growths are mostly unsatisfactory. Forced fruit is never precisely the same as wild fruit."

"Why not?"

"Because, my boy, there is a self-consciousness about all forced things, and the hallmark of the Bohemian is an absolute ingenuousness."

"But to return to your example. Suppose the tare among the wheat had always recognized itself—had always craved to be a tare with other tares—until at length its roots spread and spread and passed beyond the boundary of the wheat-field! Why should it not flourish and lift its head among the weeds?"

"Because, boy, it would have its traditions. It might live forever among the weeds, it might flourish and reign over them, but it would have a reminiscence unknown to them—the knowledge of the years in which it strove to mold itself to the likeness of the wheat before rebellion woke within it. I know! I know! I know Bohemia—love Bohemia—but at best I am only a naturalized Bohemian. I can live on a crust with these good creatures, or I can send my gold flying with theirs, but I'm hanged if, for instance, I can sin in quite the delicious, child-like, whole-hearted way that is their prerogative! I have done most of the things that they have done, but their disarming candor, their simple joy in their exploits, is something debarred to me. It isn't for nothing, I tell you, that I have countless God-fearing generations behind me!"

He spoke jestingly, but his glance, when it met the eager impetuosity of the boy's, was quiet and observant.

"I disagree with you!" Max cried, suddenly. "I disagree with you wholly! Individuality has nothing to do with environment—nothing to do with ancestry."

"Ah, that's not logical! Humanity is only a chain of which we are the last links forged. I have had my own delusions, when I sent the ideal to the right-about and made realism my god, but as time has gone on my theories have gone back on me, and tradition has come into its own, until now I see the skeleton in every beautiful body, and the heart of me craves something behind even the bones—the soul of the creature."

"But that is different, because your desire and your theory have been the common desire and theory—the things that burn themselves out. My theory is not of the body, it is of the mind. I only contend that in all the greater concerns of life I am a being perfectly competent to stand alone."

"My dear boy, by the mercy of God all the ideas of youth are reversible! My fire has been extinguished; your ice will hold until the sun is in the zenith, and not one moment longer."

"I deny it! I deny it!"

He spoke with a fine defiance. He paused, the more convincingly to express himself; but even as he paused, his eyes and his mind were suddenly opened to a fresh impression, were lured from the moment of gravity, caught and held by the lights and crowds into which they had abruptly emerged—lights and crowds through which the pervading sense of a pleasure-chase stole like a scent borne on a breeze.

"Where are we?" he said, sharply. "What place is this?"

"The Boulevard de Clichy. Come, boy! Discussions are over. The curtain is up; the play is on!" Without apology, Blake caught his shoulder and swung him out into the roadway, as he had swung him across the Esplanade des Invalides that morning. "Come! I'm going to insist upon a new medicine; my first prescription was not the right one. You're too theoretical to-night for a place of traditions. We'll shelve our little *cabaret* till some hour when genius burns, and instead I'll plunge you straight into common frivolity, as though you were some Cockney tourist getting his week-end's worth! Have you ever heard of the Bal Tabarin?"

"Never. And I would much—- much rather—"

"No, you wouldn't! I have spoken. Come along!"

Before Max could resist he was swept across the wide roadway, round a corner, and through what looked to him like the entrance to a theatre.

There were many people gathered about this entrance: men in evening dress, men in shabby, insignificant clothes, women in varying types of costume. Max would have lingered to study the little crowd, but Blake looked upon his hesitancy with distrust, and still retaining the grip upon his shoulder, half led, half pushed him through a short passage straight into the dancing-hall, where on the instant his ears were assailed by a flood of joyous sound in the form of a rhythmic, swinging waltz—his eyes blinked before the flood of light to which the Parisian pins his faith for public pleasures— and his nostrils were assailed by a penetrating smell of scent and smoke. Dazed and a little frightened he drew back against a wall, overwhelmed by the atmosphere. Superficially there was little astonishing in the Bal Tabarin; but to the uninitiated being with wide eyes it seemed in very truth the gay world, with its stirring music, its walls flaunting their mirrors and their paintings, its galleries with their palms and railed-in boxes, and beneath—subtly suggestive adjunct—- the bars, with their countless bottles of champagne, bottles of every conceivable size built up in serried rows as though Venus would raise an altar to Bacchus.

Leaning back against the wall, Max surveyed the scene, fascinated and confused. A thousand questions rose to his lips, but not one found utterance. Again and yet again his bright glance ranged from the gay red of the bandsmen's coats to the lines of spectators sitting at the little tables under the galleries, returning inevitably and persistently to the pivot of the scene—a space of pale-colored, waxed floor in the centre of the hall, where innumerable couples whirled or glided to the tune of the waltz.

He had seen many a ball in progress, but never had he seen dancing as he saw it here, where grace rubbed shoulders with absolute *gaucherie*, and wild hilarity mingled unashamed with a curious seriousness—one had almost said iciness—of demeanor. The women, who formed the definite interest of the picture, were for the most part young, with a youth that lent slimness and suppleness to the figure and permeated through the freely used paint and powder like some unpurchasable essence. Among this crowd of women some were fair, some brown, a few red-haired, but the vast majority belonged to the type that was to become familiar to Max as the true *Montmartroise*—the girl possessed of the dead white face, the red, sensual lips, the imperfectly chiselled nose, attractive in its very imperfection, and the eyes—black, brown, or gray—that see in a single glance to the bottom of a man's soul. Richness of apparel was not conspicuous among them, but all wore their clothes with the sense of fitness that possesses the *Parisienne*. Each head was held at the angle that best displayed the well-dressed hair and cleverly trimmed hat; each light skirt was held waist-high with a dexterity that allowed the elaborate petticoat to sweep out from the neat ankles in a whirl of lace.

Some of these girls danced with pleasure-seeking young Englishmen or Americans in conventional evening dress, others with little clerks in ill-fitting clothes and bowler hats, while many chose each other for partners, and glided over the waxed floor in a perfection of motion difficult to excel.

Leaning back against the wall, he watched the picture, gaining courage with familiarity, and unconsciously a little gasp of regret parted his lips as the waltz crashed to a finish and the dancers moved in a body toward the tables and the bars. Then for the first time he remembered Blake, and, looking round, saw his green eyes fixed upon him in a quizzical, satirical glance.

"Well, the devil has a pleasant way with him, there's no denying it! Come and find a seat! The next will be one of the special dances—a *can-can* or a Spanish dance. I'd like you to see it."

"Who will dance it?"

"Who? Oh, probably, if it's the *can-can*, half a dozen of the best-looking of those girls with the elaborate *lingerie*. They're paid to dance here. They're part of the show."

"I see!" Max was interested, but his voice did not sound very certain. "And the others?" he added. "That fair girl, for example, sitting at the table with the hideous, untidy little man in the brown suit?"

Blake's eyes sought out the couple. "What! The two smiling into each other's eyes? Those, my boy, are true citizens of the true Bohemia. She is probably a little dressmaker's assistant, whose whole available capital is sunk in that Pierrot hat and those pretty shoes; and he—well, he might be anything with that queer, clever head! But he's probably a poet, in the guise of a journalist, picking up a few francs when he can and where he can. A precarious existence, but lived in Elysium! Wish I were twenty—and unanalytical! Come along! It's to be a Spanish dance. You mustn't miss it!"

They made their way forward, pushing toward the open space, upon which a shaft of limelight had been thrown, the better to display the faces and figures of eight Spanish women who, dressed in their national costume, stood preening themselves like vain birds, tossing their heads and showing their white teeth in sudden smiles of recognition to their friends among the audience. While Max's interested eyes were travelling from one face to another, the signal was given, and with an electric spontaneity the dance began. It was a wonderful dance—a dance of sensuous contortion crossed and arrested at every moment by the fierce flash of pride, the swift gesture of contempt indicative of the land that had conceived it—a dance that would diminish to the merest sway of the body accompanied by the slow, hypnotic enticement of half-closed eyes, and then, as a fan might shut or open, leap back in an instant to a barbaric frenzy of motion in which loosened hair and flaming draperies carried the beholder's senses upon a tide of intoxication.

Max was conscious of quickened heart-beats and flushed cheeks as the dancers paused and the high, shrill call that indicated an encore pierced through the smoke-laden air; and without question he turned and followed Blake to one of the many tables standing in the shadow of the galleries.

The table was packed tightly between other tables, and in the moment of intoxication he had no glance to spare for his neighbors. Even Blake's voice when it came to him sounded far away and impersonal.

"Sit down, boy! What will you drink?"

"What you drink, *mon ami*, I will drink."

He sat down and, with a new exuberance, threw himself back in his seat. It was a moment of bravado that reckoned not at all with circumstance;

his gesture was imperiously reckless, the space about him was crowded to suffocation; by a natural sequence of events his head came into sharp contact with the waving plumes of a hat at the table behind him.

With volubility and dispatch the owner of the hat expressed her opinion of his awkwardness; one or two people near them laughed, and, flushing a desperate red, he turned, raised his hat, and offered an apology.

The possessor of the feathers was a woman of thirty who looked ten years older than her age; her face was unhealthily pale even beneath its mask of powder, and her eyes were curiously lifeless, but her clothes were costly and her figure fine, if a trifle robust. At sound of the boy's voice she turned. Her movement was slow and deliberate; her gaze, in which a dull resentment smouldered, passed over his confused, flushed face, and rested upon Blake's; then a light, if light it might be called, glimmered in her eyes, and her immobile face relaxed into a smile.

"'Allo, mon cher! But I thought you had dropped out of life!"

The boy, with a startled movement, turned his eyes on Blake; but Blake was smiling at the woman with the same pleasant smile—half humorous, half satirical—that he had bestowed dispassionately upon the young Englishman in the train the night before, and upon the little *café* proprietress of the rue Fabert—the smile that all his life had been a passport to the world's byways.

"What! you, Lize!" he was saying easily, and with only the faintest shadow of surprise. "Well, if I have been dead, I am now resurrected! Let's toast old times, since you are alone. *Garçon! Garçon!*"

Out of the crowd a waiter answered his call. Wine was brought, three glasses were brought and filled, while Max watched the performance—watched the ease and naturalness of it with absorbed wonder.

"Lize," said Blake, as the waiter disappeared, "my friend who dared to interfere with that marvellous hat is called Max. Won't you smile upon him?"

Max blushed again, he could not have told why, and the lady smiled—a vague, detached smile.

"A pretty boy!" she said. "He ought to have been a woman." Then, sensible of having discharged her duty, she turned again to Blake.

"And the world, *mon cher*? It has been kind to you?"

Blake laughed and drank some of his wine. "Oh, I can't complain! If it isn't quite the same world that it was, the fault's in me. I'm getting old, Lize! Eight-and-thirty come next March!"

A palpable chill touched the woman; she shivered, then laughed a little hysterically, and finished her wine.

"Ssh! Ssh! Don't say such things!"

Blake refilled her glass. "I was jesting. A man is as old as he feels; a woman—" He lifted his own glass and smiled into her eyes with a certain kindliness of understanding. "Come, Lize! The old times aren't so far behind us! 'Twas only yesterday that Jacques Aujet painted you as the Bacchante in his 'Masque of Folly.' Do you remember how angry you were when he used to kiss you, and the grape juice used to run into your hair and down your neck? Why, 'twas hardly yesterday!"

The woman looked down, and for a moment a shadow seemed to rest upon her—a something tangible and even fearful, that lent to her mask-like face a momentary humanity.

"*Mon ami*," she said, in a toneless voice, "do you remember that Jacques is ten years dead?"

Then suddenly, as if fleeing from her own fear, she looked up again, surfeiting her senses with the crowds, the lights, the smoke and scent and crashing music.

"But what folly!" she cried. "Life goes on! The same round, is it not so? Life and love and jealousy! Come, little monsieur, what have you to say?"

She turned to Max, sitting silent and attentive; but even as she turned, there was a flutter of interest among the tables behind her, and a young girl ran up, laying her hand upon her arm.

"Lize!" she said, with a little gasp. "Lize! He is here—and I am afraid."

Max looked up. It was the girl he had pointed out to Blake as sitting at the table with the ugly, clever-looking man; and his eyes opened wide in fresh surprise, fresh interest as he studied the details of her appearance. She was of that most attractive type, the fair *Parisienne*; her complexion was of wax-like paleness, her blonde hair broke into little waves and tendrils under her Pierrot hat, while her eyes, clear and blue, proclaimed her extreme youth. As she stood now, clinging to the elder woman's arm, her mind showed itself in an utter naturalness, an utter disregard of the fact that she was observed. Max remembered Blake's words—"These are true citizens of the true Bohemia."

But the woman Lize had turned at her cry, and laid a plump, jewelled hand over her slim, nervous fingers.

"Jacqueline! My child, what is wrong?"

"He is here! And Lucien is here! And I am afraid!"

The words were vague, but the elder woman asked for no explanation.

"Does Lucien know?"

The girl shook her head.

"And this beast—where is he?"

The girl, silent from emotional excitement, nodded toward the opposite bar, and a light flickered up into Lize's eyes as she scanned the crowd divided from them by the space of waxed floor, from which the Spanish dancers had just retreated.

Max raised his glass and drank some of his champagne. His first dread of the place was gripping him again—exciting him, confusing him. All about him, like the scent-laden atmosphere itself, moved the crowd— the girls of Montmartre and their cavaliers. Everywhere was that sense of conscious enjoyment—that grasping of the mere moment that the Parisian has reduced to a science. It enveloped him like a veil—the artless artificiality of Paris! Everywhere fans emblazoned with the words Bal Tabarin fluttered like butterflies, everywhere cigar smoke mingled with the essences from the women's clothes, but beneath it all lurked a something unanalyzed, dimly understood, that chained his imagination. It hung about him; it crouched behind the women's expectant eyes; then suddenly it sprang forth like an ugly beast into a perfumed garden.

It came in a moment: a little scuffle at the bar opposite, as a heavy, fair-bearded man disengaged himself from the crowd about him, a little flutter of interest as he made an unsteady way across the waxed floor, a little smothered scream from the girl as he lurched up to the table and paused, gazing at her with angry, bloodshot eyes.

For a second of silence the two looked at each other—the girl with a frightened, fascinated gaze, the man with the slow insolence that drink induces. At last, muttering some words in a guttural tongue unknown to the boy, he swayed forward and laid a heavy red hand upon her shoulder.

The gesture was brutal, masterful, expressive. A sense of mental sickness seized upon Max; while the woman Lize suddenly braced herself, changing from the inert, half-hypnotized creature of a moment before into a being of fury.

"*Sapristi!*" she cried aloud. "A pretty lover to come wooing!" And she added a phrase that had never found place in Max's vocabulary, and at which the surrounding people laughed.

The words and the laugh were tow to the fire of the man's rage. He freed the girl's arm and struck the table with a resounding violence that made the glasses dance.

It was the signal for a scene. In a second people at the neighboring tables rose to their feet, chairs were overturned, a torrent of words poured forth from both actors and spectators, while through everything and above everything the band poured forth an intoxicating waltz.

Max, forgetful of himself, stood with wide eyes and white, absorbed face. He saw the climax of the scene—saw the bearded man lean across the table and seize the girl by the waist—saw, to his breathless amazement, the woman Lize suddenly grasp the champagne bottle and fling it full into his face; then, abruptly, out of the maze of sensations, he felt some one grip him by the shoulder and march him straight through the crowd, into the vestibule, on into the open air.

Outside, in the glare of the lights, in the cold fresh air of the street, he turned, white and shaking, upon Blake.

"Why did you do it?" he demanded. "I think you were a coward! I would not have run away!"

Blake laughed, though his own voice was a little uneven, his own face looked a little pale. "There are some battle-fields, boy, where discretion is obviously the better part of valor! I'm sorry I brought you here, though they generally manage to avoid this sort of thing."

Max still looked indignant.

"But she was a friend of yours!"

"A friend! My God!"

"But she called you her friend!"

"Friendship is a much-defaced coin that poverty-stricken humanity will always pass! Our friendship, boy, consists in the fact that she once loved and was loved by a man I knew. Poor Lize! She had a bit too much heart for the game she played. And the heart is there still, for all the paint and powder and morphine she fights the world with! Poor Lize!"

Max's eyes were still wide, but the anger had died down.

"And the girl?" he questioned. "The girl, and the brute, and the man with the clever head? What have they all to do with each other and with her?"

Blake's lips parted to reply, but closed again.

"Never mind, boy!" he said, gently. "Come along back to your hotel; you've seen enough life for one night."

CHAPTER X

WITH a new day began a new epoch. On the morning following the night, of first adventure Max woke in his odd, mountainous bed at the Hôtel Railleux kindling to fresh and definite sensations. In a manner miraculously swift, miraculously smooth and subtle, he had discovered a niche in this strange city, and had elected to fit himself to it. A knowledge of present, a pledge of future interests seemed to permeate the atmosphere, and he rose and dressed with the grave deliberation of the being who sees his way clear before him.

It was nine o'clock when he entered the *salle-à-manger*, and one sharp glance brought the satisfying conviction that it was deserted save for the presence of the assiduous young waiter, who came hurrying forward as though no span of hours and incidents separated yesterday's meal from to-day's.

His attentive attitude was unrelaxed, his smile was as deferential as before, but this morning he found a less responsive guest. Max was filled with a quiet assurance that debarred familiarity; Max, in fine, was bound upon a quest, and the submissive young waiter, the bare eating-room, Paris itself, formed but the setting and background in his arrogant young mind to the greatness of the mission.

The thought—the small seed of thought that was responsible for the idea had been sown last night, as he leaned over the parapet fronting the Sacré-Coeur, looking down upon the city with its tangle of lights; and later, in the hours of darkness, when he had tossed on his heavy bed, too excited to lure sleep, it had fructified with strange rapidity, growing and blossoming with morning into definite resolve.

He drank his coffee and ate his roll in happy preoccupation, and, having finished his meal, left the room and went quietly down the stairs and through the glass door of the hotel.

The frost still held; Paris still smiled; and, buttoning up his coat, he paused for a moment on the doorstep to turn his face to the copper-red sun and breathe in the crisp, invigorating air; then, with a quaintly decisive manner that seemed to set sentiment aside, he walked to the edge of the footpath and hailed a passing *fiacre*.

"To the church of the Sacré-Coeur," he commanded.

The *cocher* received the order with a grumble, looked from his unreliable horse to the frosty roadway, and was about to shake his head in definite negation when Max cajoled him with a more ingratiating voice.

"The rue Ronsard, then? Will you take me to the corner of the rue Ronsard?"

The man grumbled again, and shrugged his shoulders until his ears disappeared in the shaggy depths of his fur cape; but, when all hope seemed fled, he laconically murmured the one word *"Bon!"* whipped up his horse, and started off with a fine disregard of whether his fare had taken his seat or been left behind upon the footpath.

To those who know Montmartre only as an abode of night—a place of light and laughter and folly—Montmartre in the day, Montmartre at half-past nine in the morning, comes as a revelation. The whole picture is as a coin reversed. The theatres, the music-halls, the *cabarets* all lie with closed eyes, innocently sleeping; the population of pleasure-seekers and pleasure-mongers has disappeared as completely as if some magician had waved his wand, and in its place the streets teem with the worker—the early, industrious shopkeeper and the householder bent upon a profitable morning's marketing. Max, gazing from the *fiacre* with attentive eyes, followed the varying scenes, while his horse wound a careful and laborious way up the cobble-paved streets, and noted with an artist's eye the black, hurrying figures of the men, cloaked and hooded against the cold, and the black, homely figures of the women, silhouetted against the sharp greens and yellows of the laden vegetable stalls at which they chattered and bargained.

It was all noisy, interesting, alive; and as he watched the pleasant, changing pictures, his courage strengthened, his belief in his own star mounted higher; the decision of last night stood out, as so few nocturnal decisions can stand out, unashamed and justified in the light of day.

At the corner where the rue André de Sarte joins the rue Ronsard he dismissed his cab, and with a young inquisitiveness in all that concerned the quarter, paused to look into the old curio shop, no longer closed as on the previous night, but open and inviting in its dingy suggestion of mysteries unsolved.

Now—at this moment of recording the boy's doings—the curio shop no longer exists at the corner of the rue André de Sarte; it has faded into the unknown with its coppers and brasses, its silver and tinsel, its woollen and silk stuffs; but on that January morning of his first coming it still held place, its musty perfumes still conjured dreams, its open doorway, festooned with antique objects, still offered tempting glimpses into the long and dim interior, where an old Jew, presiding genius of the place, lurked like a spider in the innermost circle of his web.

Max lingered, drawn into self-forgetfulness by the blending of faded hues, the atmosphere of must and spices, the air of age indescribable that veiled the place. He loitered about the windows, peeped in at the doorway, would even have ventured across the threshold had not a ponderous figure, rising silently from a heap of cushions upon the floor of the inmost room, sent him hastening round the corner, guiltily conscious that it was new lamps and not old he was here to light.

The interest of his mission flowed back, sharpened by the momentary break, and it was with very swift steps that he ran up the Escalier de Sainte-Marie to the rue Müller; there, in the rue Müller, he paused, his back to the green plantation, his face to the row of houses rising one above the other, each with its open doorway, each with its front of brick and plaster, its iron balcony from which hung the inevitable array of blankets, rugs, and mattresses absorbing the morning air.

To say that, in the mystic silence of the previous night and restless hours of the dawn, Max had vowed to himself that here in the rue Müller he would make a home, and to add that, coming in the light of day, he found a door open to him, sounds at the least fabulous; yet, as he stood there—eager, alert, with face lifted expectantly, and bright gaze winging to right and left—fable was made fact: the legend '*Appartement à louer*' caught his glance like a pronouncement of fate.

It sounds fabulous, it sounds preposterous, and yet it obtains, to be accounted for only by the fact that in this curious world there are certain beings to whom it is given to say of all things with naïve faith, not 'I shall seek,' but 'I shall find.'

Max had never doubted that, if courage were high enough to undertake the quest, absolute success awaited him. He read the legend again, '*Appartement à louer 5ième étage. Gaz: l'eau,*' and without hesitation crossed the rue Müller and passed through the open door.

The difference was vast between his nervous entry thirty-six hours ago into the Hôtel Railleux and the boldness of his step now. The difference between secret night and candid morning lay in the two proceedings—the difference between self-distrust and self-confidence. Then he had been a creature newly created, looking upon himself and all the world with a sensitive distrust; now he was an individual accepted of others, assured of himself, already beginning to move and have his being in happy self-forgetfulness.

He stepped into the hallway of the strange house and paused to look about him, his only emotion a keen interest that kept every nerve alert. The hallway round which he looked displayed no original features: it was a lofty, rather narrow space, the walls of which—painted to resemble marble—were defaced by time, by the passing of many skirts and the rubbing of many shoulders. In the rear was a second door, composed of glass, and beyond it the suggestion of a staircase of polished oak that sprang upward from the dingy floor in a surprising beauty of panelled dado and fine old banister.

Max's eyes rested upon this staircase: in renewed excitement he hurried down the hall and, regardless of the consequence, beat a quick tattoo with his knuckles upon the glass door.

Silence greeted his imperative summons, and as he waited, listening intently, he became aware of the monotonous hum of a sewing-machine coming through a closed door upon his left.

The knowledge of a human presence emboldened him; again he knocked, this time more sharply, more persistently. Again inattention; then, as he lifted his hand for the third time, the hum of the machine ceased abruptly, the door opened, and he turned to confront a small woman with wispy hair and untidy clothes, whose bodice was adorned with innumerable pins, and at whose side hung a pair of scissors large as shears.

"Monsieur?" Her manner was curt—the manner of one who has been disturbed at some engrossing occupation.

Max felt rebuffed; he raised his hat and bowed with as close an imitation as he could summon of Blake's ingratiating friendliness.

"Madame, you have an *appartement* to let?"

"True, monsieur! An *appartement* on the fifth floor—gas and water." There was pride in the last words, if a grudging pride.

"Precisely! And it is a good *appartement*?"

"No better in Montmartre."

"A sufficiency of light?"

'Light?' The woman smiled in scorn. 'Was it not open to the skies—with those two windows in front, and that balcony?'

Max's excitement kindled.

"Madame, I must see this *appartement*! May I mount now—at once?"

But the matter was no such light one. Madame shook her head. 'Ah, that was not possible!'

'Why not?'

'Ah, well, there was the *concierge*! The *concierge* was out.'

'But the *concierge* would return?'

'Oh yes! It was true he would return!'

The little woman cast a wistful eye on the door of her own room.

'At what hour?'

'Ah! That was a question!'

'This morning?'

'Possibly!'

'This afternoon?'

'Possibly!'

'But not for a certainty?'

'Nothing was entirely certain.'

Anger broke through Max's disappointment. Without a word he turned on his heel and strode down the hall with the air of an offended prince.

The woman watched him with an expressionless face until he reached the door, then something—perhaps his youth, perhaps his brave carriage, perhaps his defiant disappointment—moved her.

"Monsieur!" she called.

He stopped.

"Monsieur, if it is absolutely necessary that you see the *appartement*—"

"It is. Absolutely necessary." Max ran back.

"Then, monsieur, I will conduct you up-stairs."

The suggestion was greedily seized upon. This *appartement* on the fifth floor had grown in value with each moment of denial.

"Thank you, madame, a thousand times!"

"Shall we mount?"

"On the moment, if you will."

Through the glass door they went, and up the stairs, mounting higher and ever higher in an unbroken silence. Half way up each flight of stairs there was a window through which the light fell upon the bare oak steps, proving them to be spotless and polished as the floor of a convent. It was an unexpected quality, this rigid cleanliness, and the boy acknowledged it with a mute and deep satisfaction.

Upon each landing were two doors—closed doors that sturdily guarded whatever of secrecy might lie behind, and at each of these silent portals Max glanced with that intent and searching look that one bestows upon objects that promise to become intertwined with one's daily life. At last the ascent was made, the goal reached, and he paused on the last step of the stairs to survey the coveted fifth floor.

It was as bare, as scrupulously clean as were the other landings; but his quick glance noted that while the door upon the left was plain and unadorned as the others he had passed, that upon the right bore a small brass plate engraved with the name 'L. Salas.'

This, then, was his possible neighbor! He scanned the name attentively.

"This is the fifth floor, madame?"

"The fifth floor, monsieur!" Without ceremony the little woman went forward and, to his astonishment, rapped sharply upon the door with the brass plate.

Max started. "Madame! The *appartement* is not occupied?"

The only reply that came to him was the opening of the door by an inch or two and the hissing whisper of a conversation of which he caught no word. Then the lady of the scissors looked round upon him, and the door closed.

"One moment, monsieur, while madame throws on a garment!"

A sudden loss of nerve, a sudden desire for flight seized upon Max. He had mounted the stairs anticipating the viewing of empty rooms, and now he was confronted with a furnished and inhabited *appartement*, and commanded to wait 'while madame threw on a garment'! A hundred speculations crowded to his mind. Into what *milieu* was he about to be hurled? What sordid morning scene was he about to witness? In a strange confusion of ideas, the white face of the woman Lize sprang to his imagination, coupled with the memory of the empty champagne bottle and the battered tray of the first night at the Hôtel Railleux. A deadly sensitiveness oppressed him; he turned sharply to his guide.

"Madame! Madame! It is an altogether unreasonable hour to intrude—"

The reopening of the door on the right checked him, and a gentle voice broke across his words:

"Now, madame, if you will!"

He turned, his heart still beating quickly, and a sudden shame at his own thoughts—a sudden relief so strong as almost to be painful—surged through him.

The open door revealed a woman of forty-five, perhaps of fifty, clothed in a meagre black skirt and a plain linen wrapper of exquisite cleanliness. It was this cleanliness that struck the note of her personality—that fitted her as a garment, accentuating the quiet austerity of her thin figure, the streaks of gray in her brown hair, the pale face marked with suffering and sympathy and repression.

With an instinctive deference the boy bared his head.

"Madame," he stammered, "I apologize profoundly for my intrusion at such an hour."

"Do not apologize, monsieur. Enter, if you will!" She drew back, smiling a little, and making him welcome by a simple gesture. "We are anxious, I assure you, to find a tenant for the *appartement*; my husband's health is not what it was, and we find it necessary to move into the country."

He followed her into a tiny hall; and with her fingers on the handle of an inner door, she looked at him again in her gentle, self-possessed way.

"You will excuse my husband, monsieur! He is an invalid and cannot rise from his chair."

She opened the inner door, and Max found himself in a bedroom, plain in furniture and without adornment, but possessing a large window, the full light from which was falling with pathetic vividness on the shrunken figure and wan, expressionless face of a very old man who sat huddled in a shabby leathern arm-chair. This arm-chair had been drawn to the window to catch the wintry sun, and pathos unspeakable lay in the contrasts of the picture— the eternal youth in the cold, dancing beams—the waste, the frailty of human things in the inert figure, the dim eyes, the folded, twitching hands.

The old man looked up as the little party entered, and his eyes sought his wife's with a mute, appealing glance; then, with a slight confusion, he turned to Max, and his shaking hand went up instinctively to the old black skullcap that covered his head.

"He wishes to greet you, monsieur, but he has not the strength." The woman's voice dropped to tenderness, and she stooped and arranged the rug about the shrunken knees. "If you will come this way, I will show you the *salon*."

She moved quietly forward, opening a second door.

"You see, monsieur, it is all very convenient. In summer you can throw the windows open and pass from one room to the other by way of the balcony."

She moved from the bedroom into the *salon* as she spoke, Max and the lady of the pins following.

"See, monsieur! It is quite a good room."

Max, still subdued by the vision of age, went forward silently, but as he entered this second room irrepressible surprise possessed him. Here was an atmosphere he had not anticipated. A soft, if faded, carpet covered the floor; a fine old buffet stood against the wall; antique carved chairs were drawn up to a massive table that had obviously known more spacious surroundings; while upon the walls, from floor to ceiling, were pictures— pictures of all sizes, pictures obviously from the same hand, on the heavy gold frames of which the name 'L. Salas' stood out conspicuously in proof of former publicity.

"Madame!" He turned to the sad-faced woman, the enthusiasm of a fellow-craftsman instantly kindled. "Madame! You are an artist? This is your work?"

The woman caught the sympathy, caught the fire of interest, and a faint flush warmed her cheek.

"Alas, no, monsieur! I am not artistic. It is my husband who is the creator of these." She waved her hand proudly toward the walls. "My husband is an artist."

"A renowned artist!"

It was the woman of the pins and scissors who spoke, surprising Max, not by the sudden sound of her voice, but by her sudden warmth of feeling. Again Blake's words came back—'These are the true citizens of the true Bohemia!'—and he looked curiously from one to the other of the women, so utterly apart in station, in education, in ideals, yet bound by a common respect for art.

"It is my loss," he said, quietly, "that I did not, until to-day, know of M. Salas."

"But no, monsieur! What would you know of twenty years ago? It is true that then my husband had a reputation; but, alas, time moves quickly— and the world is for the young!"

She smiled again, gently and patiently, and a sudden desire seized Max to lift and kiss one of her thin, work-worn hands. The whole pitiful story of a vogue outlived, of a generation pushed aside, breathed in the silence of these fifth-floor rooms.

"They must be a great pride to you, madame—these pictures."

"These, monsieur—and the fact that he is still with me. We can dispense with anything save the being we love—is it not so? But I must not detain you, talking of myself! The other rooms are still to see! This, monsieur, is our second bedroom! And this the kitchen!"

Max, following her obediently, took one peep into what was evidently her own bedroom—a tiny apartment of rigid simplicity, in which a narrow bed, with a large black crucifix hanging above it, seemed the only furniture, and passed on into the kitchen, a room scarce larger than a cupboard, in which a gas-stove and a water-tap promised future utility.

"See, monsieur! Everything is very convenient. All things are close at hand for cooking, and the light is good. And now, perhaps, you would wish to pass back into the *salon* and step out upon the balcony?"

Still silent, still preoccupied, he assented, and they passed into the room so eloquent of past hours and dwindled fortunes.

"See, monsieur! The view is wonderful! Not to-day, perhaps, for the frost blurs the distances; but in the spring—a little later in the year—"

Crossing the room, she opened the long French window and stepped out upon the narrow iron balcony.

Max followed, and, moving to her side, stood gazing down upon the city of his dreams. For long he stood absorbed in thought, then he turned and looked frankly into her face.

"Madame," he said, softly, "it is a place of miracle. It is here that I shall live."

She smiled. She had served an apprenticeship in the reading of the artist's heart—the child's heart.

"Yes, monsieur? You will live here?"

"As soon, madame, as it suits you to vacate the *appartement*."

Again she smiled, gently, indulgently. "And may I ask, monsieur, whether you have ascertained the figure of the rent?"

"No, madame."

"And is not that—pardon me!—a little improvident?"

Max laughed. "Probably, madame! But if it demanded my last franc I would give that last franc with an open heart, so greatly do I desire the place."

The quiet eyes of the woman softened to a gentle comprehension.

"You are an artist, monsieur."

The color leaped into the boy's face, his eyes flashed with triumph.

"Madame, how did you guess?"

"It is no guessing, monsieur. You tell me with every word."

"Ah, madame, I thank you!" With a charming, swift grace he bent and caught her hand. "And, madame"—he hesitated naïvely and colored again. "Madame, I would like to say that when my home is here it will be my care never to desecrate the atmosphere you have created." He bent still lower, the sun caressing his crisp, dark hair, and very lightly his lips touched her fingers.

"*Adieu*, madame!"

"*Adieu*, monsieur!"

CHAPTER XI

IT seemed to Max, as the door closed behind him and he found himself upon the bare landing, that he had dreamed and was awake again; for in truth the *ménage* into which he had been permitted to peep seemed more the fabric of a dream than part of the new, inconsequent life he had elected to make his own. A curious halo of the ideal—of things set above the corroding touch of time or fortune—surrounded the old man forgotten of his world, and the patient wife, content in her one frail possession.

He felt without comprehending that here was some precious essence, some elixir of life, secret as it was priceless; and for an instant a shadow, a doubt, a question crossed his happy egoism. But the sharp, inquisitive voice of his guide brought him back to material things.

"You like the *appartement*, monsieur?"

He threw aside his disturbing thoughts.

"Undoubtedly, madame!" he said, quickly. "It is here that I shall live." Without conscious intention he used the phrase that he had used to Blake—that he had used to Madame Salas.

"You are quick of decision, monsieur?"

"It is well, at least, to know one's own mind, madame! And now tell me who I shall have for my neighbor." As they moved toward the head of the stairs, he indicated the second door on the landing—the door innocent of name, bell, or knocker.

"For neighbor, monsieur? Ah, I comprehend! That is the *appartement* of M. Lucien Cartel, a musician; but his playing will not disturb you, for the walls are thick—and, in any case, he is a good musician."

A conclusion, winged with excitement, formed itself in the mind of Max.

"Madame!" he cried. "He plays the violin—this M. Cartel?"

"Both violin and piano, monsieur. He has a great talent."

"And, madame, he played last night? He played last night between the hours of ten and eleven?"

"He plays constantly, monsieur, but of last night I am not sure. Last night was eventful for M. Cartel! Last night—But I speak too much!"

She glanced at Max, obviously desiring the question that would unloose her tongue. But Max was not alert for gossip, he was listening instead to a faint sound, long drawn out and fine as a silver thread, that was slipping through the crevices of M. Cartel's door.

"Ah, there he goes!" interjected the little woman. "Always at the music, whatever life brings!"

"And I am right! It was he who played last night. How curious!"

The woman glanced up, memory quickening her expression.

"But, yes, monsieur, you are perfectly correct," she said. "M. Cartel did play last night. I remember now. I was finishing the hem of a black dress for Madame Dévet, of the rue des Abesses, when my husband came in at eleven o'clock. He walked in, leaving the door open—the door I came through this morning at your knock—and he stood there, blowing upon his fingers, for it was cold. 'Our good Cartel is in love, Marthe!' he said, laughing. 'He is making music like a bird in spring!' And then, monsieur, the next thing was a great rush of feet down the stairs, and who should come flying into the hallway but M. Cartel himself. He paused for an instant, seeing our door open, and he, too, was laughing. 'What a fellow that Charpentier is!' he cried to my husband. 'His *Louise* has kept me until I am all but late for my *rendezvous*!' And he ran out through the hall, singing as he went. That was all I saw of M. Cartel until two o'clock this morning, when some one knocked upon our door—"

But she was permitted to go no further. The silvery notes of the violin had dwindled into silence, and Max abruptly remembered that he had an appointment with Blake on the Boulevard des Italiens.

"You are very good, madame, but it is necessary that I go! When can I see the *concierge*?"

"The *concierge*, monsieur, is my husband. He will be here for a certainty at one o'clock."

"Good, madame! At one o'clock I shall return."

He smiled, nodded, and ran down the first flight of stairs; but by the window at the half-landing he stopped and looked back.

"Madame, tell me something! What is the rent of the *appartement*?"

"The rent? Two hundred and sixty francs the year."

"Two hundred and sixty francs the year!" His voice was perfectly expressionless. Then, apparently without reason, he laughed aloud and ran down-stairs.

The woman looked after him, half inquisitively, half in bewilderment; then to herself, in the solitude of the landing, she shook her head.

"An artist, for a certainty!" she said, aloud, and, turning, she retraced her steps and knocked with her knuckles on the door of M. Lucien Cartel.

Meanwhile, Max finished his descent of the stairs, his feet gliding with pleasant ease down the polished oak steps, his hand slipping smoothly down the polished banister. Already the joy of the free life was singing in his veins, already in spirit he was an inmate of this house of many histories. He darted across the hall, picturing in imagination the last night's haste of M. Cartel of the violin. What would he be like, this M. Cartel, when he came to know him in the flesh? Fat and short and negligent of his figure? or lean and pathetic, as though dinner was not a certainty on every day of the seven? He laughed a little to himself light-heartedly, and gained the street door with unnecessary, heedless speed—gained it on the moment that another pedestrian, moving swiftly as himself, entered, bringing him to a sharp consciousness of the moment.

Incomer and outgoer each drew back a step, each laughed, each tendered an apology.

"*Pardon*, monsieur!"

"*Pardon*, mademoiselle!"

Then simultaneously a flash of recognition leaped into both faces.

"Why," cried the girl, "it is the little friend of the friend of Lize! How droll to meet like this!"

Her candor of speech was disarming; reticence fled before her smile, before her artless friendliness.

"What a strange chance!" said Max. "What brings you to the rue Müller, mademoiselle?"

She smiled, and in her smile there was a little touch of pride—an indefinite pride that glowed about her slender, youthful person like an aura.

"Monsieur, I live in this house—now."

"Now?" Sudden curiosity fired him.

"Ah, you do not comprehend! Last night was sad, monsieur; to-day—" She stopped.

"To-day, mademoiselle?"

For a second the clear, childish blue of her eyes flashed like a glimpse of spring skies.

"It is too difficult, monsieur—the explanation. It is as I say. Last night was dark; to-day the sun shines!" She laughed, displaying the dazzling whiteness of her teeth. "And you, monsieur?" she added, gayly. "You also live here in the rue Müller? Yes? No?" She bent her head prettily, first to one side, then to the other, as she put her questions.

"I hope to live here, mademoiselle."

"Ah! Then I wish you, too, the sunshine, monsieur! Good-day!"

"Good-day, mademoiselle!"

It was over—the little encounter; she moved into the dark hallway as light, as joyous, as inconsequent as a bird. And Max passed out into the sharp, crisp air, sensible that the troubling memories of the Bal Tarbarin had in some strange manner been effaced—that inadvertently he had touched some source whence the waters of life bubbled in eternal, crystal freshness.

In the rue Ronsard he found a disengaged cab, and in ten minutes he was wheeling down into the heart of Paris. It was nearing the hour of *déjeuner*, the boulevards were already filling, and the cold, crisp air seemed to vibrate to the bustle of hurrying human creatures seriously absorbed in the thought of food.

He smiled to himself at this humorously grave homage offered up so untiringly, so zealously to the appetite, as he made his way between the long line of tables at the restaurant where he had appointed to meet Blake. Like all else that appertains to the Frenchman, its very frankness disarmed criticism or disgust. He looked at the beaming faces, smiling up from the wide-spread napkins in perfect accord with life, and again, involuntarily, he smiled. It was essentially a good world, whatever the pessimists might say!

From a side-table he heard his name called, and with an added glow of pleasure, he turned, saw Blake, and made his way through the closely ranged chairs and the throng of hurrying waiters.

"Well, boy! Dissipation suits you, it seems! You're looking well. Just out of bed, I suppose?"

Max laughed. Words were brimming to his lips, until he knew not how to speak.

"And now, what 'll you eat? I waited to order until you came."

"I do not know that I can eat."

"God bless my soul, why not? Sit down!"

Max laughed again, dropped obediently into a chair, rested his arms on the table, and looked full at Blake.

"May I speak?"

"From now till Doomsday! *Garçon!*"

But Max laid an impulsive hand upon his arm.

"Wait! Do not order for one moment! I must tell you!" He gave a little gasp of excitement. "I have seen an *appartement* in the rue Müller—an *appartement* with a charming *salon* opening upon a balcony, a nice little bedroom, another room with an excellent painting light, a kitchen with water and gas, all—all for what do you imagine?"

"What in God's name are you raving about?" Blake laid down the *menu* just handed to him.

Max paid not the slightest heed.

"All for two hundred and sixty francs the year! Figure it to yourself! Two hundred and sixty francs the year! What one would pay in a couple of days for a suite of hotel rooms! I am mad since I have seen the place—quite mad!" He laughed again so excitedly that the people at the neighboring table stared.

"I can subscribe to that!" said Blake, satirically.

"Listen! Listen! You have not heard; you have not understood. I have found an *appartement* in the rue Müller, at Montmartre—the *appartement* I had set my heart upon, the place where I can live and paint and make my success!"

Blake stared at him in silence.

"Yes! Yes!" Max insisted. "And it is all quite settled. And you are coming back with me to-day at one o'clock to interview the *concierge!*"

Blake threw himself back in his chair. "I'm hanged if I am!"

Yesterday the boy would have drawn back upon the instant, armored in his pride, but to-day his reply was to look direct into Blake's face with fascinating audacity.

"Then you will leave me to contend alone against who can say what villain—what *apache*?"

"It strikes me you are qualified to deal with any *apache*."

"You are angry!"

"Angry! I should think not!"

"Oh yes, you are!" Max's eyes shone, his lips curled into smiles.

"And why should I be angry? Because your silly little wings have begun to sprout? I'm not such a fool, my boy! I knew well enough you'd soon be flying alone."

Max clapped his hands. "Oh yes, you are! You are angry—angry—angry! You are angry because I found my way to Montmartre without you, and made a little discovery all by myself! Is it not like a—" He stopped, laughed, reddened as though he had made some slip, and then on the instant altered his whole expression to one of appeal and contrition.

"*Mon ami!*"

Blake's reply was to pick up the *menu* and turn to the attending waiter.

"Monsieur Ned!"

Blake glanced at him reluctantly, caught the softened look, and laughed.

"You're a young scamp—and I suppose I'm a cross-grained devil! But if I was angry, where's the wonder? A man doesn't pick up a quaint little book on the *quais*, and look to have it turning its own leaves!"

"But now? Now it is all forgiven? You will not cast away your little book because—because the wind came and fluttered the pages?"

Once again Max spoke softly, with the softness that broke so alluringly across the reckless independence of look and gesture.

A sudden consciousness of this fascination—a sudden annoyance with himself that he should yield to it—touched Blake.

"I can't go with you to Montmartre," he said, abruptly. "It's McCutcheon's last day in Paris, and I promised to give him the afternoon."

"Who? The long, spider man who disliked me?"

"A spider who weaves big webs, I can tell you! You ought to be more respectful to your elders."

"And I ought to have a studio across the river? Oh, Monsieur Ned, order some food, for the love of God! I am perishing of hunger."

Blake ordered the *déjeuner*, and talked a great deal upon indifferent subjects while they ate; but each felt jarred, each felt disappointed, though neither could exactly have said why. At last, with a certain relief, they finished their coffee and made a way between the long lines of tables to the door.

There they halted for a moment in mutual hesitation, and at last the boy held out his hand.

"And now I must wish you good-bye! Shall I see you any more?"

Blake seemed lost in thought; he took no notice of the proffered hand.

"Are you going to drive or walk?" He put the question after a considerable pause.

"I thought to drive, because—"

Without permitting him to complete the sentence Blake crossed the footpath and hailed a passing cab.

"Come on! In you get!"

Max obeyed uncertainly, and as he took his seat a sudden fear of loss crushed him—life became blank, the brightness of the sun was eclipsed.

"Monsieur Ned!" he called. "Monsieur Ned! I shall see you again?"

Blake was speaking to the *cocher*. 'Rue Ronsard!' he heard him say. 'The corner of the rue André de Sarte!'

He leaned out of the window.

"Monsieur Ned! Monsieur Ned! I shall see you again? This is not good-bye?"

Blake turned; he laid his hand on the door of the cab and suddenly smiled his attractive, humorous smile.

"Little fool!" he said. "Didn't you know I was coming with you?"

PART II

CHAPTER XII

FROM a distinctly precarious perch—one foot on the back of a chair, the other on an oak chest—Blake surveyed the unfurnished *salon* of the fifth-floor *appartement*. His coat was off, in one dusty hand he held a hammer, in the other a picture, while from between his lips protruded a brass-headed nail.

"If I drive the nail here, boy, will you be satisfied? Upon my word, it's the last place I'll try!" He spoke with what dignity and distinctness he could command, but the effect was lost upon Max, who, also dusty, also bearing upon his person the evidences of manual labor, was crouching over a wood fire, intent upon the contents of a brass coffee-pot.

"Max! Do you hear me?"

"No, I do not hear. Take the nail from your mouth."

"Take it for me! I haven't a hand."

Max left the coffee-pot with some reluctance, crossed the room, and with the seriousness known only to the enthusiastic amateur in house-furnishing, removed the nail from Blake's mouth.

"It is a shame! You will spoil your nice teeth."

"What is a tooth or two in such a cause! Have you a handkerchief?"

"Yes."

"Then, for the love of God, wipe my forehead for me!"

Still without a smile, Max produced a handkerchief that had obviously played the *rôle* of duster at an earlier hour and, passing it over Blake's face, removed the dew of heat, leaving in its place a long black streak.

"Thanks! I'm cooler now—though probably dirtier!"

"Dirtier! On the contrary, *mon ami*! You have the most artistic scar of dust that makes you as interesting as a German officer! Oh!" His voice rose to a cry of sharp distress, and he ran back to the fire. "Oh, my coffee! My beautiful coffee! Oh, Ned, it has over boiled!"

Blake eyed the havoc from his coign of vantage with a philosophy tinged with triumph.

"Didn't I tell you that coffee-pot was a fraud the very first day old Bluebeard tried to palm it off on us! You will never distinguish between beauty and utility."

"Beauty is utility!" Max, in deep distress, was using the much-taxed handkerchief to wipe the spilt coffee from the hearth.

"Should be, my boy, but isn't! I say, give me that business to see to!" Regardless of the picture still dangling from his hand, he jumped to the ground and strode through a litter of papers, straw, and packing-cases.

"Give me that rag!" He took the sopping handkerchief and flung it into a distant corner. "A wisp of this straw is much more useful—less beautiful, I admit!"

Max glanced up with wide eyes, extremely wistful and youthful in expression. "I do not believe I care about either the use or the beauty," he said, plaintively. "I only care that I am hungry and that my coffee is lost."

"Hungry, boy? Why, bless my soul, you must be starving! What time is it at all?" Blake pulled out his watch. "Eleven! And we've been at this hard since eight! Hungry! I should think you are. Look here! You just sit down!" He pushed aside the many objects that encumbered the floor, and began impatiently to strip the packing from a leather arm-chair.

Max laughed a little.

"But, *mon cher*, I prefer the ground—this nice warm little corner close to the fire. One day I think I shall have two cushions, like your Bluebeard of the curio shop, and sit all day long with my legs crossed, imagining myself a Turk. Like this!" He drew back against the wall, curling himself up with supple agility, and smiled into his companion's eyes.

Blake looked down, half amused, half concerned.

"Poor little *gamin*! Tired and dirty and hungry. Just you wait!" Nodding decisively, he crossed the room, opened the door softly, and disappeared.

Left to himself, Max drew farther back into his warm corner and clasped his hands about his knees. Max was enjoying himself. The fact was patent in the lazy ease of his pose, in the smile that hovered about his lips, in the slow, pleased glance that travelled round and round the bare room and the furniture still standing ghostly in its packing. It was still the joyful beginning of things: the clean white paper upon the walls spoke of first hours as audibly as the bunch of jonquils peeping from a dark corner spoke of spring. It was still the beginning of things—the salt before the sweet, the ineffable, priceless moment when life seems malleable and to be bent to the heart's desire.

One month had passed since his first visit to this fifth floor; one month since he had entered Paris, armored in his hopes; one month since Blake had crossed his path.

The smile upon his lips deepened, then wavered to seriousness, and his gaze turned from the white wall to the fire, where the flames from the logs spurted copper and blue.

One month. A dream—or a lifetime?

Gazing into the fire, questioning his own fancy, he could scarce decide which; a dream in the quick moving of events—the swift viewing of new scenes; a lifetime in alteration of outlook and environment—the severing and knitting of bonds.

The happy seriousness was still enfolding him, his eyes were still intent upon the fire, when Blake entered, triumphant, carrying a coffee-pot, and followed by a demure girl with blonde hair and delicate pale skin.

"Monsieur is served!"

Max, startled out of his reverie, jumped to his feet.

"What is this? Oh, but you should not! You should not!"

"And why not, in the name of God? If you insist upon having antique brass coffee-pots, your neighbors must expect to suffer, eh, Jacqueline?"

The little Jacqueline laughed, shaking her fair head. "Ah, well, monsieur, it is an art—the keeping of an establishment—and must be learned like any other!"

"And you think we ought to go to school?"

"I did not say that!" She laid down the loaf of bread, the butter, and the milk-jug that she was carrying, and took the coffee from Blake's hands with an air of pretty gravity. "And now, monsieur, where are the cups?"

Blake turned to Max. "Cups?" he said in English. "I know we bought something quite unique in the matter of cups, but where the deuce we put them—For the love of God and the honor of the family, boy, tell me where they are!"

Max's eyes were shining. "They are in the chest, *mon cher*. We put them there for safety as we went out last night."

"Good! Give me the key."

"The key, *mon ami*, I have left at the Hôtel Railleux!"

Consternation spread over Blake's face, then he burst out laughing and turned to Jacqueline, relapsing into French.

"Monsieur Max would have you to know, mademoiselle, that he possesses an altogether unusual and superior set of Oriental china, which he bought from a certain villanous Jew at the corner of the rue André de Sarte; that for safety he has locked that china into the artistic and musty dower-chest standing against the wall; and that for greater safety he has forgotten the key in an antique hotel near the Gare du Nord!"

He laughed again; Max laughed; the little Jacqueline laughed, and ran to the door.

"Oh, *la! la*! What a pair of children!" She flitted out of the room, returning with two cups, which she set beside the coffee and the milk.

"And now, messieurs, it is possible you can arrange for yourselves!" She shot a bright, quizzical look from one to the other. "I know you would wish me to stay and measure out the milk and sugar, and it would flatter me to do so, but, unhappily, I have a dish of some importance upon my own fire, and it is necessary that one is domestic when one is only a woman—is it not so, Monsieur Max?" She wrinkled her pretty face into a grimace of mischief, and nodded as if some idea infinitely amusing, infinitely profound lurked at the back of her blonde head.

"Good-day, Monsieur Edouard. Good-day, Monsieur Max!"

"Strange little creature!" said Blake, as the door closed upon her. "Frail as a butterfly, with one capacity to prevent her taking wing!"

"And that capacity—what is it?" Max had returned to his former position, and was pouring out the coffee as he crouched comfortably by the fire.

"The capacity, boy, for the *grande passion*. Odd that it should exist in so light a vessel, but these are the secrets of Nature! There are moments, you know, when this little Jacqueline isn't laughing at life—rare, I admit, but still existent—and then you see that the corners of her mouth can droop. She may live to find existence void, but she'll never live to find it shallow. Thanks, boy!" He took his cup of coffee, and, walking to the table, cut a slice of bread, which he carried back to the fire. "Now, don't say a word! I'm going to make you the finest bit of toast you ever saw in your life!"

Max, preserving the required silence, watched him make the toast, carefully balancing the bread on the tip of a knife, carefully browning, carefully buttering it.

"Now! Taste that, and tell me if there wasn't a great *chef* lost in me!"

He carried the toast back to the fire and watched Max eat the first morsel.

"Nice?"

"Delicious!"

"Ah! Then it's all fair sailing! I'll cut myself a bit of bread and sit down on my heels like you. There's something in that Turkish idea, after all! But, as I was saying"—he buttered his bread and dropped into position beside the boy—"as I was saying awhile ago, that child next door, with all her innocent air and her blue eyes, has climbed the slippery stairs and reached the seventh heaven. And not only reached it herself, mind you, but dragged that ungainly Cartel with her by the tip of her tiny finger! Wonderful! Wonderful! Enviable fate!"

Max's eyes laughed. "M. Cartel's?"

"M. Cartel's. Oh, boy, that seventh heaven! Those slippery steps!"

"And the tip of a tiny finger?" Max was jesting; but Blake, lost in his own musings, did not perceive it.

"For Cartel—yes!" he said. "For me, no! I think I'd like the whole hand."

Here Max picked up a tongs and stirred the logs until they blazed.

"Absurd!" he said. "The tip of a finger or the whole of a hand, it is all the same! It is a mistake, this love! That old story of the Garden and the Serpent is as true as truth. Man and Woman were content to live and adorn the world until one day they espied the stupid red Apple—and straightway they must eat! Look even at this Cartel! He is an artist; he might make the world listen to his music. But, no! He sees a little butterfly, as you call her— all blonde and blue—and down falls his ambition, and up go his eyes to the sky, and henceforth he is content to fiddle to himself and to the stars! Oh, my patience leaves me!" Again he struck the logs, and a golden shower of sparks flew up the chimney.

"I don't know!" said Blake, placidly. "I'm not so sure that he isn't getting the best of it, when all's said and done!"

Max reddened. "You make me angry with this 'I do not know!' and 'I am not so sure!' The matter is like day. You cannot submerge your personality and yet retain it."

"I don't know! I'd submerge mine to-morrow if I could find an *alter ego*!"

"Then, *mon cher*, you are a fool!"

Blake drank his coffee meditatively. "Some say the fools are happier than the wise men! I remember a poor fool of a boy at home in Clare who used to say that he danced every night with the fairies on the rath, and I often thought he was happier than the people who listened to him out of pity, and shook their heads and laughed behind his back!"

Max looked up, and as he looked the anger died out of his eyes.

"Ned, *mon cher*, you are very patient with me!"

Blake turned. "What do you mean?"

"What I say—that you are patient. Why is it?"

"Oh, I don't know. I'm fond of you, I suppose."

"I am, then, a good comrade?"

"The best."

"What is it you find in me?"

"I don't know! You are you."

"I amuse you?"

"You do—and more."

"More! In what way more?" Max drew nearer.

"Oh, I don't know! You're as amusing and spirited and generous as any boy I've known, and yet you're different from any boy. You sometimes fit into my thoughts almost like a woman might!" He hesitated, and laughed at his own conceit.

Max, with an odd little movement of haste, drew away again.

"Do not say that, *mon ami*! Do not think it! I am your good comrade, that is all."

"Of course you are! Sorry if I hurt your pride."

"You did not. It was not that." With an inexplicable change of mood Max drew near again, and suddenly slipped his hand through Blake's arm.

They laughed in unison at the return to amity, and then fell silent, looking into the fire, watching the blue spurt of the flames, the feathery curls of ash on the charred logs.

"Ned! Make me one of your stories! Tell me what you are seeing in the fire!"

Blake settled himself more comfortably.

"Well, boy, I was just seeing a castle," he began in the accepted manner of the story-teller, and in his pleasant, soothing voice. "A great big castle on the summit of a mountain, with a golden flag fluttering in the sunset; and I think it must be the 'Castle of Heart's Desire,' because all up the craggy path that leads to it there are knights urging their horses—"

"Good!" Max smiled with pleasure and pressed his arm. "Continue! Continue!"

"Well, they're all sorts of knights, you know," Blake went on in the dreamy, singsong voice—"fair knights and red knights and black knights, every one of them in glittering armor, with long lances, and wonderful devices on their shields—"

"Yes! Yes!"

"—wonderful devices on their shields, and spurs of gold and silver, and waving plumes of many colors; and the flanks of their horses—cream-colored and chestnut and black—shine in the light."

"Continue, *mon cher*! Continue! I can see them also!" Max, utterly absorbed, charming as a child, bent forward, staring into the heart of the fire.

"Well, they mount and mount and mount, and sometimes the great horses refuse the craggy path and rear, and sometimes a knight is unseated and the others look back and laugh at his discomfiture and ride on until they themselves are proved unfit; and so, on and on, while the way gets steeper and more perilous, and the company smaller and still smaller, until the sun drops down behind the mountain and the gold flag flutters as gray as a moth, and in all the windows of the castle torches spring up to greet the knight who shall succeed."

"And which is he—the knight who shall succeed?"

"Don't you see him?"

"No! Where is he? Where?"

"Why, there—riding first, on the narrowest verge of the craggy path! A very young knight with dark hair and a proud carriage and gray eyes with flecks of gold in them."

For an instant Max gazed seriously into the flames, then turned, blushing and laughing.

"Ah! But you are laughing at me! What a shame! For a punishment you shall go straight back to work." He jumped up and handed Blake his discarded hammer.

Blake looked reluctantly at the hammer, then looked back at the enticing flame of the logs.

"Oh, very well! Have it your own way!" he said, getting slowly to his feet. "But if I were you, I'd like to have heard what awaited the knight in the tapestried chamber of the castle tower!"

CHAPTER XIII

TO the zest of the amateur, Blake added knowledge of a practical kind in the arrangement of household gods, and long ere the February dusk had fallen, the fifth-floor *appartement* had assumed a certain homeliness. True, much of the 'old iron,' as he termed the coppers and brasses for which Max had bartered in the rue André de Sarte, still encumbered the floor, and most of the windows cried aloud for covering; but the little *salon* was habitable, and in the bedroom once occupied by Madame Salas a bed and a dressing-table stood forth, fresh and enticing enough to suggest a lady's chamber, while over the high window white serge curtains shut out the cold.

At seven o'clock, having torn the canvas wrappings from the last chair, the two workers paused in their labors by common consent and looked at each other by the uncertain light of half a dozen candles stuck into bowls and vases in various corners of the *salon*.

"Boy," said Blake, breaking what had been a long silence, "I tell you what it is, you're done! Take a warm by the fire for a minute, while I tub under the kitchen tap, then we'll fare forth for a meal and a breath of air!"

Max, who had worked with fierce zeal if little knowledge, made no protest. His face was pale, and he moved with a certain slow weariness.

"Here! Let's test the big chair!" Blake pulled forward the deep leathern arm-chair, that had been purchased second-hand in the rue de la Nature, and set it in front of the blazing logs. Without a word, Max sank into it.

"Comfortable?"

"Very comfortable." The voice was a little thin.

The other looked down upon him. "You're done, you know! Literally done! Why didn't you give in sooner?"

"Because I was not tired—and I am not tired."

"Not tired! And your face is as white as a sheet! I don't believe you're fit to go out for food."

"How absurd! You talk as though I were a child!" Max lifted himself petulantly on one elbow, but his head drooped and the remonstrance died away before it was finished.

"I talk as if you were a child, do I? Then I talk uncommon good sense! Well, I'm off to wash."

"There is some soap in my bedroom." The voice seemed to come from a great distance, the elbow slipped from the arm of the chair, the dark head drooped still more, and as the door shut upon Blake, the eyelids closed mechanically.

Blake's washing was a protracted affair, for the day had been long and the toil strenuous; but at last he returned, face and hands clean, hair smooth, and clothes reduced to order.

"Sorry for being so long," he began, as he walked into the room; but there he stopped, his eyebrows went up, and his face assumed a curious look, half amused, half tender.

"Poor child!" he said below his breath, and tiptoeing across the room, he paused by the arm-chair, in the depths of which Max's slight figure was curled up in the pleasant embrace of sleep.

The fire had died down, the pool of candle-light was not brilliant, and in the soft, shadowed glow the boy made an attractive picture.

THE IMPRESSION OF A MYSTERY FLOWED BACK UPON HIM

One hand lay carelessly on either arm of the chair; the head was thrown back, the black lashes of the closed eyes cast shadows on the smooth cheeks.

Blake looked long and interestedly, and his earliest impression—the impression of a mystery—flowed back upon him strong as on the night of the long journey.

The beauty and strength of the face called forth thought; and Max's own declaration, so often repeated, came back upon him with new meaning, 'I am older than you think!'

For almost the first time the words carried weight. It was not that the features looked older; if anything they appeared younger in their deep repose. But the expression—the slight knitting of the dark brows, the set of the chin, the modelling of the full lips, usually so mobile and prone to laughter—suggested a hidden force, gave warranty of a depth, a strength irreconcilable with a boy's capacities.

He looked—puzzled, attracted; then his glance dropped from the face to the pathetically tired limbs, and the sense of pity stirred anew, banishing question, causing the light of a pleasant inspiration to awaken in his eyes.

Smiling to himself, he replenished the fire with exaggerated stealth; and, creeping out of the room, closed the door behind him.

He was gone for over half an hour, and when he again entered, the fire had sprung into new life, and fresh flames—blue and sulphur and copper-colored—were dancing up the chimney, while the candles in their strange abiding-places had burned an inch or two lower. But his eyes were for Max, and for Max alone, and with the same intense stealth he crept across the room to the bare table and solemnly unburdened himself of a variety of parcels and a cheery-looking bottle done up in red tissue-paper.

Max still slept, and, drawing a sigh of satisfaction, he proceeded with the task he had set himself—the task of providing supper after the manner of the genius in the fairy-tale.

First plates were brought from the new-filled kitchen shelves; then knives were found, and forks; then the mysterious-looking parcels delivered up their contents—a cold roast chicken, all brown and golden as it had left the oven, cheese, butter, crisp rolls, and crisp red radishes, finally a little basket piled with fruit.

It was a very simple meal, but Blake smiled to himself as he set out the dishes to the best advantage, placed the wine reverentially in the centre to crown the feast, and at last, still tiptoeing, came round to the back of Max's chair and laid his hands over the closed eyes.

"Guess!" he said, as if to a child.

Max gave a little cry, in which surprise and fear struggled for supremacy; then he sprang to his feet, shaking off the imprisoning hands.

"What is it? Who is it?" Then he laughed shamefacedly, and, turning, saw the spread table.

"Oh, *mon ami*!" His eyes opened wide, and he gazed from the food to Blake. "*Mon ami!* You have done this for me while I was sleeping!"

His gaze was eloquent even beyond his words, and Blake, finding no fit answer, began to move about the room, collecting the vases that held the candles and carrying them to the table.

"*Mon ami!*"

"Nonsense, boy! It's little enough I do, goodness knows!"

"This is a great deal."

"Nonsense! What is it? You were fagged and I was fresh! And now I suppose I must knock the head off this bottle, for we haven't a corkscrew. The Lord lend me a steady hand, for 'twould be a pity if I shook the wine!"

He carried the bottle to the fireplace, and with considerable dexterity cracked the head and wiped the raw glass edges. "Now, boy, the glasses! Oh, but have we glasses, though?" His face fell in a manner that set Max laughing.

"We have one glass—in my room."

"Bravo! Fly for it!"

Max laughed again—his sleep, his surprise, his gratitude equally routed; he flew, in literal obedience to the command, across the little hall and, groping his way to the dressing-table, searched about in the darkness for the tumbler.

"Ned! A candle!"

Blake brought the desired light, and together they discovered the coveted glass. Max seized upon it eagerly, but as he delivered it up a swift exclamation escaped him:

"My God! How dirty I am! Regard my hands!"

"What does it matter! You can wash after you've eaten."

"Oh, but no! I pay more compliment to your feast."

"Very well, then! We may hope to sup in an hour or so. I know you and the making of your toilet!"

"Impertinent!" Max caught him by the arm and pushed him, laughing, toward the door. "Go back and complete the table. I will delay but four—three—two minutes in the making of myself clean."

"But the table is complete—"

"It is incomplete, *mon ami*; it is without flowers."

Before Blake's objections could form into new words, he found himself in the little hallway with the bedroom door closed upon him, and, being a philosopher, he shook his head contentedly and walked back into the *salon*, where he obediently brought to light the bowl of jonquils that was still perfuming the air from its dark corner, and set it carefully between the wine and the fruit.

Ten minutes and more slipped by, during which, still philosophical, he walked slowly round and round the table, straightening a candle here, altering a dish there, humming all the while in a not unmusical voice the song from *Louise*.

He was dwelling fondly upon the line

"Depuis le jour où je me suis donnée"—

when the door of the bedroom was flung open as by a gale, and at the door of the *salon* appeared Max—his dark hair falling over his forehead, a comb in one hand, a brush in the other.

"*Mon cher!* a hundred—a thousand apologies for being so long! It is all the fault of my hair!"

Blake looked at him across the candles. "Indeed I wouldn't bother about my hair, if I were you! A century of brushing wouldn't make it respectable."

"Why not?"

"Look at the length of it!"

"Ah, but that pleases me!"

Blake shook his head in mock seriousness. "These artists! These artists!" he murmured to himself.

Max laughed, threw the comb and brush from him into some unseen corner of the hall, and ran across the *salon*.

"You are very ill-mannered! I shall box your ears!"

Blake threw himself into an attitude of defence. "I'd ask nothing better!" he cried. "Come on! Just come on!"

Max, laughing and excited, took a step forward, then paused as at some arresting thought.

"Afraid? Oh, *la, la*! Afraid?"

"Afraid!" The boy tossed the word back scornfully, but his face flushed and he made no advance.

"You'll have to, now, you know!"

Max retreated.

"Oh, no, you don't!" With a quick, gay laugh, touched with the fire of battle, Blake followed; but ere he could come to close quarters, the boy had dodged and, lithe and swift as a cat, was round the table.

"No! No!" he cried, with a little gasp, a little sob of excitement that caught the breath. "No! No! I demand grace. A starving man, *mon ami*! A starving man! It is not fair."

He knew his adversary. Blake's hands dropped to his sides, he yielded with a laugh.

"Very well! Very well! Another time I'll see what you're made of. And now 'we'll exterminate the bread-stuffs,' as McCutcheon would say!"

And laughing, jesting—content in the moment for the moment's sake—they sat down to their first serious meal in the little *salon*.

CHAPTER XIV

THE meal was over; the candles had burned low; in the quiet, warm room the sense of repose was dominant.

Blake took out his cigarette-case and passed it across the table, watching Max with lazy interest as he chose a cigarette and lighted it at a candle-flame.

"Happy?"

"Absolutely!"

He had wanted in a vague, subconscious way to see the flash of the white teeth, the quick, familiar lifting of the boy's glance, and now he smiled as a man secretly satisfied.

"I know just exactly what you're feeling," he said, as Max threw himself back in his chair and inhaled a first deep breath of smoke. "You feel that that little white curl from the end of your cigarette is the last puff of smoke from the boats you have burned; and that, with your own four walls around you, you can snap your fingers at the world. I know! God, don't I know!"

Max smiled slowly, watching the tip of his cigarette. "Yes, you know! That is the beautiful thing about you."

The appreciation warmed Blake's soul as the good red wine had warmed his blood.

"I believe I do—with you. I believe I could tell you precisely your thoughts at this present moment." With a pleasant, meditative action, he drew a cigar from his case.

"Tell me!"

"Well, first of all, there's the great contentment—the sense of a definite step. You're strong enough to like finality."

"I hope I am. I think I am."

"You are! Not a doubt of it! But what I mean is that you've left an old world for a new one; and no matter how exciting the voyaging through space may have been, you like to feel your feet on terra firma."

Max leaned forward eagerly. "That is quite true! And I like it because now I can open my eyes, and say to myself, 'not to-morrow, but to-day I live.' I have put—how do you say in English?—my hand upon the plough."

"Exactly! The plough—or the palette—it's all the same! You're set to it now."

The boy's eyes flashed in the candle-light, and for an instant something of the fierce emotion that can lash the Russian calm, as a gale lashes the sea, troubled his young face.

"You comprehend—absolutely! I have made my choice; I have come to it out of many situations. I would die now rather than I would fail."

In his voice was a suppressed fervor akin to some harsh or cruel emotion; and to Blake, watching and listening, there floated the hot echo of stories in which Russians had acted strange parts with a resolve, a callousness incomprehensible to other races.

"When you talk like that, boy, I could almost go back to that first night, and adopt McCutcheon's theory. You might feasibly be a revolutionary with those blazing eyes."

Max laughed, coming back to the moment.

"Only revolutionary in my own cause! I fight myself for myself. You take my meaning?"

"Not in the very least! But I accept your statement; I like its brave ring. You are your own romance."

"I am my own romance."

"Let's drink to it, then! Your romance—whatever it may be!" He raised the half-empty tumbler, drank a little, and handed it across the table.

Max laughed and drank as well. "My romance—whatever it may be!"

"Whatever it may be! And now for that breath of air we promised ourselves! It's close on ten o'clock."

So the meal ended; coats were found, candles blown out, and a last proprietary inspection of the *appartement* made by the aid of matches.

They ran down the long, smooth staircase, and, stepping into the quiet, starlit rue Müller, linked arms and began their descent upon Paris with as much ease, as nice a familiarity as though life for both of them had been passed in the shadow of the Sacré-Coeur.

On the Boulevard de Clichy the usual confusion of lights and humanity greeted them like welcoming arms, and with the same agreeable nonchalance they yielded to the embrace.

Conscious of no definite purpose, they turned to the right and began to breast the human tide with eyes carelessly critical of the thronging faces, ears heedlessly open to the many tangled sounds of street life. Outside the theatres, flaunting posters made pools of color; in the roadway, the network of traffic surged and intermingled; from amid the flat house fronts, at every few hundred yards, some *cabaret* broke upon the sight in crude confusion of scenic painting and electric light; while dominating all—a monument to the power of tradition—the sails of the time-honored mill sprang red and glaring from a background of quiet sky.

But the two, walking arm-in-arm, had no glance for revolving mill-sails or vivid advertisement, and presently Blake halted before a house that, but for a certain prosperity of stained-glass window and dark-green paint, would have seemed a common wine shop.

"Max," he said, "do you remember the famous night when we went to the Bal Tabarin, and saw much wine spilled? It was here I was first going to bring you then."

"Here?"

"This very place! 'Tis one of the old artistic *cabarets* of Paris—grown a bit too big for its shoes now, like the rest of Montmartre, but still retaining a flavor. What do you say to turning in?"

"I say 'yes.'"

"Come along, then! I hope 'twon't disappoint you! There's a good deal of rubbish here, but a scattering of grain among the chaff. Ah, messieurs! Good-evening!"

This last was addressed with cordiality to a knot of men gathered inside the doorway of the *cabaret*, all of whom rose politely from their chairs at Blake's entry.

Max, peering curiously through the tobacco smoke that veiled the place, received an impression of a room—rather, of a shop—possessed of tables, chairs, a small circular counter where glasses and bottles winked and gleamed, and of walls hung with a truly Parisian collection of impressionist studies and clever caricatures.

"Monsieur is interested?"

He turned, to meet the eyes of the host, a stout and affable Frenchman, who by right divine held first place among the little group of loungers; but before he could frame a reply, Blake answered for him.

"He is an artist, M. Fruvier, and finds all life interesting."

M. Fruvier bowed with much subtle comprehension.

"Then possibly it will intrigue him to step inside, and hear our little concert. We are about to commence."

Blake nodded in silent acquiescence; the knot of men bowed quickly and stiffly; and Max found himself being led across the bare, sawdust-strewn floor into an inner and larger room—a holy of holies—where the light was dimmer and the air more cool.

Here, a scattered audience was assembled—a score or so of individuals, sober of dress, unenthusiastic of demeanor, sitting in twos and threes, sipping beer or liqueurs and waiting for the concert to begin.

Max's eyes wandered over this collection of people while Blake sought for seats, but his glance and his interest passed on almost immediately to the walls, where, as in the outer room, pictures ranged from floor to ceiling.

The seats were chosen; a white-aproned waiter claimed an order, and Blake gave one as if from habit.

"And now, boy, a cigarette?"

"If you please—a cigarette!" Max's voice had the quick note, his eyes the swift light that spoke excitement. "*Mon ami*, I like this place! I like it! And I wonder who painted that?" He indicated a picture that hung upon the wall beside them.

"I don't know! Some chap who used to frequent the place in his unknown days. We can ask Fruvier."

"It is clever."

"It is."

"It has imagination."

They both looked at the picture—a study in black and white, showing an attic room, with a *pierrette* seated disconsolate upon a bed, a *pierrot* gazing through a window.

"*Pierrot* seeking the moon, eh?"

Max nodded.

"Yes. It has imagination—and also technique!"

But their criticism was interrupted; a piano was opened at the farther end of the room by an individual affecting the unkempt hair and velveteen coat of past Bohemianism, who seated himself and ran his fingers over the keys as though he alone occupied the room.

At this very informal signal, the curtain rose upon a ridiculously small stage, and an insignificant, nervous-looking man stepped toward the footlights at the same moment that M. Fruvier and his followers entered and seated themselves in a row, their backs to the wall.

This appearance of the proprietor was the sole meed of interest offered to the singer, the audience continuing to smoke, to sip, even to peruse the evening papers with stoic indifference.

The song began—a long and unamusing ditty, topical in its points. Here and there a smile showed that it did not pass unheard, and as the singer disappeared a faint *roulade* of applause came from the back of the room.

Max turned to his companion.

"But I believed the Parisians to be all excitement! What an audience! Like the dead!"

"They are excitable when something excites them."

"Then they dislike this song?"

"Oh no! 'Not bad!' they'd say if you asked them; but they're not here to be excited—they're not here to waste enthusiasm. Like ourselves, they have worked and have eaten, and are enjoying an hour's repose. The song is part of the hour—as inevitable as the *bock* and the cigar, and you can't expect a smoker to wax eloquent over a familiar weed."

"How strange! How interesting!" The boy looked round the scattered groups that formed to his young eyes another side-show in the vast theatre of life.

No one heeded his interest. The women, young and elderly alike, conversed with their escorts and sipped their liqueurs with absorbed quiet; the men smoked and drank, talked or read aloud little paragraphs from their papers with whispering relish.

Then again the piano tinkled, and the same singer appeared, to sing another song almost identical with the first; but now his nervousness was less, he won a laugh or two for his political innuendoes, and when he finished Max clapped his hands, and Blake laughingly followed suit.

"He's a new man," he said; "this is probably his first night."

"His first? Oh, poor creature! What a *début*! Clap your hands again!"

"Poor creature indeed! He's delighted with himself. Many a better man has been driven from the stage after his first verse. Your Paris can be cruel."

Their example had been tepidly followed, and the singer, beaming under the relaxed tension of his nerves, was smiling and bowing before entering upon the perils of a third song.

"And what do they pay him?"

"Oh, a couple of francs a song! The fees will grow with his success."

Max gasped. "A couple of francs! Oh, my God!"

"What do you expect? We're not in Eldorado."

"But a couple of francs!"

"Ssh! Don't talk anarchy. Here come the powers that be!"

M. Fruvier was coming toward them, making his way between the seats with many bows, many apologetic smiles.

"Well, messieurs, and what of our new one? Not a Vagot, perhaps"— mentioning a famous *comique* whose star had risen in the firmament of the *cabaret*—"not a Vagot, perhaps, but not bad! Not bad?"

"Not bad!" acquiesced Blake.

"Very good!" added Max, pondering hotly upon the wage of the singer, and regarding M. Fruvier with doubtful glance.

"No! No! Not bad!" reiterated that gentleman, as if viewing the performance from a wholly impersonal standpoint. "Not bad!" And, still bowing, still smiling, he wandered on to exchange opinions with his other patrons, while a new singer appeared, a man whose vast proportions and round red face looked truly absurd upon the tiny stage, but whose merry eye and instant friendly nod gained him a murmur of welcome.

With the appearance of the new-comer a little stir of life was felt, and in obedience to some impulse of his own, Max took a sketch-book and a pencil from his pocket, and sat forward in his seat, with glance roving round and round the room, pencil poised above the paper.

"I heard this fellow here twelve years ago," said Blake. "He and Vagot were young men then. Shows the odd lie of things in this world! There's Vagot making his thousands of francs a week next door at the Moulin Rouge, and this poor fat clown still where he was!"

Max did not reply. His head was bent, his face flushed; he was sketching with a furious haste.

"What are you doing?"

Still no reply. The song rolled on; and Blake, leaning back in his seat, smoking with leisurely enjoyment, felt for perhaps the first time in his life the sense of complete companionship—that subtle condition of mind so continuously craved, so rarely found, so instantly recognized.

"Boy," he said at last, "let me come up sometimes when you're messing with your paints? I won't bother you."

Max looked up and nodded—a mere flash of a look, but one that conveyed sufficient; and the two relapsed again into silence.

At the end of an hour the boy raised his head, tossed a lock of hair out of his eyes, and closed his sketch-book.

Blake met his eyes comprehendingly. "Will we go?"

"Yes. But one more glance at this black-and-white!"

He jumped up, unembarrassed, unconscious of self, and looked at the picture closely; then stepped back and looked at it from a little distance, eyes half closed, head critically upon one side.

"Satisfied?" Blake rose more slowly.

"Perfectly. It is clever—this! It has imagination!" He slipped his arm confidingly through Blake's, and together they made a way to the door.

A new song began as they stepped into the outer room—the tinkle of the piano came thinly across the smoke-laden air. Blake paused and looked back.

"Well, and what do you think of it? A trifle dull, perhaps, but still—"

"Dull? But no! Never! I could work here. Others have worked here. It is in the atmosphere—- the desire to create."

They passed into the street, Blake raising his hat to a stout lady, presumably Madame Fruvier, who sat wedged behind the counter, Max glancing greedily at the bold rough sketches, the brilliantly Parisian caricatures adorning the walls.

"It is in the atmosphere! One breathes it!" he said again, as they walked down the cool, lighted boulevard. "I feel it to-night as I have not felt it before—the artist's Paris. Mon ami" —he raised a glowing face—"*mon ami*, tell me something! Do you think I shall succeed? Do you think I possess a spark of the great fire—a spark ever so tiny?"

His earnestness was almost comical. He stopped and arraigned his companion, regardless of interested glances and passing smiles.

"Ned, tell me! Tell me! Have you faith in me?"

Blake looked into the feverishly bright eyes, and a swift conviction possessed him.

"I know this, boy, whatever you do, you'll do it finely! More I cannot say."

Max fell silent, and they proceeded on their way, each preoccupied with his own thoughts. At the turning to the heights Blake paused.

"I'll say good-bye here! I have letters to write to-night; but I'll be up to-morrow to spirit you off to lunch. I won't come too early, for I know what you'll be doing all the morning."

Max laughed, coming back out of his dream. "And what is it I shall be doing all the morning?"

"Why, carting canvases and paint tubes, and God knows what, up those steps till your back is broken, and then settling down with your temper and your ambition at fever heat to begin the great picture at the most inopportune moment in the world! Think I don't know you?"

Max laughed again, but more softly.

"*Mon ami!*"

"I'm right, eh? That sketch at the *cabaret* is meant to grow?"

Instantly Max was diffident. "Oh, I am not so sure! It is only an idea. It may not arrive at anything."

"Let's have a look?"

Max's hand went slowly toward his pocket. "I am not sure that I like it; it is not my theory of life. It's more of your theory—it is ironical."

"Let's see!"

The sketch-book came reluctantly to light, and as Max opened it, the two stepped close to a street lamp.

"As I tell you, it is ironical. If it becomes a picture I shall give it this name—*The Failure.*" He handed it to Blake, leaning close and peering over his shoulder in nervous anxiety.

"Understand, it is but an idea! I have put no work into it."

Blake held the book up to the light, his observant face grave and interested.

"What a clever little beggar you are!" he said at length.

Max glowed at the words, and instantly his tongue was loosed.

"Ah, *mon cher*, but it is only a sketch! That atmosphere—that dim, smoky atmosphere—is so difficult with the pencil. The audience is, of course, but suggested; all that I really attempted was the singer—the failure with the merry eyes."

"And well you've caught him too, by gad! One would think you had seen the antithesis—Vagot, the success, long and lean and yellow, the unhappiest-looking man you ever saw."

"Ah, but you must not say that!" cried Max unexpectedly. "I told you it was not my theory. To me success is life, failure is death! This is but a reflected impression of yours—- an impression of irony!" He took the sketch-book from Blake's hands and closed it sharply; then, to ask pardon for his little outburst, he smiled.

"*Mon cher*! Forgive me! Come to-morrow, and we will see if day has thrown new light."

They shook hands.

"All right—to-morrow! Good-night, boy—and good luck!"

"Good-night!"

Max stood to watch the tall figure disappear into the tangle of traffic, then with a light step, a light heart, a light sense of propitiated fate, he began the climb to his home.

CHAPTER XV

THAT night the pencil-sketch obsessed the brain of Max. Tossing wakeful upon his bed, he saw the pageant of the future—touched the robe, all saffron and silver, of the goddess Inspiration—and, with the brushes and colors of imagination, gained to the gateway of fame.

It was a wild night that spurred to action, and with the coming of the day, Blake's prophecy was fulfilled. Before the Montmartre shops were open, he was seeking the materials of his art; and long ere the sun was high, he was back in the room that had once been the bedroom of M. Salas, surrounded by the disarray of the inspired moment.

The room was small but lofty, and a fine light made his work possible. The inevitable wood fire crackled on the hearth, but otherwise the atmosphere spoke rigidly of toil.

Zeal, endeavor, ambition in its youngest, divinest form—these were the suggestions dormant in the strewn canvases, the tall easel, the bare walls; and none who were to know, or who had known, Max—none destined to kindle to the flame of his personality, ever viewed him in more characteristic guise than he appeared on that February morning clad in his painting smock, the lock of hair falling over his forehead, his hands trembling with excitement, as he executed the first bold line that meant the birth of his idea.

So remarkable, so characteristic was the pose that chance, ever with an eye to effect, ordained it an observer, for scarcely had he lost himself in the work than the door of his studio opened with a Bohemian lack of ceremony, and his neighbor, Jacqueline—dressed in a blue print dress that matched her eyes—came smiling into the room.

"Good-day, monsieur!"

He glowered with complete unreserve.

"You are displeased, monsieur; I intrude?"

"You do, mademoiselle."

The tone was uncompromising, but Jacqueline came on, softly moving nearer and nearer to the easel, looking from the canvas to Max and back again to the canvas in an amused, secret fashion comprehensible to herself alone.

"You feel like my poor Lucien, when an interruption offers itself to his work; but, as I say, *ennui* is the price of admiration! Is it not so, Monsieur Max?"

She leaned her blonde head to one side, and looked at him with the naïve quality of meditation that so became her.

"Do not permit me to disturb you, monsieur! Continue working."

"Thank you, mademoiselle!" A flicker of irony was observable in the tone and, with exaggerated zeal, he returned to his task.

The girl came softly behind him, looking over his shoulder.

"What is the picture to be, monsieur?"

"It is an idea caught last night in a *cabaret*. It would not interest you."

"And why not?"

Max shrugged his shoulders, and went on blocking in his picture.

"Because it is a psychological study—a side-issue of existence. Nothing to do with the crude facts of life."

"Oh!" Jacqueline drew in her breath softly. "I am only interested, then, in the crude facts? How do you arrive at that conclusion, monsieur?"

"By observation, mademoiselle."

"And what have you observed?"

"It is difficult to say—in words. In a picture I would put it like this—a blue sky, a meadow of rank green grass, a stream full of forget-me-nots, and a girl bending over it, with eyes the color of the flowers. Conventionality would compel me to call it *Spring* or *Youth*!" He spoke fast and he spoke contemptuously.

She watched him, her head still characteristically drooping, the little wise smile hovering about her lips.

"I comprehend!" she murmured to herself. "Monsieur is very worldly-wise. Monsieur has discovered that there is—how shall I say?—less atmosphere in a blue sky than in a gray one?"

Max glanced round at her. He had the uncomfortable feeling that he was being laughed at, but her clear azure eyes met his innocently, and her mouth was guiltless of smiles.

"I have had a sufficiency of blue sky," he said, and returned to his work.

"One is liable to think that, monsieur, until the rain falls!"

"So you doubt the endurance of my philosophy?"

She shrugged; she extended her pretty hands expressively.

"Monsieur is young!"

The words exasperated Max. Again it had arisen—the old argument. The anger smouldering in his heart since the girl's invasion flamed to speech.

"I could wish that the world was less ready with that opinion, mademoiselle! It knows very little of what it says."

"Possibly, monsieur! but you admit that—that you are scarcely aged." There was a quiver now about the pretty lips, a hint of a laugh in the eyes.

"Mademoiselle,"—he wheeled round with unexpected vehemence,—"I should like you, to tell me exactly how old you think I am."

"You mean it, monsieur?"

"I mean it. Is it seventeen—or is it sixteen?" His voice was edged with irony.

"It is neither, monsieur!" Jacqueline was very demure now, her eyes sought the floor. "Granted your full permission, monsieur, I would say—"

"You would say—?"

"I would say"—she flashed a daring look at him and instantly dropped her eyes again—"I would say that you have twenty-four, if not twenty-five years!"

The confession came in a little rush of speech, and as it left her lips she moved toward the door, contemplating flight.

An immense surprise clouded Max's mind, a surprise that brought the blood mantling to his face and sent his words forth with a stammering indecision.

"Twenty-four—twenty-five! What gave you that idea?"

"Oh, monsieur, it is simple! It came to me by observation!"

Leaving Max still red, still confused, she slipped out of the room noiselessly as she had come, and as the door closed he heard the faint, exasperating sound of a light little laugh.

CHAPTER XVI

AFTER Jacqueline had closed the door and the light laugh had died into silence, Max stood before his easel, hands inert, the flush still scorching his face. For the first time since the birth of the new life he had been made sensible of personal criticism—the criticism winged with fine ridicule, that leaves its victim strangely uncertain, curiously uneasy. The immemorial subtlety of woman had lurked in the girl's eyes as she cast her last penetrating glance at him. He felt now, as he stood alone, that his soul had been stripped and was naked to the bare walls and gaping canvas, and his start was one of purely unbalanced nerves when a knock fell upon the door, telling of a new intruder.

He had all but cried out in protest when the door opened, but at sight of the invader the cry merged into an unstrung laugh of welcome.

"Ned! You?"

Blake walked into the room, talking as he came. "Well, upon my word! Wasn't I right? Here he is, easel and canvas and all—even the temper isn't wanting!"

Max ran forward, caught and clung to his arm.

"*Mon ami*! *Mon cher*! I have wanted you—wanted you."

"Anything wrong?"

"No! No! Nothing. It was only—"

"What?"

Again Max laughed nervously, but his fingers tightened.

"Only this—I have wanted to hear you say that I am your friend—your boy, Max—as I was yesterday and the day before and the day before. Say it! Say it!" His eyes besought Blake's.

"What! Tell you you are yourself?"

He nodded quickly and seriously.

The other looked into his face, and for some unaccountable reason his amusement died away.

"What a child it is!" he said kindly; and, putting his hands upon the boy's shoulders, he shook him gently. "Who has been putting notions into your head? Whoever it is, just refer him to me; I'll deal with him."

It was Max's turn to laugh. "Ah, but I am better now! I am quite all right now! It was only for the moment!" He made a little sound, half shy, half relieved. "It was, I suppose, as you expected; I tired myself with carrying up these things, and then I still more tired myself with trying to block in my picture, and then—"

"Yes, then?"

"No more—nothing."

"I'm sceptical of that."

Max glanced up. "Well, to you I always say the truth. The girl Jacqueline came in and chattered to me, and—"

"Oh, ho!"

"Do not say that! I cannot bear it."

"Nonsense! I'm only teasing you! Though why a little girl with hair like spun silk and skin like ivory—"

"Ah! You admire her, then?"

"I do vastly—in the abstract."

"And what does that mean—in the abstract?"

"Oh, I don't know! I suppose it means that if I were a painter I might use her as a model, or if I were a poet I might string a verse to her; but being an ordinary man, it means—well, it means that I don't feel drawn to kiss her. Do you see?"

"I see." Max grew thoughtful; he disengaged the hands still lying lightly on his shoulders and walked back to his easel.

"You don't a bit! But it doesn't matter! What is it you're doing?"

Max, idle before his canvas, did not reply.

"*Mon ami?*" he said, irrelevantly.

"What?"

"Tell me the sort of woman you want to kiss."

Blake looked round in surprise.

"Well, to begin with, I used the word symbolically. I'm a queer beggar, you know; the kiss means a good deal to me. To me, it's the key to the idealistic as well as the materialistic—the toll at the gateway. I never kiss the light woman."

"No?" Max's voice was very low, his hands hung by his sides, the look in his half-veiled eyes was strange. "Then what is she like—the woman you would kiss?"

"Oh, she has no bodily form. One does not say 'her hair shall be black' or 'her hair shall be red' any more than one makes an image of God. She dwells in the mysterious. Even when the time comes and she steps into reality, mystery will still cling to her. There must always be the wonder—the miracle." He spoke softly, as he always spoke when sentiment entrapped him. His native turn of thought found vent at these odd times and made him infinitely interesting. The slight satire that was ordinarily wont to twist his smile was smoothed away, and a certain sadness stole into its place; his green eyes lost their keenness of observation and looked into a space obscure to others. In these rare moments he was essentially of his race and of his country.

"No," he added, as if to himself, "a man does not say 'her hair shall be red' or 'her hair shall be black'!"

"It is very curious—very strange—a dream like that!" Max's voice was a mere whisper.

"Without his dreams, man would be an animal."

"And you, then, wait for this woman? In seriousness you wait, and believe that out of nothing she will come to you?"

Blake turned away and walked slowly to the window, the sadness, the aloofness still visible in his face like the glow from a shrouded light.

"That's the hardship of it, boy—the faith that it wants and the patience that it wants! Sometimes it takes the heart out of a man! There're days when I feel like a derelict; when I say to myself, 'Here I am, thirty-eight years old, unanchored, unharbored.' Oh, I know I'm young as the world counts age! I know that plenty of men and women like me, and that I pass the time of day to plenty as I go along! But all the same, if I died to-morrow there isn't one would break a heart over me. Not a solitary one."

"Do not say that!"

"It's true, all the same! Sometimes I say to myself, 'Wha a fool you are, Ned Blake! The Almighty gives reality to some and dreams to some, and who knows but your lot is to go down to your grave hugging empty hopes, like your forefathers before you!' It's terrible, sometimes, the way the heart goes out of a man!"

"Ned! Ned! Do not say that!" Max's voice was strangely troubled, strangely unlike itself, so unlike and troubled that it wakened Blake to self-consciousness.

"I'm talking rank nonsense! I'm a fool!"

"You are not!" The boy ran across to him impulsively; then paused, mute and shy.

"What is it, boy?"

"Only that what you say is not the truth. If you were to die, there is one person who would—"

Blake's face softened. He was surprised and touched.

"What? You'd care?"

Max nodded.

"Thank you, boy! Thank you for that!"

They stood silent for a moment, looking through the uncurtained window at the February breezes ruffling the holly bushes in the plantation, each unusually aware of the other's presence, each unusually self-conscious.

"But if it comes to pass—your miracle—you will forget me? You will no longer have need of me, is that not so?"

Max spoke softly, a disproportionate seriousness darkening his eyes, causing his voice to quiver.

Blake turned to answer in the same vein, but something checked him— some embarrassment, some inexplicable doubt of himself.

"Boy," he said, sharply, "we're running into deep waters. Don't you think we ought to steer for shore? I came to smoke, you know, and watch you at your work."

The words acted as a charm. Max threw up his head and gave a little laugh, a trifle high, a shade hysterical.

"But, of course! But, of course! I believe I, too, was falling into a dream; and the dream comes after, the work first, is it not so? The work first; the work always first. Place another log upon the fire and begin to smoke, and I swear to you that before the day is finished I will make you proud of me. I swear it to you!"

CHAPTER XVII

THERE is impetus, if not necessarily inspiration in a goading thought, and Max returned to his interrupted task with a zeal almost in excess of his protestations. He worked with vigor—with an exuberant daring that seemed to suggest that the creation of his picture was rather the creation of a mental narcotic than the expression of an idea.

He had given rein to sentiment in the moment with Blake, and now he was applying the curb, working incessantly—- never pausing to speak— never casting a glance at the corner where his companion was smoking and dreaming over the fire.

To the casual observer it might have seemed a scene of ideal comradeship; yet in the minds of the comrades there lurked an uneasiness, an uncertainty not lightly to be placed—not easily to be clothed in words. A certain warmth was stirring in Blake's heart, coupled with a certain wonder at his sudden discovery of the depth of the boy's regard; while in the boy's own soul a tumult of feelings ran riot.

Shame burned him that he should have confessed himself; amazement seared him that the confession had been there to make. A bewildering annoyance filled him—a first doubting of the ego he was cherishing with so fine a care.

It is indeed a black moment when an egoist doubts himself; it is as if the god within the temple became self-conscious; more, it is as if the god rent down the veil before the shrine and showed himself a thing of clay to his astonished worshippers.

The mind of Max was a complex study as he worked with his new-found vehemence, expressing or crushing a thought with each bold stroke. He prided himself upon his powers of self-analysis; and, being possessed as well of honesty and of a measure of common sense, the mental picture that confronted him was scarcely pleasant seeing. Doubt of himself—of his own omnipotence—- had assailed him; and, being young, being spoiled of the world, it found expression in bitter resentment.

Having continued his onslaught upon the canvas until midday was close at hand, he suddenly astonished the unoffending Blake by flinging his charcoal from him to the furthest end of the room, where it broke rudely against the spotless wall-paper.

"God bless my soul!" Blake turned, to see an angry figure striding to the window, his hair ruffled, his hands thrust deep into his trouser pockets.

"What in God's name is the matter with you?"

There was no answer and, being a wise man, he did not press the point.

Presently, as he expected, the boyish figure wheeled round.

"I cannot work. It is all bad! All wrong!"

He rose slowly and began to walk toward the easel, but with a cry the boy ran forward and intercepted him.

"No! No! No! It is bad, I tell you—you must not see. Look! This is what I shall do. This!" He turned and, swift as lightning, snapped up a knife, and before Blake could find a gesture or a word, ripped his canvas from end to end.

"Upon my word! Well, upon my word! There's an extravagant young devil! Why, in the name of God, would you destroy your canvas like that?"

"Why? Because, my friend, I am I! I do not work again upon a thing that I have marred!" His voice shook, trembling between excited laughter and tears.

Blake looked at him. "Bless my soul, if he isn't crying! Come here to me! You're a baby!"

But Max turned on him, so furious that the hot anger in his eyes scorched the tears that hung there.

"A baby? This much a baby, that I love my work so truly that I have set it upon an altar and made it my religion! And when I find, as to-day, that it fails me I am damned—my soul is lost!"

"And why does it fail you—to-day?"

"I do not know!"

"Is that the truth?"

"Yes, it is."

"Are you perfectly sure? Are you perfectly sure that 'tisn't I—my presence here—?"

"You?" Max withered him with a scorn meant for himself as well. "You rate yourself high, my friend, and you imagine my work a very trivial thing!"

"Nonsense! Plenty of artists must have solitude."

"Plenty of fools! An artist is engrossed in his art so perfectly that when he stands before his canvas no world exists but the world of his imagination. Do you suppose me to be affected because you sit somewhere in the background, smoking over the fire? Oh, no! I trust I have more capacity to concentrate!"

He shrugged his shoulders to the ears; he raised his eyebrows in the very elaboration of indifference.

Blake, hot as he in pride or anger, caught sudden fire.

"Upon my soul, you're damned complimentary! I think, if you have no objection, I'll be wishing you good-day!" He picked up his hat, and strode to the door.

"LOOK! THIS IS WHAT I SHALL DO. THIS!"

The action was so abrupt, the offence so real, that it sobered Max. With a sudden collapse of pride, he wheeled round.

"Ned! Oh, Ned!"

But the banging of the outer door was his only answer; and he drew back, his face fallen to a sudden blankness of expression, his hand going out as if for support to the tattered canvas.

Minutes passed—how many or how few he made no attempt to reckon—then a tap fell on the door and his blood leaped, leaped and dropped back to a sick pulsation of disappointment, as the door opened and Jacqueline's fair head appeared.

For an instant a fierce resentment at this new intrusion fired him, then the absorbing need for human sympathy welled up, drowning all else.

"Mademoiselle," he cried out, "I am the most unhappy person in all the world; I have tried to make a picture and failed, and I have quarrelled with my best friend!"

Jacqueline nodded sagely. "That, M. Max, is my excuse for intruding. Of the picture, of course, I know nothing"—she shrugged expressively—"but of the quarrel I understand all—having passed M. Blake upon the stairs!"

At any other moment Max would have resented in swift and explicit terms this probing of his private concerns; but the soreness at his heart was too acute to permit of pride.

"Then you are sorry for me, mademoiselle?"

"Yes, monsieur!"

"Because of my spoiled picture?" Waywardness flickered up momentarily.

"No, monsieur!"

"Then why?"

Jacqueline glanced up swiftly, then dropped her eyes.

"Because, monsieur—being but a woman—I say to myself 'life is long, and other pictures may be painted; but with love—or friendship—'"

"Mademoiselle, that is sufficient! You are charming—you are sympathetic—- but, like many others, you place too great a value upon those words 'love' and 'friendship.' It is like this! If I quarrel with my friend it is doubtless sad, but it only affects myself; if, on the contrary, I paint a bad picture I am making a blot upon a beautiful world!"

"And what of the heart, monsieur? May there not be sad stains upon the heart—even if no eyes see them?"

"Now, mademoiselle, you are talking sentiment!"

"And you, monsieur, are materialistic?" For a second a flash of mischief showed in the blue eyes.

Max stiffened his shoulders; made brave show to hide the detestable ache in his soul.

"Yes, mademoiselle," he said. "I think, without pride, I may claim to see life wholly, without idealization."

Quite unexpectedly Jacqueline clapped her hands and laughed, stepping close to him with an engaging air of mystery.

"Then all is well! I have a physic for all your ills!"

He looked distrustful.

"A physic?"

"This, monsieur—that you put aside the great sorrow of your picture, and the little sorrow of your friend—and step across and partake of *déjeuner* with Lucien and me. A very special *déjeuner*, I assure you; no less than a *poulet bonne femme*, cooked with a care—"

She threw out her hands in an ecstasy of expression, a portrayal of the artless greed that had more than once brought a smile to the boy's lips. But this time no amusement was called up; disgust rose strong within him and, accompanying it, a certainty that were Jacqueline's chicken to be laid before him, he must assuredly choke with the first morsel. One does not eat when one has failed in one's art—or quarrelled with one's best friend!

"Mademoiselle," he said, unsteadily, "you are kind—and I am not without appreciation. But to-day I have no appetite—food does not call to me. Doubtless, there are days when M. Cartel cannot eat." He strove to force a laugh.

Jacqueline looked humorously grave.

"When Lucien cannot work, monsieur, he eats the more! It is only on the days when work flows from him that I am compelled to drag him to the table—those days or, perhaps, the days—" She stopped discreetly.

"What days, mademoiselle?"

For the gratification of a curiosity he condemned, Max put the question.

"Oh, monsieur, when some little affair arises upon which he and I dispute—when some cloud, as it were, darkens the sun." She continued to look down demurely; then quickly she looked up again. "But I waste your time! And, besides, I have not finished what I would say."

"Oh, mademoiselle, I beg—"

"It is not of the *poulet* that I would speak, monsieur! I understand that artists are not all alike; and that, whereas bad work gives Lucien an appetite, it gives you a disgust! Still, you are a philosopher, and will allow others to eat, even if you will not eat yourself."

Max looked bewildered.

"Good!" Jacqueline clapped her hands again softly. "I knew I would find success! I said I would find success!"

"But, mademoiselle, I do not understand."

"No, monsieur! Neither did M. Blake, when I met him upon the stairs, and told him of my *poulet*. He also, it seems, had lost his appetite. Your picture must have been truly bad!"

She discreetly toyed with her belt during the accepted space of time in which a brain can conceive—a heart leap—to an overmastering joy; then she looked again at Max.

"It is a little idea of my own, monsieur, that you and M. Édouard should make the acquaintance of my Lucien. M. Édouard already consents; I hope that you, monsieur—"

For answer, Max caught her hand. From that moment he loved her—her prettiness, her mischief, her humanity.

"Mademoiselle! I do not understand—and I do understand!"

"But you will come, monsieur?"

"I will eat your chicken, mademoiselle—even to the bones!"

CHAPTER XVIII

COMRADESHIP in its broader sense is Bohemianism at its best; Bohemianism, not as it is imagined by the *dilettante*—a thing of picturesque penury and exotic vice—but a spontaneous intermingling of personalities, an understanding, a fraternity as purely a gift of the gods as love or beauty.

It is true that the sense of regained happiness beat strong in the mind of Max when he followed Jacqueline into her unpicturesque living-room with its sparse, cheap furniture, its piano and its gas stove, and that the happiness budded and blossomed like a flower in the sun at the one swift glance exchanged with Blake; but even had these factors not been present, he must still have been sensible of the pretty touch of hospitality patent in the girl's manner the moment she crossed her own threshold, conscious of the friendly smile of M. Lucien Cartel, typical artist, typical Frenchman of the southern provinces—short, swarthy, alive from his coarse black hair to the square tips of his fingers. It was in the air—the sense of good-will—the desire for conviviality; and in the first greeting, the first hand-shake, the relations of the party were established.

But the true note of this Bohemianism is not so much spontaneous friendship as a spontaneous capacity for the interchange of thought—that instant opening of mind to mind, when place becomes of slight, and time of no importance.

Such an atmosphere was created by M. Lucien Cartel in his poor Montmartre *appartement*, and under its spell Max and Blake fell as surely, as luxuriously as they might have fallen under the spell of a summer day. It was not that M. Cartel was brilliant; his only capacity for brilliance lay in his strong, square hands; but he was a good fellow and possessed of a philosophy that at once challenged and interested. For Church and State he had a wide contempt, a scoffing raillery, a candid blasphemy that outraged orthodoxy: for humanity and for his art he owned an enthusiasm touching on the sublime. Upon every subject—the meanest and the most profound—he held an opinion and aired it with superb frankness and incredible fluency. So it was that, when the *poulet bonne femme* had been picked to the bones and Jacqueline had retired to some sanctum whence the clatter of plates and the sound of running water told of domestic duties, the three pushed their chairs back from the table and fell to talk.

Precisely how they talked, precisely what they talked of in that pleasant period subsequent to the meal is not to be related. They thrashed the paths of morality, science, religion until their contending voices filled the room and the tobacco smoke hung in clouds about them. They talked until the last drop of Jacqueline's coffee had been drained; they talked until Jacqueline herself came silently back into the room and seated herself by Cartel's side, slipping her hand into his with artless spontaneity.

Morality, science, religion, and then, in natural sequence, art—music! The brain of M. Cartel tingled, his fingers twitched as the rival merits of composers—the varying schools of thought—were touched upon, warmed to, or torn by contending opinions. One end only was conceivable to that last discussion. The moment arrived when the brain of M. Cartel cried vehemently for expression, when his hand, imprisoned in the small fingers of Jacqueline, was no longer to be restrained, when he sprang from his chair and rushed to the piano, his coarse black hair an untidy mat, his ugly face alight with God's gift of inspiration.

'What had he said? Was this, then, not magnificent—wonderful?'

And, seating himself, he unloosed into the common room a beauty of sound more adorning than the rarest devices of the decorator's art—a mesh of delicate harmonies that snared the imaginations of his three listeners and sent them winging to the very borders of their varying realms.

M. Lucien Cartel in every-day life and to the casual observer was a good fellow with a fund of enthusiasm and a ready tongue; M. Lucien Cartel to the woman he loved and in the enchanted world of his art was a mortal imbued warmly and surely with a spark of the divinity he derided. There is no niggardliness in Bohemia: it made him as happy to give of his music as it made his listeners to receive, with the consequence that time was dethroned and that four people sat entranced, claiming nothing from the world outside, more than content in the knowledge that the world had no eyes for the doings of a little room on the heights of Montmartre.

From opera to opera M. Cartel wandered, now humming a passage under his breath in accompaniment to his playing, again raising his soft, southern voice in an abandonment of enthusiasm.

It was following close upon some such enthusiastic moment that Max rose, crossed the room, and taking a violin and bow from where they lay upon a wooden bench against the wall, carried them silently to the piano.

As silently M. Cartel received them and, lifting the violin, tucked it under his chin and raised the bow.

There is no need to detail the magic that followed upon that simple action. The world—even his own Paris—has never heard of M. Lucien Cartel, and cares not to know of the pieces that he played, the degree of his technique, the truth of his interpretation; but when at last the hand that held the violin dropped to his side and, lifting his right arm, he wiped his damp forehead with the sleeve of his coat, the faces of his audience were pale as the faces of those who have looked upon hidden places, and in the eyes of the little Jacqueline there were tears.

A moment of silence; then M. Cartel laid down his violin and laughed. The laugh broke the spell: Jacqueline, with a childish cry of excitement, flew across the room and, throwing her arms about his neck, kissed him with unashamed fervor; Blake and Max pressed round the piano, and in an instant the room was humming again to the sound of voices, and some one made the astounding discovery that it was five o'clock.

This was Blake's opportunity—the opportunity loved beyond all others of the Irishman, when it is permissible to offer hospitality. The idea came to him as an inspiration, and was seized upon as such. Eager as a boy, he laid one hand on Max's shoulder, the other on that of M. Cartel.

'He had a suggestion to make! One that admitted of no refusal! M. Cartel had entertained them regally; he must suffer them to make some poor return. There was a certain little *café* where the *chef* knew his business and the wine really was wine—' He looked from one face to another for approval, and perhaps it was but natural that his eyes should rest last and longest on the face of Max.

So it was arranged. A dinner is a question readily dealt with in the quarter of Montmartre, and soon the four—laughing, talking, arguing— were hurrying down the many steps of the Escalier de Sainte-Marie, bent upon the enjoyment of the hour.

CHAPTER XIX

THEY dined with a full measure of satisfaction; for with his invitation to a feast, your Parisian accepts an obligation to bring forth his best in gayety, in conversation, in good-will; and it might well have happened that Blake, spending ten times as much money upon guests of his own world, might have lacked the glow, the sense of success, that filled him in the giving of this dinner to an unknown musician and a little blonde-haired *Montmartroise*.

They dined; and then, because the winds were still wintry and coffee could not yet be sipped outside *café* doors, they betook themselves to the little theatre of the 'Trianon Lyrique' on the Boulevard Rochechouart, where for an infinitesimal sum the *bourgeoisie* may sit in the stalls and hear light opera conscientiously sung.

As it was a gala evening, Blake reserved a box, and the little Jacqueline sat in the place of honor, neat and dainty to the point of perfection, with a small black jacket fitting closely to her figure, and a bunch of violets, costing ten centimes, pinned coquettishly into her lace *jabot*. They sat through the performance in a happy mood of toleration, applauding whenever applause might be bestowed, generously silent when anything tempted adverse criticism; and between the acts they smoked and drank liqueurs in company with the good Montmartre shopkeepers—the soldiers—the young clerks and the young girls who formed the crowd in the lounge.

But all things end; the curtain fell on the last act of *Les Cloches de Corneville*, and not without a pleasant, passing sigh, the four left the theatre.

The boulevard teemed with life as they made their way into the open; a certain intoxication seemed blown along the thoroughfare on the light spring wind; a restless energy tingled in the blood.

On the steps of the little theatre, Blake looked back at his party.

'The night was young! What would they say to supper?'

Jacqueline's eyes sparkled, but she looked at M. Cartel, and regretfully M. Cartel shook his head.

'Alas! He was expecting a friend—a composer, to call upon him before midnight.'

Jacqueline betrayed no disappointment; with a charming air she echoed the regret, the shake of the head, and slipped a confiding hand through M. Cartel's arm.

Then followed the leave-taking—the thanks and disclaimers—the promises of future meetings—and at last the lovers moved out into the crowd—M. Cartel, cheery and brisk, humming the tunes of 'Les Cloches,' the little Jacqueline clinging to his arm, smiling up into his ugly face.

Max watched them for a moment with a deep intentness, then wheeled round swiftly and caught Blake's arm.

"Ned! Take me somewhere! I would forget myself!"

"What troubles you, boy? Not the thought of the picture?"

"No! A something of no consequence. Do not question me. Be kind to me, and take me where I can see life and forget myself."

"Where will I take you?"

"To some place of gayety—where no one thinks."

"Very well! We'll go over and have supper at the Rat Mort. You won't be over-troubled with thought there. We can sit in a corner and observe, and I give you my word there will be no encounters with old friends this time! I'll be blind and deaf and dumb if anything is washed up from the past!"

Guiding the boy across the crowded roadway, he passed through the narrow door and up the steep stair that ends so abruptly into the long, low supper-room of the Rat Mort.

Max felt the abruptness of this entry, as so many climbers of the ladder-like stairs have felt it before him; and a dazed sensation seized upon him as the wild *Ztigane* music of the stringed orchestra beat suddenly upon his ears and the intense white light struck upon his sight.

He felt it as others have felt it—the excitement, the consciousness of an emotional atmosphere—as he followed Blake down the dazzlingly bright room. It was in the air, as it had been at the Bal Tabarin.

As they seated themselves, the barbaric music ceased; the orchestra broke forth afresh with a light Parisian waltz, and down between the lines of tables came a negro and a negress—properties of the place, as were the glasses and the table linen—waltzing with the pliant suppleness, the conscious sensuality of their race, and close behind them followed a second couple—a Spaniard, restless and lithe, small of stature and pallid of face, and a young Spanish girl of splendid physique.

Max sat silent, attentive to this dance, while Blake ordered supper; but when the wine was brought, he lifted his glass and drank, as if some strong sensation had dried his throat.

Blake turned and looked at him.

"Well? Is it amusing?"

"It is—and it is not. Those black creatures are extraordinary. They are repulsive—like figures in a nightmare."

"Oh! Repulsive, are they? And what about a certain picture we once looked at—when I was swept off the face of the earth for using that same word? I believe, you know, that points of view are changing! I believe I'm coming to part two of my little book! These niggers aren't a bit more disgusting than the monkey sucking the fruit."

Max glanced at him, laughed a trifle self-consciously and drank some more wine. "Let us forget monkeys and little books and all such stupidities. There is a pretty woman over there! Make me a story concerning her." He nodded toward a table in the middle of the room.

Blake, looking, saw a slim woman in white, whose large hat threw a becoming shadow on auburn hair and red-brown eyes.

"Ah, now," he said, thoughtfully, "you've given me too much to do! At a first glance I'd say she's just the ordinary better-class *cocotte*; but at a second glance it seems to me I'd pause. There's something about the eyes—there's something about the mouth that puzzles me. You'll have to wait, my boy, and let fate tell you your fairy tale!"

Trained in the consciousness of regard, the woman they discussed looked across at them as Blake ceased, and the flicker of a smile touched her lips—a smile of interest in which there lurked no hint of invitation.

"Ah, wasn't I right! She discriminates—our auburn lady! We'll see something interesting before the night is out, mark my words!"

They half forgot her and her possible story in the hour that followed, though Max noted that the woman who wanders from party to party at the Rat Mort, distributing roses, paused twice by her table and spoke to her, each time departing without unburdening herself of her wares; also, he noted that the pallid little Spaniard, who had been scattering his attentions among the ladies unprovided with companions, came and bowed before her, and that, contrary to her impression of aloofness, she rose and danced a waltz with him.

At this episode of the dance, Blake's eyes as well as the boy's were attracted; and, as she glided up and down between the tables, cool, unmoved, seemingly indifferent to the world about her, his interest reawakened, and he cast a sidelong glance at Max.

"Wait!" he said. "When you see that guarded look in a woman's eyes, you may always know she's expecting something."

Even as he spoke, she returned to her solitary table, dismissing the Spaniard with an inclination of the head and, as she seated herself, both observers saw a change pass over her face—saw her gaze narrow and turn toward the door—saw a faint flush touch her cheeks and recede, leaving them paler than before.

It was a controlled emotion, almost imperceptible—differing in essence from either the latent violence of the woman Lize or the artless impulsiveness of the little Jacqueline; but with certain intuition it sent Max's glance winging to the door of the supper-room, assured that some issue in the subtle war of sex was about to be fought out.

A new party was entering the room—a small dark *Parisienne*, bringing in her wake two Englishmen—one brown—the other fair, with the accepted Saxon fairness.

Down the long room the little lady came, ushered by obsequious waiters, the recipient of many glances, admiring or envious; close behind her followed the brown-haired Englishman and, a little in the rear, her second cavalier—reserved of demeanor, distinguished of carriage, obviously upholding the tradition of *sang-froid* that clings to his countrymen.

Max's instinct was fully awake now; and when, in passing her table, the fair man inclined his head to the auburn-haired lady, the matter merely fitted with his expectations.

What brief emotional past lay in the mists of the unknown, linking this woman to this man? Nothing was to be read from her face—no expression of pleasure, none of chagrin; but in her half-veiled eyes a certain brilliance was observable and her long, white fingers began softly to drum upon the table in time to the music.

No explanation was demanded; in a clear, disconcerting flash, the situation was laid bare. Here was woman desiring the love of man; woman determined to reap her spoil. It was one issue in the deathless, relentless struggle—the struggle wherein the little Jacqueline clung to her M. Cartel, tenacious as the frail fern to the ungainly rock—wherein Madame Salas had fought sickness and neglect to protect a fading life. It was a truth—arresting as truth must ever be; and stricken with a tingling fear, the boy drove it from him, and turned his eyes from the fateful, shadowed face and the light, drumming fingers.

A new dance had begun: the grinning negro had seized upon the Spanish girl and was whirling her down the room to the laughter of the company, while her countryman looked round the tables in indifferent search for a partner.

His glance skimmed the white figure at the lonely table, the eyes of the woman were lifted for an instant, revealing a flash of their new light, and in a moment the two were dancing again, moving up and down the room, in and out between the tables with their original easy grace; but this time the woman's lips were parted and her eyelids drooped in a clever simulation of enjoyment.

Up and down they glided, passing and repassing the table where the little dark lady supped with her two cavaliers, but never once did the woman raise her eyes to the Englishman's or seem aware of the cold, close glance that followed her movements; but once, as the music faded to silence, and her white skirt swept past his table for the last time, she murmured something softly in Spanish to her partner, and allowed one level, effective glance to fall on his pallid face.

That was all; the waltz stopped, she disengaged herself gently, and walked back alone to her table.

This waltz was followed by another and yet another, and again she fell to her old attitude of lowered eyes and drumming fingers.

The Englishman at his table made pretence to eat his supper, poured himself out a fresh glass of champagne, drank it, and with a suddenly achieved decision, gave a cool laugh of excuse, rose and walked straight toward the solitary figure.

Max, momentarily *clairvoyant*, felt the violent heartbeat, the caught breath, that told the woman of his presence—felt to a nicety the control of her expression, the rigidity of her body, as she slowly raised her head and met his eyes; then he saw the man bow, making some suggestion, and he leaned back in his seat with a little sigh of satisfaction as the woman smiled and rose and the two began to dance.

Both tall above the ordinary, they were a well-suited couple, and a certain pleasure filled the beholder's mind as they moved decorously up and down the long aisle formed by the double row of tables—the man entirely indifferent to his surroundings, dancing in this Parisian supper-place precisely as he would have danced in a London ball-room; the woman following his every movement with a passivity—a oneness—that gave no hint of the definite purpose at work within her brain.

The dance over, he led her back to her table, drew her chair forward with elaborate politeness, bowed and, with a murmured word, strolled back to his own table.

So sure had been her triumph, so abrupt its collapse, that Max—smoking his cigarette, sipping his coffee—turned, with a little exclamation, to Blake.

"Have you observed, *mon ami*? Oh, why was that?"

Blake was carefully lighting a cigar.

"'Twould be hard to say," he answered, meditatively. "In a matter of emotion, an Englishman has a way of getting frightened of himself. This particular specimen has come over to Paris to play—and he doesn't fancy fire for a toy!"

"And what will happen? What will be the end?" Max had laid his cigarette aside; his fingers were interlaced, sure sign that his emotions were running high; and his eyes, when he fixed them on Blake's, held a touch of their rare sombre fire.

"How will it end, you say? Guess, my child!"

Max shook his head.

"Well, boy, Eve will be Eve to the end of time—and Adam will be Adam!"

"You mean—? Oh, but look!"

This last was called forth by the rising from table of the trio—the quiet passing from the room of the fair man in the train of his friend and the little dark lady.

It seemed so final, so sharp an answer to his question, that Max could feel—as things personal and close—the sick sinking of the heart, the accompanying whiteness of cheek that must fall upon the woman sitting immovable and alone.

"I am sorry!" he cried. "Oh, but I am sorry!"

Blake looked thoughtfully at the tip of his cigar.

"Wait!"

Even as he said it, the fair man reappeared alone. "What did I say? Eve will be Eve—Adam will be Adam!"

But Max was not listening. Excited, lifted beyond himself, he was watching the Englishman thread a way between the tables—watching the woman thrill to his approach without lifting an eyelid, moving a muscle. Rigid as a statue she sat, until he was quite close; then, curiously, as if nature demanded some symbol of the fires within, her lips opened and she began to hum the tune the orchestra was playing.

It was a strange form of self-expression, and as she yielded to it her cheeks burned suddenly and her eyes shone between their narrowed lids.

She did not speak when the man seated himself at her table, she did not even look up; she went on humming in a strange ecstatic reverie, but she smiled—a very slow, a very subtle smile.

A waiter came, and wine was brought; she drank, laid down her glass and continued her strange song. The seller of flowers hovered about the table, smiling at the Englishman, and laid a sheaf of pink roses on the white cloth; still the humming continued, though mechanically the woman's long, white fingers gathered up the flowers and held them against her face. At last, unexpectedly, she raised her head, looked at the man whose eyes were now fixed in fascination upon her, looked away beyond him, and, lifting her voice from its murmuring note, began to sing aloud.

It was a scene curious beyond description—the hot, white room, the many painted faces, the many jewelled hands, the grotesque black forms of the negro dancers, and in the midst a woman hypnotized by her own triumph into absolute oblivion.

She sat with the roses in her hands, her eyes looking into space, while her voice, pure and singularly true, gathered strength until gradually the chattering of voices and the clinking of glasses lessened, and the musicians lowered their music to a deliberate accompaniment.

Nowhere but in Paris could such a scene take place; but here, although the faces turned toward the singer's were flushed with wine, they were touched with comprehension. The gathered roses—the high, sweet voice—the rapt face composed a picture, and even when his eyes are glazed, your Parisian is a connoisseur.

The last note quivered into silence; a little ripple of applause followed; and with the same concentrated, hypnotized gaze, the woman's eyes turned from space and rested again upon the man.

It was the glance ancient as tradition—significant as fate. At his distant table, Max rose and laid a trembling hand upon Blake's arm.

"Ned! May we go?"

"Oh, why? The night is young!"

"Please!"

"But why?"

"I desire it."

Blake looked more closely, and his expression changed.

"Why, you're ill, boy!" he said. "You're as white as a sheet!"

Max tried to laugh. "It is the heat—nothing more."

"Of course it is! The place is like a hot-house! You want a breath of air!"

Again Max tried to laugh, but it was a laugh oddly broken.

"That is it!" he said. "I want the air."

CHAPTER XX

MAX passed down the long, low room, blind to the white light, blind to the flowers and faces, deaf to the voices and laughter and swaying sound of stringed instruments.

One glance he permitted himself—one only—at the table where the man and woman still looked into each other's eyes and where the sheaf of pink roses still shed its incense: then he passed down the steep, short stairs, halting at the door of the *café*, hesitating between two atmospheres—outside, the sharp street lights, the cold, wind-swept pavement—within, the hot air, the close sense of humanity, powerful as a narcotic.

"Ned!" he said, looking back for Blake, "I need a favor. Will you grant it?"

"A hundred!" Blake was buttoning up his coat.

"Then wish me good-night here. I would go home alone."

"Alone? What nonsense! You don't think I'd desert you when you're seedy? What you want is air. We'll take a stroll along the boulevards."

Max shook his head. He seemed rapt in his own thoughts; his pale face was full of purpose.

"I am quite well—now."

"Then all the more reason for the stroll! Come along!"

But the boy drew away. "Another time! Not to-night."

"Why not?"

"I cannot tell you."

Blake looked more closely at the nervously set lips, the dark eyebrows drawn into a frown.

"I say, boy, it hasn't got on your nerves—this place? I know what a queer little beggar you are."

"No; it is not that."

"Then what? Another inspiration?"

"No."

"Very well! I won't probe. I'm old enough to know that the human animal is inexplicable. Good-night—and good luck! I'll see you to-morrow."

"To-morrow, yes!"

There was relief in the readiness of the response, relief in the quick thrusting forth of the boy's hand.

"Good-night!"

"Good-night! And go to bed when you get home. You're very white."

"Yes."

His voice seemed to recede further into its distant absorbed note, his fingers were withdrawn from Blake's close pressure with a haste that was unusual, and turning away, he crossed the boulevard as though the vision of some spectre had lent wings to his feet.

No impression of romance touched him as he hastened up the narrow streets toward his home. He had no eyes for the secret shadows, the mysterious corners usually so fruitful of suggestion; his whole perceptions were turned inward; his self-consciousness was a thing so living, so acute that he went forward as one bereft of sight or hearing.

Reaching the foot of the Escalier de Sainte-Marie, he quickened his already hurried pace, and began to run up the uneven steps. The door of his house stood open, and he plunged into the dark well of the hall without waiting to strike a match. By instinct his hand found the smooth banister, and he began his climb of the stairs.

Up he went, and up, living in himself with that perfect absorption that comes in rare and violent moments—moments of sorrow, of pleasure or, it may be, of surprise, when a new thought suspends the action of the brain.

In obedience to some unconsidered instinct he softened his steps on reaching the fifth floor, and crept across the bare corridor to the door of his own rooms.

He entered quietly, and still ignoring the need for light, groped a way to his bedroom.

It was the room that had once belonged to Madame Salas; and, like the kitchen, it looked upon the network of roofs and chimneys that spread away at the rear of the house. Now, as he entered, closed the door, and stood leaning against it, breathing quickly, these roofs and chimneys, seen through the uncurtained window, made a picturesque medley of lines and curves startlingly distinct against the star-powdered sky.

The ethereal light of a Parisian spring night filled the room, touching the white walls—the white bed—a bowl of flowers upon the dressing-table and its fairy-like reflection in the mirror—to a subtly insidious fragility that verged upon the unreal; and the boy, quivering to his tangled sensations, felt this unreality quicken his self-distrust, touch and goad him as a spur.

Physical action became imperative; he walked unsteadily across the room, pulled the serge curtains across the window, abruptly shutting out both stars and roofs, and turning to the dressing-table, groped for matches and struck a light.

Four candles stood in an old silver candelabra; he touched them with the match-flame, they flickered, spat, rose to a steady glow. In the new light the room looked warmer, more in touch with human things and, moving with the inevitableness of a pendulum, his mind swung to a definite desire.

Impulse seized him; questions, doubts, fears were submerged; trembling to a loosed emotion, he ran across the room and bent over his narrow bed.

He was alone now; alone in the absolutely primal sense of the word, when the individual ceases to act even to himself. The instinct he had denied was dominating him, and he was yielding with a sense of intoxication.

With hands that shook in excitement, he raised the mattress and, searching beneath, drew forth an object—a flat packet, bound and sealed—the packet, in fine, that had lain so deep and snug in the pocket of his overcoat on the night of his entry into Paris.

His hand—his whole body—was trembling as he brought it to light and walked back to the dressing-table.

There, he pulled forward a chair and sat down before the mirror. For a full minute he sat, as if enchained, then at length—in obedience to the force that was dominating him—his fingers crept under the string, there came to the ear a faint, sharp crackle, and the seals broke.

The seals broke, a gasp slipped from between his parted lips, and in his hands lay the symbol of all the imaginings, all the pretty mockery wherewith he purported to cheat nature.

It lay in his hands—a simple thing, potent as simple things ever are. No rare jewel, no state paper, merely the long, thick strands of a woman's hair.

The paper fell away, and he lifted it shakingly to the light. Stiff-coiled from its long imprisonment, it unwound slowly, allowing the candle-light to filch strange hues from its dark length—glints of bronze, tinges of copper-color that gleamed elusively from the one end, where it had been roughly clipped from the head, to the other, where it still curled and twisted into little tendrils like a living thing.

A woman's hair! A weapon old as time—as light, as destructible, as possessed of subtle powers as woman herself. Strand upon strand, he drew it out, following the glints of light with dazed, questioning eyes.

A woman's hair! A woman's hair, woven to blind men's eyes!

Max leaned forward, quivering to a new impulse, and, raising the heavy coils, twisted them swiftly about his head. With the action, the blood rushed into his cheeks, a flame of excitement sprang into his eyes and, drawing the candles closer, he peered into the mirror.

There are moments when a retrospective impression is overwhelming—when a scent, a sight, a sound can quicken things dead—things buried out of mind.

Max looked and, looking, lost himself. The boy with his bravery of ignorance, his frankly arrogant egoism was effaced as might be the writing from a slate, and in his place was a sexless creature, rarely beautiful, with parted, tremulous lips and wide eyes in which subtle, crowding thoughts struggled for expression.

He looked, he lost himself, and losing, heard nothing of a sound, faint and undefined, that stole from the region of the outer door—nothing of a light step in the little hall outside his room. Leaning closer to the mirror, still gazing absorbed, he began to twist the short waves of his own hair more closely into the strands that resembled them so nearly in texture and hue.

It was then, quietly—with the appalling quietude that can appertain to a fateful action—that the handle of the bedroom door clicked, the door itself opened, and the little Jacqueline—more child than ever in the throes of a swift amazement—stood revealed, a lighted candle in one hand, in the other a china mug.

At sound of the entry, Max had wheeled round, his hands still automatically holding up the strands of hair; at the vision that confronted him, a look of rage flashed over his face—the violent, unrestrained rage of the creature taken unawares.

At the look the little Jacqueline quailed, her lips opened and drooped, her right hand was lowered, until the candlestick hung at a perilous angle and the wax began to drip upon the floor.

"Oh!" she cried, "and I thought to find the room empty! *Pardon! Pardon! Oh, pardon, mons—madame!*"

CHAPTER XXI

IT was spoken—the one word, so brief, so significant; and Jacqueline stood hesitating, pleading, equally ready to rush forward or to fly.

At last Max spoke.

"Why do you call me that?"

The tone in which the question was put was extremely low, the gray eyes were steady almost to coldness, the strong, slight fingers began mechanically to fold up the hair, strand upon strand.

Jacqueline's candle swayed, until a stream of the melted wax guttered to the floor.

"Because—"

"Yes?"

"Because—oh, because—because—I have always known!"

Then indeed a silence fell. Jacqueline, too petrified to embellish her statement, let her voice trail off into silence; Max, folding—mechanically folding—the strands of hair, offered neither disclaimer nor acceptance. With the force of the inevitable the confession had struck home, and deep within him was the strong soul's respect for the inevitable.

"You have always known?" he said, slowly, when the silence had fulfilled itself. "You have always known—that I am a woman?"

It sounded abominably crude, abominably banal—this tardy question, and never had Max felt less feminine than in the uttering of it.

The lips of Jacqueline quivered, her blue eyes brimmed with tears of distress.

"Oh, I could wish myself dead!"

"And why?"

"Because I have made myself an imbecile!"

The humiliation, the self-contempt were so candid, so human, that something changed in Max's face and the icy rigidity of pose relaxed.

"Come here!"

The guilty child to the life, Jacqueline came timidly across the room, the candlestick still drooping unhappily from her right hand, the mysterious mug clutched in her left.

Max's first action was to take possession of both, and to set them side by side upon the dressing-table. The candle Jacqueline delivered up in silence, but as the mug was wrested from her, she cried out in sudden vindictiveness:

"And that—look you—that is the cause of all! It was Lucien's idea! I served a cup of *bouillon* to him and to his friend at midnight, for they had talked much; and finding it good, nothing would serve but I must place a cup also for Monsieur Max, to await him on his return. Alas! Alas!"

Max pushed the cup away, as if to remove a side issue.

"Answer the question I put to you! You know that I am a woman?"

"Yes; I know."

"Since when? Since the night at the Bal Tabarin?"

"Oh, but no!"

"Since the morning we met upon this doorstep?"

"No."

"Since the morning you made the coffee for M. Blake and me?"

Jacqueline was twisting the buckle of her belt in nervous perturbation.

"Answer me! It was since that morning?"

"No! Yes! Oh, it was before that morning. Oh, madame—monsieur!" She wrung her hands in a confusion of misery. "Oh, do not torture me! I cannot tell you how it was—or when. I cannot explain. You know how these things come—from here!" She lightly touched the place where she imagined her heart to be.

Max, sitting quiet, made no betrayal of the agony of apprehension at work within.

"And how many others have had this—instinct? M. Cartel? M. Blake?"

So surprising, so grotesque seemed the questions, that self-confidence rushed suddenly in upon Jacqueline. She threw back her head and laughed— laughed until her old inconsequent self was restored to power.

"Lucien! Monsieur Édouard! Oh, *la, la*! How droll!"

"Then they do not know?"

"Know? Are they not men? And are men not children?"

The vast superiority—the wordly wisdom in the babyish face was at once so comical and so reassuring that irresistibly Max laughed too; and at the laugh, the little Jacqueline dropped to her knees beside the dressing-table and looked up, smiling, radiant.

"I am forgiven?"

"I suppose so!"

"Then grant me a favor—one favor! Permit me to touch the beautiful hair!"

Without waiting for the permission, the eager little hands caught up the coiled strands, and in a moment the candlelight was again chasing the red tints and the bronze through the dark waves.

"My faith, but it is beautiful! Beautiful! And what a pity!"

"A pity—?"

"That no man may see it!" For an instant Jacqueline buried her face in the silky mass; then, like a little bright bird, looked up again. "A man would go mad for this!"

"For a thing like that? Absurd!"

"Yet a thing like that can demolish Monsieur Max, and leave in his place—"

"What?"

"How shall I say? His sister?" She looked up anew, disarming in her naïve candor: and a swift temptation assailed her listener—the temptation that at times assails the strongest—the temptation to unburden the mind.

"Jacqueline," Max cried, impetuously, "you speak a great truth when you say that! We have all of us the two natures—the brother and the sister! Not one of us is quite woman—not one of us is all man!"

The thought sped from him, winged and potent; and Jacqueline, wise in her child's wisdom, offered no comment, put forward no opinion.

"It is a war," Max cried again, "a relentless, eternal war; for one nature must conquer, and one must fail. There cannot be two rulers in the same city."

"No," Jacqueline murmured, discreetly, "that is most true."

"It is. Most true."

"Why, then, was madame adorning herself with her beautiful hair when I had the unhappiness to enter? Has not madame already waged her war—and conquered?"

The eyes were full of innocent question, the soft lips perfectly grave.

Max paused to frame the falsehood that should fit the occasion; but, like a flood-tide, the frankness, the courage of the boy nature rose up, and the truth broke forth.

"I thought until to-night, Jacqueline, that the battle was won; but to-night, while I supped with M. Blake, a little play was played out before me—a little human play, where real people played real parts, where the woman clung to her womanhood, as you cling to yours, and the man to his manhood, as does M. Cartel; where the stage effects were smiles and glances and eyes and hair—"

Jacqueline nodded, but said not a word.

"And as I watched, the thought came to me—the mad thought, that I had, perhaps, lost something—that I had, perhaps, put something from me. Oh, it was a possession! A possession of some evil spirit!"

Max sprang from the chair, and began to pace up and down the shadowed room, while the little Jacqueline, sitting back upon her heels in a stillness almost Oriental, watched, evolving some thought of her own.

"And so madame desired to strangle the evil spirit with her beautiful hair?"

The hurried steps ceased.

"I wished to see the woman in me—and to dismiss her!"

"And was she easily dismissed?"

The new question seemed curiously pregnant. Max heard it, and in swift response came back again to the dressing-table, took the hair from Jacqueline's hands and began again to intertwist it with the boyish locks.

Jacqueline raised herself from her crouching position, the more easily to gratify her curiosity.

"It is extraordinary—the change!" she murmured. "Extraordinary! Madame, let us complete it! Let us remove that ugly coat!" Excitedly, and without permission, she began to free Max of the boy's coat, while Max yielded with a certain passive excitement. "And, now, what can we find to substitute? Ah!" She gave a cry of delight and ran to the bed, over the foot of which was thrown a faded gold scarf—a strip of rich fabric such as artists delight in, for which Max had bargained only the day before in the rue André de Sarte.

"Now the tie! And the ugly collar!" She ran back, the scarf floating from her arm; and Max, still passive, still held mute by conflicting sensations, suffered the light fingers to unloose the wide black tie, to remove the collar, to open a button or two of the shirt.

"And now the hair!" With lightning-like dexterity, Jacqueline drew a handful of hairpins from her own head, reduced her short blonde curls to confusion, and in a moment had brushed the thick waves of Max's clipped hair upward and secured them into a firm foundation.

"Now! Now, madame! Close your eyes! I am the magician!"

Max's eyes closed, and the illusion of dead hours rose again, more vivid, more poignant than before. With the familiar sensation of deft fingers at work upon the business of hairdressing, a thousand recollections of countless nights and mornings—countless preparations and wearinesses—countless anticipations and disgusts, born with the placing of each hairpin, the coiling of the unfamiliar—familiar—weight of hair.

"Now, madame! Is it not a picture?"

With the gesture and pride of an artist, Jacqueline cast the wide scarf round Max's shoulders and stepped back.

Max's eyes opened, gazing straight into the mirror, and once again in that night of contrasts, emotion rose paramount.

It was most truly a picture; not the earlier, puzzling sketch—the anomalous mingling of sex—but the complete semblance of the woman—the slim neck rising from the golden folds, the proud head, seeming smaller under its coiled hair than it had ever appeared in the untidiness of its boy's locks.

"And now, madame, tell me! Is the evil spirit one lightly to be dismissed?"

All the woman in the little Jacqueline—the creature of eternal tradition, eternal intrigue—was glorying in her handiwork, in the consciousness of its potency.

But Max never answered; Max continued to stare into the glass.

"You will dismiss it, madame?"

Max still stared, a peculiar light of thought shining and wavering in the gray eyes.

"Madame, you will dismiss it?"

Max turned slowly.

"I will do more, Jacqueline. I will destroy it utterly."

"Madame!"

"I have a great idea."

"Madame!"

"If a spirit—no matter how evil—could be materialized, it would cease to affect the imagination. I shall materialize mine!"

"Madame!"

"Yes; I have arrived at a conclusion. I shall render my evil spirit powerless by materializing it. But I must first have a promise from you; you must promise me to keep my secret."

"Madame—madame!" Jacqueline stammered.

"You will promise?"

"Yes."

"And how am I to trust you?"

Jacqueline's blue eyes went round and round the room, in search of some overwhelming proof of her fidelity; then swiftly they returned to Max's.

THE COMPLETE SEMBLANCE OF THE WOMAN

"Not even to Lucien, madame, shall it be revealed!" And silently Max nodded, realizing the greatness of the pledge.

Many hours later, when all the lights were out in the rue Müller and all the doors wore closed, the slight figure of the boy Max might have been seen by any belated wanderer slipping down the Escalier de Sainte-Marie to post a letter—a letter that had cost much thought, and upon which had been dropped many blots of ink; and had the belated wanderer been possessed of occult powers and wished to probe inside the envelope, the words he would have read were these—scrawled with bold impetuosity:

> *Mon Ami,*—My idea—the true idea—has come to me. It was born in the first hour of this new day, and with it has come the knowledge that, either you were right and some artists need solitude, or I am one of the fools I talked of yesterday!
>
> All this means that I am ill of the fever of work, and that for many, many days—many, many weeks—I shall be in my studio—locked away even from you.
>
> Think no unkind thing of me! All my friendship is yours— and all my thought. Be not jealous of my work! Understand! Oh, Ned, understand! And know me, for ever and for ever, your boy.
>
> MAX.

PART III

CHAPTER XXII

OF all the ills that circumstance forces upon man, separation from a beloved object is, perhaps, the most salutary. Separation is the crucible wherein love undergoes the test absolute; in the fire of loss, grief softens to indifference or hardens to enduring need.

The pale blue sky of May smiled upon Montmartre. The shrubs in the plantation shimmered forth in green garments, the news-vender by the gate, the little old Basque peasant woman telling her beads in the shade of a holly-tree, even the children screaming at play on the gravelled pathway, were touched with the charm of the hour. Or so it seemed to Max—Max, *debonair* of carriage—Max, hastening to a *rendezvous* with fast-beating heart and nerves that throbbed alternately to a wild joy of anticipation and a ridiculous, self-conscious dread.

How he had counted upon the moment! How he had loved and feared it in ardent, varying imagination! And now, that it had at last arrived, how hopelessly his prearranged actions eluded him, how humanly his rehearsed sentences failed to marshal themselves for speech! As he climbed up the plantation, dazzled by the sun, intoxicated by the budding summer, he felt the merest unsophisticated youth—the merest novice, dumb and impotent under his own emotions.

Then, suddenly, all self-distrust—even all self-consciousness—was reft from him and he stood quite still, the blood burning his face, a strange sensation contracting his throat.

"At last! After a hundred thousand years!"

The first impression that fled across his mind was the intense familiarity of Blake's voice—the delightful familiarity of Blake's phrasing; the second, the brimming joy of regained companionship.

"*Mon ami! Cher ami!*"

His hands went out and were caught in Blake's; and all existence became a mirror to the blue, smiling sky.

No further word was said; Blake took possession of his arm in the old, accustomed fashion, and silently—in that silence which makes speech seem poor—they turned and began to pace up and down the gravelled path.

There was nothing beautiful in the plantation of the Sacré-Coeur; the shrubs, for all their valor of green, were slight things if one thought of forest trees, the grass was a mere pretence of grass. But the human mind is a great magician, weaving glories from within, and neither Blake nor Max had will for anything but the moment set precisely as it was.

For the gift of the universe, Blake could not have told why the mere holding of the boy's arm, the mere regulating of his pace to his, filled him with such satisfaction; nor, for the same magnificent bribe, could Max have explained the glow—the all-sufficing sense of fulfilment, born of the physical contact.

For long they paced up and down, wrapped in their cloak of content; then some look, some movement brought the world back, and Blake paused.

"What a selfish brute I am! What about the work? Tell me, is it done?"

Max looked up, the sun discovering the little flecks of gold in his gray eyes; Max laughed from sheer happiness.

"*Mon ami!* But absolutely I had forgotten! Figure it to yourself! I came out of the house, hot and cold for my poor picture, and immediately we met—" He laughed again. "*Mon ami!* What a compliment to you!"

"It is done then—the great work?"

"Yes; it is finished."

"Then I must see it this minute—this minute—this very minute!"

The definiteness of the tone was like the clasp of the arm, and Max glowed anew. By a swift, emotional effort, he conjured up the longings that had preyed upon him in his self-imposed solitude—conjured them for the sheer joy of feeling them evaporate before reality.

"It awaits you, *mon ami!*" He made a sweeping gesture, as though he laid the world at his friend's feet. And Blake, noting this, noted also with an odd little sense of gratification, that Max's English was a trifle more halting—a trifle more stilted for the break in their companionship.

Still arm in arm, they passed down the sloping pathway to the gate, where the children still played shrilly and the old Basque peasant still drowsed over her rosary beads. As they passed her, Blake put his hand in his pocket and slipped a silver coin into her fingers.

"They're so like my own people—these Basque peasants!" he said, by way of excuse. "They always give me a warm feeling about the heart."

The old woman looked up surprised, and both were attracted by the picture she made against the dark holly-trees—- the brown withered face, the astonishingly bright eyes like the eyes of a bird, the spare, bent figure with its scrupulous cleanliness of dress.

"The blessing of the good God rest upon you, monsieur!" she said, solemnly. "And may He provide you with your heart's desire!"

"And for me, *bonne mère*?" Max broke in. "What for me?"

The small bright eyes scanned the young face thoughtfully. "The good God, monsieur, will take you where He means that you should go!" Her thin lips closed, and she fell again to the telling of her beads, her inner vision doubtless weaving the scenes of her youth—the grave brown hills and sounding sea of her native country.

"For the moment it would seem that the good God points a way to the studio!" said Max, as they turned away. "*Mon ami*, I burn and tremble at once! Suppose it is of no use—my picture?" He stopped suddenly by the gate, to gaze with unpremeditated consternation at Blake; and Blake, touched by the happy familiarity of the action, laughed aloud.

"The same Max!" he cried. "The same, same Max! It's like turning back to the first page of my little book. Come along! I have spirit for anything to-day—even to tell you that you've made a failure. Come along, boy! It's a great world, when all's said and done! Come along! I'll race you up the steps!"

Laughing like a couple of children, they ran up the Escalier de Sainte-Marie, smiled upon indulgently by the careless passers-by, and entering the house, the race was continued up the polished stairs.

At the door of the *appartement* Max came level with Blake, his face glowing with excitement, his laughter broken by quick breaths.

"Oh, Ned, no! No! You must not enter! I am to go first. I have arranged it all. Ned, please!" He pulled Blake back and, opening the door, passed into the little hall and on into the bare, bright studio.

To Blake, following closely, the scene bore a striking resemblance to another scene—to the occasion upon which Max had blocked in, and then destroyed, his *cabaret* picture—save that now the light was no longer the silvery light of spring, but the pale gold radiance of a youthful summer.

The impression came, but the impression was summarily erased, for as he crossed the threshold, Max flew to him, his exuberance suddenly dead, the trepidation of the artist enveloping him again, chasing the blood from his cheeks.

"Oh, Ned! Dear Ned! If it is bad?" He caught and clung to Blake's arm, restraining him forcibly. "Do not look! Wait one moment! Just one little moment!"

Very gently Blake disengaged the clinging hands. "What a child he is, after all! He shuts himself away and works like a galley-slave and then, when the moment of justification comes—! Nonsense, boy! I'm not a critic. Let me see!"

As in a dream, Max saw him walk round the easel and pause full in front of it; in an agony of apprehension, a quaking eagerness, he lived through the moment of silence; then at Blake's first words the blood rushed singing to his ears.

"It's extraordinary! But who is it?"

"Extraordinary? Extraordinary?" In a wild onset of emotion, Max caught but the one word. "Does that mean good—or does it mean bad? Oh, *mon cher*, all that I have put into that picture! Speak! Speak! Be cruel! It is all wrong? It is all bad?"

"Don't be a fool!" said Blake, harshly. "You know it's good. But who is it? That's what I'm asking you. Who is it?"

Heedless, unstrung—half laughing, half crying—Max ran across the room. "Oh, *mon ami*, how you terrified me—I thought you had condemned it!"

But Blake's eyes were for the picture; the portrait of a woman seated at a mirror—a portrait in which the delicate reflected face looked out from its shadowing hair with a curious questioning intentness, a fascinating challenge at once elusive and vital.

"Who is it?"

He spoke low and with a deliberate purpose; and at his tone recklessness seized upon Max.

"A woman, *mon ami*! Just a woman!" He stiffened his shoulders, threw up his head, like a child who would dare the universe.

"Yes, but what woman?" With amazing suddenness Blake swung round and fixed a searching glance upon him. "She's the living image of you—but you with such a difference—"

He stopped as swiftly as he had begun, and in the silence Max quailed under his glance. Out of the unknown, fear assailed him; it seemed that under this mastering scrutiny his mask must drop from him, his very garments be rent. In sudden panic his thought skimmed possibilities like a circling bird and lighted upon the first-found point of safety.

"She is my sister," he said, in a voice that shook a little. "She is my sister—Maxine."

Blake's eyes still held his.

"But you never said you had a sister."

Max seized upon his bravado, flinging it round him as a garment.

"*Mon ami*," he cried, "we are not all as confiding as you! Besides, it is not given to us all to possess five aunts, seven uncles, and twenty-four first cousins! If I have but one sister, may I not guard her as a secret?"

He spoke fast; his eyes flashed with the old light, half pleading, half impertinent, his chin was lifted with the old defiant tilt. The effect was gained. Blake's severity fell from him, and with a quick gesture of affection he caught him by the shoulder.

"I'm well reproved!" he said. "Well reproved! 'Twas quite the right way of telling me to mind my own affairs. And if she were *my* sister—" He turned again to the picture, but as his eyes met the mirrored eyes with their profound, inscrutable look, his words broke off unaccountably.

"Yes, *mon ami*? If she were your sister—?" Max, with eager, stealthy glance, was following his expressions.

But he did not answer; he stood lost in contemplation, speculating, he knew not why, upon the question in the mirrored face.

CHAPTER XXIII

THE studio was in darkness; the old leathern arm-chair was drawn close to the window, and from its capacious depths Blake looked down upon the lights of Paris, while Max, leaning over the balcony, looked upward at the pale May stars clustering like jewelled flowers in the garden of the sky.

They had finished dinner—a dinner cooked by Blake in the little kitchen beyond the hall, and empty coffee-cups testified to a meal enjoyed to its legitimate end. The sense of solitude—of an intimate hour—lay upon the scene as intangibly and as definitely as did the darkness; but Max, watching the pageant of the stars, resting his light body against the iron railing, was filled with a mental restlessness, the nervous reaction of the day's triumph. More than once he glanced at Blake, a little gleam of uncertainty flashing in his eyes, and more than once his glance returned to the sky, as if seeking counsel of its immensity.

Upon what point was Blake speculating? What were the thoughts at work behind his silence? The questions tormented him like the flicking of a whip, and he marked with an untoward jealousy the profundity of Blake's calm—marked it until, goaded by a sudden loneliness, he cried his fear aloud.

"Ned! You missed me in these weeks?"

Blake started, giving evidence of a broken dream. "Missed you, boy?" he said, quietly. "I didn't know how much I missed you until I saw you again to-day."

"And you have made no new friend?"

"Not a solitary one—man, woman, or child!"

The reply would have satisfied the most suspicious; and Max gave a quick, deep sigh of relief.

"Ah! I thank God!"

In the darkness, Blake smiled, looking indulgently at the youthful figure silhouetted against the sky. "Why are you so absurd, boy?" he asked, gently. "Surely, I have proved myself!"

"Forgive me! I was jealous!" With one of his engaging impulses, the boy straightened himself and came across the balcony. "I am a strange creature,

Ned! I want you altogether for myself—I want to know you satisfied to be all mine!"

Blake looked up. "Do you know," he said, irrelevantly and a little dreamily, "do you know that is just the speech I could imagine issuing from the lips of your picture! Tell me something of this mysterious sister of yours; I've been patient until now."

Max drew back into the darkness.

"Of my sister? There is nothing to tell!"

"Nonsense! There's always something to tell. It's the sense of a story behind things that keeps half of us alive. Come! I've spun you many a yarn." With the quiet air of the man who means to have his way, he took out and lighted a cigar.

"Come, boy! I'm listening!"

Max had turned back to the railing, and once more he leaned out into the night; but now his eyes were for the meshed lights of the city and no longer for the stars, his restlessness had heightened to excitement, his heart seemed to beat in his throat. The temptation to make confession, to make confession here, isolated in the midst of the world, with the friend of his soul for confessor, caught him with the urgency of an embracing gale. To lay himself bare, and yet retain his garments! His head swam, as he yielded to the suggestion.

"There is nothing to tell!" he said again.

"That's admitted! All the best stories begin that way."

Max laughed and took a cigarette from his pocket. His nerves were tingling, his blood racing to the thought of the precipice upon which he stood. One false step and the fabric of his existence was imperilled! The adventurer awoke in him alive and alert.

"She intrigues you, then—Maxine?"

"Marvellously—as the Sphinx intrigues me! To begin with, why the name? You Max! She Maxine!"

For an instant Max scanned the dark plantation with knitted brows; then he looked over his shoulder with a peculiar smile.

"We are twins, *mon cher!*" he said, taking secret joy in the elaboration of his lie. "My mother was a Frenchwoman, by name Maxine, and when she died at our birth, my father in his grief bestowed the name upon us both—the boy and the girl—Max and Maxine!" Very carefully he lighted his cigarette. His whole nature was quivering to the dangers of this masked confession—this dancing upon the edge of the precipice. "My father was a man of ideas!" He carefully threw the match down into the rue Müller.

"Your father, I take it, was a personage of importance?" Blake was momentarily sarcastic.

"A personage, yes," the boy admitted, "but that is not the point. The point is that he was a man of ideas, who understood the body and the soul. A man who trained a child in every outdoor sport until it was one with nature, and then taught it to entrap nature and bend her to the uses of art. He was very great—my father!"

"He is dead?"

"Yes; he is dead. He died the year before Maxine married."

"Ah, she married?" Absurd as it might seem, there was a fleeting shadow of disappointment discernible in Blake's voice.

"Yes, she married. After my father's death she went to my aunt in Petersburg, and there she forgot both nature and art—and me."

"And who was the man she married?"

Max shrugged his shoulders to the ears. "Does it serve any purpose to relate? He was very charming, very accomplished; how was my sister, at eighteen, to know that he was also very callous, very profligate, very cruel? These things happen every day in every country!"

"Did she love him?" Blake was leaning forward in his chair; he had forgotten to keep his cigar alight.

"Love him?" With a vehemence electric as it was unheralded, Max's voice altered; with the passionate changefulness of the Russian, indifference was swept aside, emotion gushed forth. "Love him? Yes, she loved him— she, who was as proud as God! She loved him so that all her pride left her— all the high courage of my father left her—"

"And he—the man, the husband?"

"The man?" Max laughed a short, bitter laugh unsuggestive of himself. "The man did what every man does, my friend, when a woman lies down beneath his feet—he spurned her away."

"But, my God, a creature like that!"

Again Max laughed. "Yes! That is what you all say of the woman who is not beneath your own heel! You wonder why I disapprove of love. That is the reason of my disapproval—the story of my sister Maxine! Maxine who was as fine and free as a young animal, until love snared her and its instrument crushed her."

"But the man—the husband?" said Blake again.

"The man? The man followed the common way, dragging her with him—step by step, step by step—down the sickening road of disillusionment—down that steep, steep road that is bitter as the Way of the Cross!"

"Boy!"

"I shock you? You have not travelled that road! You have not seen the morass at the bottom! You have not seen the creature you loved stripped of every garment that you wove—as has my sister Maxine! You do well to be shocked. You have not been left with a scar upon your heart; you have not viewed the last black picture of all—the picture of your beloved as a dead thing—dead over some affair of passion so sordid that even horror turns to disgust. You do well to be shocked!"

"Dead?" repeated Blake, caught by the sound of the word. "He died, then?"

"He killed himself." Max laughed harshly. "Killed himself when all the wrong was done!"

"And your sister? Your sister? Where did she go—what did she do?"

"What does a woman do when she is thrown up like wreckage after the storm?"

"She does as her temperament directs. I think your sister would go back to nature—to the great and simple things."

With a tense swiftness the boy turned from his fixed contemplation of the sky, his glance flashing upon Blake.

"One must be naked and whole to go back to nature! One fears nature when one is wreckage from the storm!"

"Then she turned to art?"

"No, my friend! No! Art, like nature, exacts—and she had already given! She was too frightened—too hurt to meddle with great things. She dried her tears before they had time to fall; she hardened her heart, and went back to the world that gives nothing and exacts nothing."

"Poor child!" said Blake. "Poor child!"

"She went back to the world—and the world poured oil on her wounds, and soothed her fears and taught her its smiling, shallow ways."

"Poor child!"

The reiterated word had a curious effect upon the boy; his fierceness dropped from him; he turned again to the railing and, looking upward, seemed to drench himself in the coolness of the starlight.

"For years she lived her shallow life. She took lightly the light gifts the world offered; among those gifts was love—"

"Stop!" cried Blake, involuntarily. "You are tarnishing the picture!"

"I am only painting in crude colors! Much love was offered lightly to Maxine, and she took it—lightly; then one day her friend the world brought for her consideration a suitor more powerful, more distinguished, even less exigent than the rest—"

"Stop! Stop!" cried Blake, again. "I can't see her as this hard woman. She frightens me!"

"She has sometimes frightened me," said Max, enigmatically, "but that is outside the picture. She took, as I tell you, with both hands, smiling very wisely to herself, holding her head very high. But when the head is held too high, the feet sometimes fall into a trap. It came suddenly—the trapping of my sister Maxine."

"Yes! Yes! Tell me!"

"I am telling you, my friend! The date of Maxine's marriage was fixed, and she moved through her world content. One night a great court function was held; she was present, her *fiancé* was present, the atmosphere was all congratulation—like honey and wine. When it was over, the *fiancé* begged the privilege of escorting her to her home, and they drove together through the cold Russian night. They spoke little; Maxine's thoughts skimmed lightly over the future, her hands lay lightly in her *fiancé's*. All was unemotional— all was smooth and undisturbed—until they reached the street where her house stood; then, with the swiftness that belongs to mad moments, the being beside her showed himself. Quick as a flash of lightning, the dignified, distinguished, unexacting lover was effaced, and in his place was a man— an animal—a passionate egoist! He caught her in his arms, and his arms were like iron bands; his lips pressed hers, and they were like a flame. In a flash, the fabric of her illusions was scattered. She saw the truth. The world had cheated her, this second marriage was to be as the first. Terror seized my sister Maxine—terror of life, terror of herself. Her false calm broke up, as the ice breaks under the hand of spring—wells of fear gushed in her heart. She dismissed her lover at the gateway of her house; he guessed nothing— he knew nothing but that her hands were shaking and that her face was white, but when he was gone she rushed to her own room, cast off all her jewels, wrapped herself in a fur cloak and commanded her sledge and her swiftest horses."

"Boy!" cried Blake. "What a situation!"

"She drove, drove for hours, feeling nothing of the biting cold, seeing nothing of the imprisoning white world about her, goaded by one idea—the terror of life—the terror of giving herself again—"

"She fled," cried Blake, with sudden intuition. "She never returned to Petersburg!" He had risen from his chair; he was supremely, profoundly interested.

"She never returned to her own house. Three days after that wild drive she left Russia—left Russia and came—"

"To you!" cried Blake. "What a superb situation! She came back to you—the companion of her youth—to you, adventuring here in your own odd way! Oh, boy, it's great!"

"It is strange—yes!" said Max, suddenly curbing himself.

"Strange? It's stupendous!" Blake caught him by the shoulder, wheeling him round, looking straight into his face. "Boy! You know what I'm going to ask? You know what I'm wanting with all my heart and soul?"

The pressure of his hand was hard; he was the Blake of rare moments— the Blake roused from nonchalant good-nature into urgency of purpose. Max felt a doubt, a thin, wavering fear flutter across his mind.

"*Mon cher*," he stammered, "I do not know. How could I know?"

"It's this, then! With all my heart and soul I want to know this sister of yours."

CHAPTER XXIV

IT came sharply, as the crash of a breaking vessel might come to the ear—this ring of reality in Blake's voice! Abruptly, unpleasantly, Max came back to the world and the consequences of his act.

Impressions and instincts spring to the artist mind; in a moment he was armored for self-preservation—so straitly armored that every sentiment, even the vague-stirring jealousy of himself that had been given sudden birth, was overridden and cast into the dark.

With the old hauteur, the old touch of imperiousness, he returned Blake's glance.

"*Mon ami,*" he said, gravely, "what you desire is impossible."

Only a moment had intervened between Blake's declaration and his reply, but it seemed to him that the universe had reeled and steadied again in that brief interval.

"And why impossible?"

Again it was the atmosphere of their first meeting—the boy hedged behind his pride, the man calmly breaking a way through that hedge.

Max shrugged. "The word is final. It explains itself."

With a conciliatory, affectionate movement, Blake's hand slipped from his shoulder to his arm. "Don't be absurd, boy," he said, gently. "Nothing on God's earth is impossible. 'Impossibility' is a word coined by weak people behind which to shelter. Why may I not know your sister?"

Max drew away his arm, not ostentatiously, but with definite purpose.

"Can you not understand without explanation—you, who comprehend so well?"

"Frankly, I cannot."

"My sister is in Paris secretly. She would think it very ill of me to discuss her affairs—"

Blake looked quickly into the cold face. "I wonder if she would, boy?" he said. "I think I'll go and see!" With perfect seriousness he stepped back into the studio, struck a match, lighted a candle and walked deliberately to the easel, while Max, upon the balcony, held his breath in astonishment.

For long he stood before the portrait; then at last he spoke, and his words were as unexpected as his action had been.

"She loves you, boy?" he asked.

"Loves me? Oh, of course!" Max was startled into the reply.

"Then 'twill be all right!" With a touch of finality he blew out his candle and came back to the balcony. "It will be all right, or I'm no judge of human nature! That woman could be as proud as Lucifer where she disliked or despised, but she'd be all toleration, all generosity where her love was touched. Tell her I'm your friend and, believe me, she'll ask no other passport to her favor."

Max, standing in the darkness—eager of glance, quick of thought, acutely attentive to every tone of Blake's voice—suddenly became cognizant of his demon of jealousy, felt its subtle stirring in his heart, its swift spring from heart to throat. A wave of blood surged to his face and receded, leaving him pale and trembling, but with the intense self-possession sometimes born of such moments, he stepped into the studio and relighted the candle Blake had blown out.

"Why are you so anxious to know my sister?" His voice was measured—it gave no suggestion either of pleasure or of pain.

Blake, unsuspicious, eager for his own affairs, followed him into the room.

"I can't define the desire," he said; "I feel that I'd find something wonderful behind that face; I feel that"—he paused and laughed a little—"that somehow I should find *you* transfigured and idealized and grown up."

"It is the suggestion of me that intrigues you?"

"I suppose it is—in a subtle way!" He glanced up, to accentuate his words, but surprise seized him at sight of the boy's white, passionate face. "Why, Max, boy! What's the matter?"

Max made a quick gesture, sweeping the words aside. "I am not sufficient to you?"

Blake stared. "I don't understand."

"Yet I speak your own tongue! I say 'I am not sufficient to you?' I have given you my friendship—my heart and my mind, but I am not sufficient to you? Something more is required—something else—something different!"

"Something more? Something different?"

"Yes! In this world it is always the outward seeming! I may have as much personality as my sister Maxine; I may be as interesting, but you do not inquire. Why? Why? Because I am a boy—she a woman!"

Blake, uncertain how to answer this cataract of words, took refuge in banter.

"Don't be fantastical!" he said. "We are not holding a debate on sex. If we are to be normal, we must declare that man and woman don't compare!"

"Now you are gambling with words! I desire facts. It is a fact that until to-day I was enough—friend enough—companion enough—"

"My child!"

But Max rushed on, lashing himself to rage.

"I was enough; but now you desire more. And why? Why? Not because you discern more in the new personality, but because it appeals to you as the personality of a woman. There is nothing deeper—nothing more in the affair—no other reason, as you yourself would say, upon God's earth!" He ended abruptly; his arms fell to his sides; his voice held in it a sound perilously like a sob.

Blake looked at him in surprise.

"My good boy," he said, "you're forgetting the terms of our friendship; to my knowledge they never included hysterics."

The tonic effect of the words was supreme; the sob was strangled in Max's throat; a swift, pained certainty came to him that Blake would not have spoken these words in the plantation that morning, would not have spoken them as they raced together up the Escalier de Sainte-Marie.

"I understand, *mon ami*!" he said, tensely. "I understand so perfectly that, were you dying, and were this request your last, I would refuse it! I hope I have explained myself!"

The tone was bitter and contemptuous, it succeeded in stinging Blake. Up to that moment he had played with the affair; now the play became earnest, his own temper was stirred.

"Thanks, boy!" he said; "but when I'm dying I'll hope for an archangel to attend to my wants—not a little cherub. Good-night to you!" Without look or gesture of farewell, he picked up his hat and walked out of the room.

Once before this thing had happened; once before Max had heard the closing of the door, and known the blank isolation following upon it. But then weeks of close companionship, weeks of growing affection had preceded the moment, giving strength for its endurance; now it came hot upon a long abstinence from friendship, an abstinence made doubly poignant by one day's complete reunion.

For a moment he stood—pride upon his right hand, love upon his left; for a moment he stood, waging his secret war, then with amazing suddenness, the issue was decided, he capitulated shamelessly. Pride melted into the night and love caught him in a quick embrace.

Lithe and silent as some creature of the forest, he was across the studio and down the stairs, his mind tense, his desires fixed upon one point.

Blake was crossing the dim hallway as the light feet skimmed the last slippery steps; he paused in answer to a swift, eager call.

"Ned! Ned! Wait! Ned, I want you!"

Blake paused; in the dim light it was not possible to read his face, but something in the outline of his figure, in the rigidity and definiteness of his stopping, chilled the boy with a sense of antagonism.

"Ned! Ned!" He ran to him, caught and clung to his arm, put forth all his wiles.

"Ned, you are angry! Why are you angry?"

"I am not angry; I am disappointed." Some strange wall of coldness, at once intangible and impenetrable, had risen about Blake. In fear the boy beat vain hands against it.

"You are disappointed, Ned—in me?"

"I am."

"And why? Why?"

"Because you have behaved like a little fool."

In themselves, the words were nothing, but Blake's tone was serious.

"And—because of that—you are disappointed?"

Max's voice undeniably shook; and the fates, peering into the dark hallway, smiled as they pushed the little human comedy nearer the tragic verge.

"I am," answered Blake, with cruel deliberateness. "I thought until to-night that you were a reasonable being—a bit elusive, perhaps—a bit wayward and tantalizing—but still a reasonable being. Now—"

"Now?" Suddenly Max had a sensation of being very small, very insignificant; suddenly he had an impression of Blake as a denizen of a wider world, where other emotions than laughter and comradeship held place—and his heart trembled unreasonably.

"Oh, *mon cher!*" he cried. "Forgive me! Forgive me! Say I am still your boy! Say it! Say it!"

Truth lent passion to his voice—false passion Blake esteemed it, and the cold, imaginary wall became more impregnable.

"That'll do, Max! Heroics are no more attractive to me than hysterics. Good-night to you!" He freed his arm and turned to the door.

In the darkness, Max threw out both hands in despairing appeal.

"Ned! Oh, Ned!" he called. But only the sound of Blake's retreating steps responded. And here was no merciful intervention of gods and mortals, to make good the evil hour; no pretty, tactful Jacqueline, no M. Cartel with his magic fiddle. Only the dim hall, the lonely stairway, the open door with its vision of cold, pale stars and whispering trees.

His misery was a tangible thing. Like a lost child, obsessed by its own fears, he bent under the weight of his sorrow; he sank down upon the lowest step of the stairs and, resting his head against the banister, broke into pitiful, silent tears.

CHAPTER XXV

IT was the morning after the reunion—the morning after the catastrophe, and Blake was breakfasting alone in his rooms.

Typically Parisian rooms they were, rooms that stood closed and silent for more than half the year and woke to offer him a welcome when his wandering footsteps turned periodically toward Paris; typically Parisian, with their long windows and stiffly draped curtains, their marble mantelpieces and gilt-framed mirrors, their furniture arranged with a suggestion of ancient formality that by its very rigidity soothed the eye.

At the moment, evidences of Blake's unusually long occupancy broke this stiffness in many directions; intimate trifles that speak a man's presence were strewn here and there—objects of utility, objects of value and interest gathered upon his last long journey. Eminently pleasant the *salon* appeared in the sunshine of the May morning—full of air and light, its gray carpet and gray-panelled walls making an agreeably neutral setting to the household gods of a gentleman of leisure. But the gentleman in question, so agreeably situated, seemed to find his state less gratifying than it might appear; a sense of dissatisfaction possessed him, as he sat at his solitary meal, a sense of dulness and loss most tenacious of hold.

More than once he roundly called himself a fool; more than once he shook out the thin sheets of his morning paper and buried himself in their contents, but unavailingly. The feeling of flatness, the sense of dissatisfaction with the world as it stood, grew instead of diminishing. At last, throwing down the paper, he gave up the unequal struggle and yielded to the pessimistic pleasure of self-analysis. He recalled last night and its vexatious trend of events, and with something akin to shame, he remembered his anger against Max; but although he admitted its possible exaggeration, the admission brought no palliation of Max's offence. He, possibly, had behaved like a brute; but Max had behaved like an imbecile!

At this point, he fell to staring fixedly in front of him, and through the meshes of his day-dream floated a face—not the face of the boy he was condemning, but that of the mysterious cause of last night's calamity.

He conjured it with quite astonishing vividness—the face of the portrait—the face so like, so unlike, the boy's. Every detail of the picture assailed him; the subtle illusion of the mirror—the strange, reflected eyes propounding their riddle.

Looking in imagination into those eyes, he lost himself delightfully. Sensations, periods of time passed and repassed in his brain—speculation, desire, and memory danced an enchanting, tangled measure.

He recalled the hundred fancies that had held, or failed to hold him in his thirty-eight years; he recalled the women who had loved too little, the women who had loved too much; and, quick upon the recollection, came the consciousness of the disillusion that had inevitably followed upon adventure.

He did not ask himself why these dreams should stir, why these ghosts should materialize and kiss light hands to him in the blue brilliance of this May morning; he realized nothing but that behind them all—a reality in a world of shadows—he saw the eyes of the picture insistently propounding their riddle—the riddle, the question that from youth upward had rankled, inarticulate, in his own soul.

It arose now, renewed, with his acknowledgment of it—the troubling, insistent question that cries in every human brain, sometimes softly, like a child sobbing outside a closed door, sometimes loudly and terribly, like a man in agony. The eternal question ringing through the ages.

He recognized it, clear as the spoken word, in this unknown woman's gaze; and for the first time in all his life the desire to make answer quickened within him. He, who had invariably sought, invariably questioned, suddenly craved to make reply!

An incurable dreamer, the fancy took him and he yielded to its glamour. How delightful to know and study that exquisite face! How fascinating beyond all words to catch the fleeting semblance of his charming Max— to lose it in the woman's seriousness—to touch it again in some gleam of boyish humor! It was a quaint conceit, apart from, untouched by any previous experience. Its subtlety possessed him; existence suddenly took on form and purpose; the depression, the sense of loss dispersed as morning clouds before the sun.

He rose, forgetful of his unfinished meal, his vitality stirring, his curiosity kindling as it had not kindled for years.

What, all things reckoned, stood between him and this alluring study? A boy! A mere boy!

No thought came to him of the boy himself—the instrument of the desire. No thought came; for every human creature is a pure egoist in the first stirring of a passion, and stalks his quarry with blind haste, fearful that at any turn he may be balked by time or circumstance. Later, when grief has chastened, or joy cleansed him, the altruist may peep forth, but never in the primary moment.

With no thought of the clinging hands and beseeching voice of last night—with no knowledge of a mournful figure that had dragged itself up the stairway of the house in the rue Müller and sobbed itself to sleep in a lonely bed, he walked across the room to his writing-table and calmly picked up a pen.

He dipped the pen into the ink and selected a sheet of note-paper; then, as he bent to write, impatience seized him, he tore the paper across and took up a telegraph form.

On this he wrote the simple message:

Will you allow me to meet your sister?—NED.

It was brief, it was informal, it was entirely unjustifiable. But what circumstance in his relation to the boy had lent itself either to formality or justification?

He rang the bell, dispatched his message, and then sat down to wait.

His attitude in that matter of waiting was entirely characteristic. He did not arrange his action in the event of defeat; he did not speculate upon probable triumph. The affair had passed out of his hands; the future was upon the knees of the gods!

He did not finish his breakfast in that time of probation; he did not again take up the paper he had thrown aside. He made no effort to occupy or to amuse himself; he merely waited, and in due time the gods gave him a sign—a telegraphic message, brief and concise as his own:

Come to-night at ten. She will be here.—MAX.

CHAPTER XXVI

AT ten o'clock, punctual to the moment, Blake walked up the Escalier de Sainte-Marie. All day a curious agitation compounded of elation and impatience had lifted him as upon wings, but now that the hour had arrived, doubt amounting almost to reluctance assailed his spirit. He walked slowly, looking about him as though the way were strange; outside the house in the rue Müller he paused and glanced up at the fifth floor, suddenly daunted, suddenly thrilled by the faint light coming mistily through the open windows of the *salon* and the studio.

What would she be like—this sister of Max? He strove ineffectually to materialize the portrait, but it eluded him. Only the soul of the woman seemed to have place in his imagination—the soul, seen through the questioning eyes.

Still a victim to the strange, new reticence, he entered the open doorway and began the familiar ascent. Here again the thought of the woman obsessed him. How must this place appear to her? His thoughts touched the varying scenes of Max's story—scenes of the girl's free youth and sumptuous, exotic after-life. None fitted accurately with a rue Müller. Of a certainty she, as well as the boy, must have the adventuring spirit!

His senses stirred, routing his diffidence, and under their spur he ran up the remaining steps, only pausing at the fifth floor as a light voice hailed him out of the dusk, a little flitting figure darted from the shadows, and Jacqueline, brimming with suppressed excitement, caught him by the arm.

"Monsieur Édouard!"

He laughed in recognition and greeting. "Well, Jacqueline! Always the air of the grand secret! Always the air of the little bird that has discovered the topmost bough of the tree! What is it to-night?"

His feelings were running riot; it was agreeable to spend them in badinage. But Jacqueline slapped his hand in reproof.

"No pleasantries, monsieur! The affair is serious."

He smiled; he lowered his voice to the tone of hers. "You have a visitor, then, Jacqueline, to this fifth floor of yours?"

Jacqueline nodded her blonde head, and again her excitement brimmed full measure.

"Monsieur, she is here—the sister of M. Max! The princess!" She whispered the last word—a whisper delicious, tremulous with the weight of actual romance.

Blake heard it, and his own heart stirred to a joyous youthful sensation. It was so naïve, so charming, so absolutely French.

"The princess!" he whispered back in just the expected tone. "Jacqueline, is she beautiful?"

Jacqueline threw up her hands, invoked heaven with her eyes, earth with her shrugging shoulders.

"Monsieur, she is ravishing!"

Blake's expressive answer was to put her gently aside and step toward Max's door.

But she was after him with a little cry. "Monsieur, not yet! I must deliver my message! The message of M. Max!"

"Of M. Max?"

"But yes, monsieur!" Her hands, her whole body expressed apology and eager explanation. "M. Max has been called away—upon a business of much importance. M. Max desires his profoundest, his most affectionate excuses—and will monsieur place him under a debt never possible of repayment by entering the *appartement*—by entertaining the princess during his absence?"

Blake stared "In the name of Heaven—"

But Jacqueline's white hands again made free with his arm.

"Monsieur, Heaven will arrange! Heaven is bountiful in these affairs!"

"But I don't understand. He has gone upon business, you say? He never had any business."

Jacqueline laughed and clapped her hands. "Do not be too sure, monsieur! He is growing up, is M. Max!" She gave another little twittering laugh of sheer delight.

"Come, monsieur! The princess is alone. It is not gallant to keep a lady waiting!"

"But you don't understand, Jacqueline. It is impossible—impossible that I should intrude—"

"It is no intrusion, monsieur! I have explained everything to madame—and she expects you!" She flitted past him to the door, threw it open and dropped him a pretty, impertinent curtsy.

"Now, monsieur!" she commanded; and Blake, half amused, half resentful, saw nothing for it but to obey.

He stepped across the threshold; he heard Jacqueline laugh again softly and close the door; then he stood, a prey to profound trepidation.

He stood for a moment, hesitating between flight and advance, then shame at his weakness forced him to go forward and open the *salon* door.

As he opened it, another change took place within him; his diffidence forsook him, his excitement was allayed as, by a restraining hand, he was dominated by a peculiar clarity of vision.

This accentuated keenness of observation came into action even in a material sense; as he passed into the familiar room, each object appealed to him in its appointed place—in its just and proper value. The quaint odd articles of furniture that he and Max had chosen in company! The pictures that he had hung upon the white walls at Max's bidding! The Russian *samovar*, the books, the open cigarette-box, each of which spoke and breathed of Max!

Every object came to him clearly in the quiet light of the lamp upon the bureau; it seemed like the setting of a play, where the atmosphere had been carefully created, the details definitely woven into a perfect chain.

He stood, looking upon the silent room, wondering what would happen—convinced that something must happen; and at last, with the same quietness—the same intense naturalness, perfect as extreme art—a slight sound came from the balcony and a woman stepped into the subdued light.

She stepped into the quiet lamplight and paused; and Blake's first subconscious feeling was that, miraculously, the empty room had taken on life and meaning—that this sudden, gracious presence filled and possessed it absolutely and by right divine.

She seemed very tall as she stood looking down into the room, her rich hair crowning her head, her young figure clothed in white and wrapped in a cloak of soft mysterious gray that fell from her shoulders simply, yet with the dignity of a royal mantle.

She stood for a full minute, looking at him, almost it seemed sharing his own uncertainty; then, with a little gesture that irresistibly conjured Max, she stepped into the room—and into his life.

"Monsieur," she said, very softly, "I am the sister of Max; you are his friend. It is surely meant that we know each other!"

CHAPTER XXVII

IT was a perfect moment; one of those rare and delicate spaces of time in which Fate's fingers seem to strike a chord at once poignant and satisfying, faint and far-reaching. The lamp-lit room, the open window and, beyond, the balcony veiled in the obscurity of the night! It was a fair setting for romance; and romance, young, beautiful, gracious as in the fairy-tale, had emerged from it into Blake's life. A smile, a word—and an atmosphere had been created! The things of the past were obscured, and the things of the present made omnipotent.

"What a brother this is of mine!" Maxine smiled again with a little quiver of humor that set her eyes alight. "Is it not like him to invite me to criticise my portrait, and leave me to receive his friend?"

She spoke, not in the English which Max invariably used, but in French; and the sound of her voice entangled Blake's senses. It seemed the boy's voice at its lowest and tenderest, but touched with new inflections tantalizing as they were delightful. Self-consciousness fled before it; he was at one with the sister as he had been at one with the brother on the crisp white morning when comradeship had been sealed to the marching of soldiers' feet and the rattle of fife and drum.

"Princess," he said, "I shall be as frank as Max himself would be! The situation is overwhelming; do with me what you will! If I intrude, dismiss me! I know how fascinating solitude on this balcony can be."

She smiled again, but gravely with a hint of the portrait's mystery.

"Solitude is an excellent thing, monsieur, but to-night I think I need the solace of a fellow-being. Will you not stay and keep me company?"

He looked at the smiling lips, the serious, searching eyes, and he spoke his thoughts impulsively.

"I shall be the most honored man in Paris!"

"That is well! Then we will talk, and watch the stars."

Here the naïve imperiousness of the boy gleamed out, familiar and reassuring, and Maxine walked across the room, turning at the window to look back for Blake.

"He is not without appreciation—this little brother of mine?" She put the question softly, tentatively, as she and Blake leaned over the balcony railing.

"He is an artist, princess."

"You think so?" Her voice warmed and vibrated; through the vague darkness he felt her eyes search his face.

"Undoubtedly."

"Ah, you love him?" The voice dropped to a great gentleness—a gentleness that touched him in a strange degree.

"It would be difficult to tell you what he has been to me," he said. "Our friendship has been a thing of great value. Has he ever told you how we met?"

"He has told me!" Her tone was still low—still curiously attractive. "And he appreciates very highly, monsieur, the affection you have given him."

She paused; and Blake, looking down upon Paris, was conscious of that pause as of something pregnant and miraculous. It filled the moment, combining, with the soft texture of her garments and the faint scent from her hair, to weave a spell subtle as it was intangible.

"There is nothing to appreciate," he made answer. "I am merely a commonplace mortal who found in him something uncommon. The appreciation is mine entirely—the appreciation of the youth, the vitality he expresses."

"Ah, but you do yourself an injustice!" She spoke impulsively and, as if alarmed at her own eagerness, broke off and began anew in a soberer voice. "I mean, monsieur, that friendship is not a solitary affair. Whatever you discerned in Max, Max must equally have discerned in you."

"I wonder!" He turned his gaze from the lights of the city to the rustling trees of the plantation. The hour was magical, the situation beyond belief. Standing there upon the balcony, suspended as it were between heaven and earth, companioned by this wonderful, familiar, unfamiliar being, he seemed to see his own soul—to see it from afar off and with a great lucidity. "I wonder!" he said again; and the sadness, the discontent that stalked him in lonely moments touched him briefly, like the shadow of a travelling cloud.

"What do you wonder, monsieur?"

"The meaning of it all, princess! Existence is such a chase. I, perhaps, hunt friendship—and find Max; I, perhaps, dream that I have found my goal, while to him I may be but a wayside inn—a place to linger in and leave! We both follow the chase, but who can say if we mark the same quarry? It's a puzzling world!"

"Monsieur, it is sometimes a glorious world!" So swift was her change of voice, so impulsive the gesture with which she turned to him, that the vividness of a suggested Max startled him. She was infinitely like to Max—Max when life intoxicated him, when he threw out both arms to embrace it.

"When you look like that, princess," he cried, "I could forget everything—I could take your hand, and show you all my heart, for you literally *are* the boy!"

There was another pause—a pause fraught with poignant things. Standing there, between heaven and earth, they were no longer creatures of conventionality, fettered by individual worlds. They were two souls conscious of an affinity.

Briefly, sweetly, Maxine's fingers touched his hand and then withdrew. "Monsieur, in moments I *am* Max!"

Nothing of surprise, nothing of question came to him. He only knew that a touch, infinitely desired, had lighted upon him—that a comprehension born of immaterial things was luring him whither he knew not.

"You are Max, princess," he said, swiftly, "but Max suddenly made possessor of a soul! I've always fancied Max a mythical being—a creature of eternal youth, fascinating as he is elusive—a faun-like creature, peeping into the world from some secret grove, ready to dart back at any human touch. Max's lips were made for laughter; his eyes are too bright for tears."

"And I, monsieur? What am I?"

"You are the miracle! You are the elusive creature deserting the green groves—stepping voluntarily into the mortal world."

"Yet if you know of me at all, you must know that I have left the mortal world and am seeking the secret groves."

"I have been told that."

"And you disbelieve?"

"I am afraid, princess, I do." He turned and looked at her—at the slim body wrapped in its long, smooth cloak of velvet—at the shadowed, questioning eyes. "I know I am greatly daring, but there are moments when we are outside ourselves—when we know and speak things of which we can give no logical account. You have put life behind you; yet what is life but a will-o'-the-wisp? Who can say where the light may not break forth again?"

"But have we not power over our senses, monsieur? Can we not shut our eyes, even if the light does break forth?"

"No, princess, we cannot! Because nature will inevitably say, 'I have given you eyes with which to see. Open those eyes'!"

"Ah, there we differ, monsieur!"

Blake laughed. "There, princess, you are the boy! He, too, thinks he can cheat nature; but I preach my gospel to him, I tell him Nature will have her own. If we will not bend to her, she will take and break us. Ah, but listen to that!"

His discourse broke off; they both involuntarily raised their heads and looked toward the windows of the neighboring *appartement*.

"Princess!" he said, delightedly. "I wouldn't have had you miss this for ten thousand pounds! Has Max described his neighbor, M. Cartel? I tell you you will have a little of heaven when M. Cartel plays *Louise*!"

Very delicately, with a curious human clarity of sound, the violin of M. Cartel executed the first notes of Louise's declaration in the duet with Julian—'*Depuis le jour où je me suis donnée!*' One caught the whole intention of the composer in the few crystal notes—one figured the whole scene—the little house of love, the lovers in their Garden of Eden, and below Paris— symbolic Paris!

"You know *Louise*, princess?"

"Yes, monsieur, I know *Louise*."

All was clear, all was understood in that brief reply. A wide contentment, vitalized by excitement, lifted the soul of Blake. Leaning over the balcony railing, drinking in the music of M. Cartel, more than a little of heaven opened to him; a unique emotion thrilled him—a consciousness of sublimity, a sense of being part of some unfathomable yet perfect scheme. The music wove its story; the lovers became one with his own existence, as he himself was one with the stars above him and the lights below. He followed every note, and in his own brain was spun the subtle thread that bound Julian and Louise; his own fancy ran the gamut of their emotions from mere human reminiscence to overwhelming passion.

As he listened, his first hearing of M. Cartel's fiddle crept back upon the feet of memory, and with it the recollection of the boy's rapture, the boy's wayward breaking of the spell and denial of the truth of love. Cautiously he moved his head and stole a glance at his companion, summing up the contrast between the present and the past.

Maxine was leaning forward, in thrall to the music: her gray cloak had fallen slightly back, displaying her white dress—her white neck; her hands were clasped, her eyes—the woman's eyes, the eyes of mystery—gazed into profound space.

He held himself rigid; he dared not stir, lest he should brush her cloak; he scarce dared breathe, lest he should break her dream. A feeling akin to adoration awakened in him, and as if in expression of the emotion, the violin of M. Cartel cried out the supreme confession of the lovers, Louise's enraptured '*C'est le Paradis! C'est une féerie!*', and Julian's answer, intoxicating as wine, '*Non! C'est la vie! l'Eternelle, la toute-puissante vie!*'

And there, with the whimsicality of the artist, the bow of M. Cartel was lifted, and sharp, pregnant silence fell upon the night.

Blake turned to Maxine; and Maxine, with lips parted, eyes dark with thought, met his regard.

For one second her impulse seemed to sway to words, her body to yield to some gracious, drooping enchantment; then, swiftly as M. Cartel had called up silence, she recalled herself—straightened her body and lifted her head.

"Monsieur," she said, with dignity, "I thank you for your kindness and for your companionship—and I bid you good-night!"

The swiftness of his dismissal scarcely touched Blake. Already she was his sovereign lady—her look a command, her word paramount.

"As you will, princess!"

She held out her hand; and taking, he bowed over, but did not kiss it.

She smiled, conceiving his desire and his restraint.

"I shall convey to Max how charmingly you have entertained me, monsieur and, perhaps—" Her voice dropped to its softest note.

Blake looked up.

"Perhaps, princess—?"

She smiled again, half diffidently. "Nothing, monsieur! Good-night!"

"Good-night!"

He left her to the gray mystery of the stars, and passed back through the quiet, lamp-lit room and down the slippery stairs that led to the mundane world; and with each step he took, each breath he drew, the words from *Louise* repeated themselves, justifying all things, glorifying all things: '*C'est la vie! l'Eternelle, la toute-puissante vie!*'

CHAPTER XXVIII

BLAKE must have reached the last step of the Escalier de Sainte-Marie, must indeed have turned the corner of the rue André de Sarte before the creaking of a footstep or the opening of a door disturbed the silence of the fifth floor; but, due time having expired—due deference having been paid to taste and the proprieties—the handle of M. Cartel's door was very softly turned, and Jacqueline slipped forth into the shadowed landing.

Never were human curiosity and feminine craft more signally displayed than in the slim little form creeping on tiptoe, the astute, *piquante* little face thrust forth into the dark. Across the landing she stole, and with deft fingers opened Max's door without a sound.

Here, in the narrow hallway, she paused and called gently, "Monsieur Max!" But as no voice answered, she crept to the *salon* door and, with a little comedy of smiles all for her own diversion, called again with pursed lips and in a stage whisper: "Madame! Madame!"

It carried—this portentous word—across the quiet room to the balcony where Maxine was lingering; it drew from her a little 'oh,' of consternation; finally, it brought her running across the room to her visitor.

Jacqueline, lynx-eyed, stood and looked at her—noting how flushed she was, how youthful-looking, how unguarded and brimming with emotion.

"Madame!" she cried. "I know without a word! It has been a grand success."

"C'EST LA VIE! L'ETERNELLE, LA TOUTE-PUISSANTE VIE!"

Maxine laughed, a girlish laugh of self-betrayal. "A grand success! Absolutely a grand success! And, Jacqueline"—she hesitated, laughed again with charming self-consciousness, rushed afresh into speech—"Jacqueline, he thought me beautiful! Not a word was said, but I know he thought me beautiful. Tell me! Am I beautiful?" Swiftly, as might the boy, she threw off her velvet cloak, letting it fall to the ground, and showed herself tall and supple and straight in her white dress.

Jacqueline rushed forward warmly, caught and kissed her hand.

"Madame, you are ravishing!" And, with her pretty native practicality, she picked up the cloak, carefully folded and carefully laid it aside.

"Ravishing!" Maxine laughed once more. "Jacqueline, I am something more than that! I am happy!" She threw out her arms, as if to embrace the universe. "I am happier than the saints in heaven! I am living in the moment, and the moment is perfection! I care nothing that yesterday I wept, that to-morrow I may weep again. I am alive and I am happy. I feel as I used to feel at fifteen years old, galloping a spirited horse. The whole world is sublime—from the dust in the streets to the stars in the sky!" She forgot her companion, her speech broke off, she turned and began to pace the room with head thrown back, hands clasped behind her with careless, boyish ease.

For a while Jacqueline watched her, diligently sifting out every emotional sign; then, deeming that some moment of her own choosing had arrived, she slipped unobserved from the room, to return a minute later bearing a kettle full of boiling water.

Maxine looked round as she made her entry.

"A kettle, Jacqueline?"

"For madame's tea. And, my God, but it is hot!" She set it down hastily in the fireplace, and sucked her finger with a pouting smile.

Maxine smiled, too, coming back from her dream with vague graciousness. "But I do not need tea."

Jacqueline did not refute the statement, but merely began to manipulate the *samovar* in the manner learned of Max, while Maxine, yielding to her own delicious exaltation, fell again to her long, slow pacing of the floor.

Presently the inviting smell of tea began to pervade the room, and Jacqueline set out a cup and saucer—Max's first purchase from old Bluebeard of the curios.

"Madame is served!" She stood behind the chair ordained for Maxine, very sedate, very assured of her own arrangements.

Maxine paused, as though the suggestion of tea was brought to her for the first time.

"How delightful!" she said, with swift, serene pleasure. "How kind! How thoughtful!"

"Seat yourself, madame!"

The chair was drawn forward; the just and proper thrill of preparation was conveyed by Jacqueline; and Maxine seated herself, still in her smiling dream.

Half the cup of tea was consumed under Jacqueline's watchful eye, then she stole round the chair.

"Madame, a cigarette?" Her fingers crept to the cigarette-box, then found and struck a match, all with a deft, unobtrusive quiet that won its way undenied.

The cigarette was lighted, Maxine leaned back in her chair, Jacqueline's confidential moment was secured.

"And so, madame, it was a grand success?"

Maxine looked up. The first fine ecstasy was past; the after-glow of deep contentment curled round her with the cigarette smoke; she was the pliant reed to the soft wind of Jacqueline's whispering.

"It was past belief," she answered, "past all belief. We stood together in the light of the lamp and looked each other in the eyes, and he never guessed. He never guessed—he, who has—Oh, it was past belief!"

"Ah!" murmured Jacqueline, complacently. "I told madame I had a quite extraordinary talent in the dressing of hair—though madame was sceptical! And as for the purchase of clothes. Did he admire madame's velvet cloak?"

Maxine smiled tolerantly. "Of course he did not!"

Jacqueline cast up her eyes to heaven. "These English—they are extraordinary! But I tell you this, madame, he knew here"—she touched her heart—"he knew here, that madame looked what she is—a queen!"

"Absurd child!"

The reproof was gentle; Jacqueline's nimble tongue took advantage of the chance given it.

"And tell me, madame? He play his part gallantly—Monsieur Édouard?" Never before had she dared so much; but never before had Maxine's eyes looked as they looked to-night.

Before replying, Maxine leaned her elbows on the table and took her face between her hands.

"It was past belief—that also!" she said at last. "He seemed a different being. I cannot understand it."

"He seemed of a greater interest, madame?"

"Of a strangely greater interest."

"In what manner, madame? Looks? Words?" Cunning as a monkey, little Jacqueline was all soft innocence in the method of her questioning.

"In every way—manner—speech—expression of thought. And, Jacqueline"—she turned her face, all radiant and unsuspicious, to her interlocutor—"I made a discovery! He loves Max!"

Jacqueline, with downcast eyes and discreet bearing, carefully removed the empty tea-cup.

"Yes, he loves me as Max! He told me so. It has made me marvellously happy—marvellously happy and, also"—she sighed—"also, Jacqueline, just a little sad!"

"Sad, madame?"

"Yes, sad because he loves Max as one loves a child, expecting no return; and—I would be loved as an equal."

"Assuredly, madame."

"I *must* be loved as an equal!" Fire suddenly kindled her dreaming voice; a look, clear and alert, suddenly crossed her eyes. "Jacqueline," she cried, "I have set myself a new task. I shall make him respect Max as well as love him; Max shall become his equal. Now, suppose you set yourself a task like that, how would you begin?"

"Oh, madame!" Jacqueline was all deprecation.

"Do not fear. Tell me!"

"Madame, it is not for me—" Jacqueline's triumph in the moment, and her concealing of the triumph, were things exquisitely feminine.

"Tell me!"

"I may speak from the heart, madame?"

Maxine bent her head in gracious condescension.

"Then, madame, I would make of Monsieur Édouard a book of figures. The princess would learn the rules; Monsieur Max would shut the book, and make up the sum. It would be quite simple."

The hot color scorched Maxine's face; she rose quickly. "Jacqueline! I had not expected this!"

"Madame desired me to speak from the heart. The heart, at times, is unruly!"

"True! Forgive me. But you should not suggest a thing that you know to be impossible."

"Pardon, madame! I was thinking of the many impossibilities performed in a good cause!"

"Say no more, Jacqueline! To-night was to-night! To-night is over!" She walked across the room and passed out upon the balcony, leaning over the railing at the spot where Blake had stood.

Jacqueline, swift and guileful, was instantly beside her.

"Madame, at its most serious, to-night was a little comedy. Is it so criminal to repeat a little comedy—once, or even twice—in a good cause? It is not as if madame were not sure of herself! Besides, the comedy was charming!"

"Yes; the comedy was charming!" Maxine echoed the sentiment, and in her heart called 'charming' a poor word. "But even if I were weak,

Jacqueline," she added, "how could I banish Max? Max could scarcely continue to have important business."

"Perhaps not, madame; but Monsieur Max might continue to display temper! Do not forget that he and Monsieur Édouard did not part upon the friendliest terms."

Maxine smiled.

"But even granted that, I could not be here again—alone."

Jacqueline, with airiest scorn, tossed the words aside.

"That, madame? Why, that arranges itself! The princess loves her brother! His quarrel is her grief. Is not woman always compassionate?"

The tone was irresistible. Maxine laughed. "Jacqueline, you were the Serpent in Adam's Garden! There is not a doubt of it! No wonder poor M. Cartel has taken so big a bite of the Apple."

She laughed again, and Jacqueline laughed too, in mischievous delight.

"Madame!" she coaxed. "Madame!"

"No!" said Maxine, with eyes fixed determinately upon the lights of the city; while somewhere above her in the cool, clear starlight, a hidden voice—her own, and not her own—whispered a subtle 'Yes!'

CHAPTER XXIX

THE universe is compounded of the miraculous; but love is the miracle of miracles. Again the impossible had been contrived; again Maxine and Blake were standing together on the balcony. The Parisian night seemed as still as a held breath, and as palpitating with human possibilities; the domes of the Sacré-Coeur loomed white against the sky, dumb witnesses to the existence of the spirit. The scene was undoubtedly poetic; yet, placed in the noisiest highway of London or the most desolate bog-land of Blake's native country, these two would have been as truly and amply cognizant of the real and the ideal; for the cloak of love was about them, the vapor of love was before their eyes, and for the hour, although they knew it not, they were capable of reconstructing a whole world from the material in their own hearts.

But they were divinely ignorant; they each tricked themselves with the age-old fallacy of a unique position, each wandered onward in the dream-like fields of romance, content to believe that the other knew the hidden way.

The scene bore a perfect similarity to the scene of the first meeting—about them, the darkness and the quiet—behind them, the little *salon* lit by the familiar lamp, showing all the reassuring evidences of the boy's occupation. For close upon an hour they had enjoyed this intimacy of the balcony, at first talking much and rapidly upon the ostensible object of their meeting—Max's quarrel with Blake, later falling to a happy silence, as though they deliberately closed their lips, the more fully to drink in the secrets of the night through eyes and ears. Strange spells were in the weaving, and no two souls are fused to harmony without much subtle questioning of spirit, many delicate, tremulous speculations compounded of wordless joy and wordless fear.

Some issue, it was, in this matter of fusing personalities, that at last caused Maxine to turn her head and find Blake studying her.

The circumstance was trivial—a mere crossing of glances, but it brought the color to her face as swiftly as if she had been taken in some guilty act.

Blake saw the expression, and interpreted it wrongly.

"You are displeased, princess? I am a bad companion to-night?" He spoke impulsively, with an anxiety in his voice that spurred her to a desire to comfort him.

"When people are sympathetic, monsieur, they are companions, whether good or bad. Is it not so?"

He moved a little nearer to her; neither was aware of the movement.

"Do you find me sympathetic?"

"Indeed, yes!" Her luminous glance rested on him thoughtfully.

"But you scarcely know me."

"Monsieur, I do know you."

"Through the boy, perhaps—" He spoke with a touch of impatience, but she stopped him with upraised hand.

"You are angry with Max, therefore you must be silent! Anger does not make for true judgment."

"Ah, that's unfair!" He laughed. "'Tis Max who is angry with me! You know I came here to-night with open arms—to find him flown! Still, I am willing to keep them open, and give the kiss of peace whenever he relents—to please you."

"Ah, no, monsieur! To please him. To please him."

"Indeed, no! To please you—and no one else. If I followed my own devices, I'd wait till he comes back, and box his ears. He'd very well deserve it."

Maxine laughed; then, swift as a breeze or a racing cloud, her mood changed.

"Monsieur, you care for Max?"

"What a question! I love Max. He's a star in my darkness—or was, until the sun shone."

He paused, fearful of where his impulses had led him; but Maxine was all sweetness, all seriousness.

"Am I, then, the sun, monsieur?"

In any other woman the words must have seemed a lure; but here was a fairness, a frankness and dignity that lifted the question to another and higher plane. Blake, comprehending, answered simply with the truth.

"Yes, you are the sun; and all my life I have been a sun-worshipper."

She made no comment; she accepted the words, waiting for the flow of speech that she knew was close at hand—the speech, probably irrelevant, certainly delightful, that he invariably poured forth at such a moment.

"Princess, do you know my country?"

She shook her head, smiling a little.

"Ah, then you don't understand my worship! In Ireland, nature condemns us to a long, black, wet winter and a long, gray, wet spring, so that the heart of a man is nearly drowned in his body, and he grows to believe that his country is nothing but a neutral-tinted waste; but one day, when even hope is dying, a miracle comes to pass—the sun shines out! The sun shines out, and he suddenly sees that his waste land is the color of emeralds and that his dripping woods are gardens, tinted like no stones that jewellers ever handle. Oh, no wonder I am a sun-worshipper!"

Maxine, glowing to his sudden enthusiasm, clasped her hands, as when she heard the music of M. Cartel.

"Ah, and that is your country?"

"That is my country, princess."

"I wish——" She stopped.

"That you could see it?"

She nodded.

"And why not? Why not—when this boy sees reason? How I would love to show it to you! You would understand."

"When would you show it to me?" She spoke very low.

"When? Oh, perhaps in April—April, when the washed skies are a blue that even Max could not find in his color-box, and the bare boughs tremble with promise. In April—or, better still, in the autumn. In October, when the lights are cool and white and the sea is an opal; when you smell the ozone strong as violets, and at every turn of the road a cart confronts you, heaped with bronze seaweed and stuck with a couple of pikes that rise stark against the sky-line, to suggest the taking of the spoils. Yes, in October! In October, it should be!"

He was carried away, and she loved him for his enthusiasm.

"You care for your country?" she said, very softly.

"Yes—in an odd way! When wonder or joy or ambition comes to me, I always have a craving to walk those roads and watch the sea and whisper my secrets to the salt earth, but I never gratify the desire; it belongs to the many incongruities of an incongruous nature. But I think if great happiness came to me, I should go back, if only for a day; or if—" He paused. "—If I were to break my heart over anything, I believe I'd creep back, like a child to its mother. We're odd creatures—we Irish!"

"I understand you," said Maxine. "You have the soul."

He looked down into the rue Müller, and a queer smile touched his lips.

"A questionable blessing one is apt to say, princess—in one's bad moments!"

"But only in one's bad moments!" Her tone was warm; her words came from her swiftly, after the manner of Max—the manner that Blake loved.

"You are quite right!" he said, "and I despise myself instantly I have uttered such a cynicism. The capacity to feel is worth all the pain it brings. If one had but a single moment of realization, one should die content. That is the essential—to have known the highest."

Once again Maxine had the sense of lifting a tangible veil, of gaining a glimpse of the hidden personality—not the half-sceptical, pleasant, friendly Blake of the boy's acquaintance, but Blake the dreamer, the idealist who sought some grail of infinite holiness figured in his own imagination, zealously guarded from the scoffer and the worldling. A swift desire pulsed in her to share the knowledge of this quest—to see the face of the knight illumined for his adventure—to touch the buckles of his armor.

"Monsieur," she whispered, "if you were to die to-night, would you die satisfied?"

In the silence that had fallen upon them, Blake had turned his face to the stars, but now again his glance sought hers.

"No, princess," he said, simply.

No weapons are more potent than brevity and simplicity. His answer brought the blood to her face as no long dissertation could have brought it; it was so direct, so personal, so compounded of subtle values.

"Then you have not known the highest?" It was not she who framed the question; some power outside herself constrained her to its speaking.

"I have recognized perfection," he said, "but I have not known it. And sometimes my weaker self—the primitive, barbaric self—cries out against the limitation; sometimes—"

"Sometimes—?"

"Nothing, princess—and everything!" With a sudden wave of self-control he brought himself back to the moment and its responsibilities.

"Forgive me! And, if you are merciful, dismiss me! They say we Irish talk too much. I am afraid I am a true Irishman." He laughed, but there was a sound behind the laughter that brought tears to her eyes.

"Monsieur, it has been happy to-night?"

"It has been heaven."

"We are not wholly a trouble to you—Max and I?"

She put out her hand, and he took it.

"Max is my friend, princess; you are my sovereign lady."

The night was close about them; Paris was below, gilding the rose of human love; the church domes were above, tending whitely toward the stars. Maxine moved nearer to him, her heart beating fast, her whole radiant being dispensing fragrance.

"Monsieur, if I am your lady, pay me homage!"

The enchantment was delicate and perfect; her voice wove a spell, her slight, strong fingers trembled in his. He had been less than man had he refused the moment. Silently he bent his head, and his lips touched her hand in a swift, ardent kiss.

CHAPTER XXX

MAXINE was in high exaltation—the exaltation that makes no count of cost. Yesterday mattered not at all; to-morrow might never dawn! As the outer door closed upon Blake, she turned back into the lighted *salon*—the little *salon* of Max's books, of Max's boyish tastes—the little *salon* loved beyond all rooms in Paris!

In a smiling dream she passed through it, on into the studio where no light was, save the light from a shred of crescent moon that had lately climbed into the sky. It had a curious effect—this bare, white room with its gaunt easel, upon which the portrait still stood, and to superstitious eyes, it might well have suggested a ghost-chamber, peopled by dead thoughts, dead impressions: but Maxine was in no morbid mood, happiness ran too high—too red and warm—to permit of shadows disputing its high place.

Smiling, smiling, she passed from the studio to the bedroom. The room that had witnessed her first weakness; the room that had brought her strength. How infinitely wise had been the conduct of that night! How irrevocably fate had created doubt and dispersed it by inspiration. If she had not twisted her hair about her head—if the little Jacqueline had not entered at the critical moment—if, for that matter, M. Cartel and his friend had not talked late and partaken of *bouillon*—

She laughed; she wandered round the room, touching, appraising the little familiar trifles associated with that past hour; at last she sat down before her mirror, and there Jacqueline found her ten minutes later, when curiosity could no longer be withheld and she came creeping across the landing for news of the night's doings.

Maxine heard her enter; heard her search the *salon* and then the studio; finally called to her.

"Jacqueline!"

"Madame!"

The door opened, and Maxine looked round, the smile still upon her lips.

"No soup for me to-night, Jacqueline? Not even tea?"

Jacqueline caught the happy lightness of the tone, and silently nodded her blonde head as she tiptoed into the room.

"Ah, madame has had a banquet of the mind! Madame has no need of my poor food."

Maxine picked up a comb and arranged the tendrils of hair that curled about her temples.

"Jacqueline," she said, after a silence, "what do you consider the highest thing?"

The question might have been astonishing, but her visitor did not betray surprise by even the quiver of an eyelash.

"Love, madame," she said.

And Maxine did not flash round upon her in one of her swift rages, did not even draw her brows together into their frowning line. She merely gazed into the mirror, as if weighing the statement judicially.

"All people do not hold that opinion," she said, at last.

Jacqueline shrugged her shoulders in the exercise of an infinite patience. "No, madame?"

"No. M. Blake talked to-night of 'the highest thing,' and he did not mean love."

"No, madame?" Jacqueline was very guileless.

But guileless as her tone was—nay, by reason of its guilelessness—it touched Maxine in some shadowy corner of her woman's consciousness; and spurred by a subtle, disquieting suggestion, she turned in her chair, and fixed her serious gray eyes upon her visitor.

"What are your thoughts, Jacqueline?"

Jacqueline, taken unawares, deprecated.

"Oh, madame—"

But Maxine was set to her point. "Answer my question," she insisted. "I wish to know. I am, above all things, practical."

It was to Jacqueline's credit that she did not smile, that she simply murmured: "Who doubts it, madame?"

"Yes; I am, above all things, practical. In this affair of the woman, I know exactly where I stand."

The girl made no comment; but even to Maxine's own ears, her declaration left a little suggestion of over-vehemence vibrating in the air; and startled by this suggestion, she did the least wise, the most human thing possible, she accentuated it.

"If I were different—if M. Blake were different, I grant that, perhaps—" She stopped abruptly. "Jacqueline, what are your thoughts?"

"Oh, madame, I have none!"

And here Maxine made a change of front, became very grave, touched the gracious, encouraging note of the being to whom life is an open book.

"You must not say that," she corrected, sweetly. "You always have ideas—even if they are sometimes a little in the air. Come! Tell me. What are your thoughts?"

But Jacqueline was wary, as befitted one who made no pretence of scholarship, but who knew the old human story by heart, and daily recited it to one ardent listener.

"Oh, madame, it is not fitting—"

"Absurd! Tell me."

Jacqueline, hard pressed, sought refuge in a truth.

"My thoughts might displease madame."

Maxine sat straighter in her chair. Here was another matter!

"Ah, so that is it! Well, now I am determined. Now I will have the thoughts at any cost."

When Maxine spoke like this, when her lips closed upon her words, when her eyes rested unflinchingly upon her listener, she was wont to have her questions answered. Jacqueline recognized the moment, saw Maxine in all her proud foolishness, loved her with that swift intermingling of pity and worship that such beings as she inevitably call forth, finally tossed her little head in her most tantalizing manner and laughed.

"With madame's permission," she said, "I will wish her good-night!"

"The permission is not granted."

"Nevertheless, madame!" Her hand was on the door.

"Wait!" cried Maxine, peremptorily. "I have asked you a question and you must answer it."

Jacqueline stopped half-way through the doorway, and looked back, her flower-like face alight with mischief.

"Pardon, madame! 'Must' is the word for the ruler. Lucien says 'must' to me; M. Blake says 'must' to"—she paused, with maddening precision; she dropped a little impertinent curtsy—"to M. Max!"

She tossed the word upon the air, as a child might blow thistle-down; she laughed and was gone, leaving Maxine conscious of a strange new sensation that whipped her to anger and yet, most curiously, left her bereft of words.

CHAPTER XXXI

NOTHING less than absolute conviction can shake a strong nature. A wave of doubt swept over Maxine as her little neighbor's words died out and the door closed, leaving her to silence and solitude; but for all her folly, she was strong, and strength such as hers is not shaken by the shaft of a Jacqueline, however cunningly sped.

She sat for long, troubled, perplexed—almost, it might have seemed, fearful of herself—- but gradually the strength asserted itself, the fine, blind faith within her asserted itself in a wave of reaction.

Some small weakness had been hers, she admitted—some small shrinking from the truth of things! She had been remiss in the application of her test, allowing the dream to oust the reality in that fascinating hour with Blake. Remiss, but no more!

At this stage in her meditations, she returned to the balcony, studying the sky anew—drinking in confidence from the glory of the stars, the slight grace of the crescent moon.

She became the boy again in mind and heart, enthusiastic, assured, thirsting for action; she looked down upon Paris frankly and without defiance—or so she deemed; and the old, wild suggestions of 'liberty, equality, brotherhood,' seemed to rise, ghostly, from its stones.

Enthusiasm is ever a gracious, pardonable thing, because in its essentials are youth and zeal and all high, white-hot qualities whose roots strike not in the base earth. Any sage, nay, any simpleton, seeing Maxine upon the balcony, could have told her what a fool she was; but who would have told it without a pause, without a sigh for the divinity of such folly?

Next day she rose, refreshed of body, because refreshed of soul; and arrayed in the garments of her strength, went forth to prove her faith.

Max it was—Max of the quick, lithe feet and eager glance—who left the rue Müller, heedless of breakfast, and began his descent upon Paris, making straight for the heart of the citadel with the true instinct of the raider.

Up to this moment, Blake's rooms had been a mere name, lying as they did within the forbidden precincts of the fashionable world, but to-day no corner of Paris offered terrors, for the simple reason that Paris itself had come to be incorporated in Blake, and that, being strong enough to dare Blake, Max was strong enough to dare the city.

Self-analysis played no part in his mental process as he swung down the steep, familiar streets. A singleness of purpose, high as it was foolish, possessed and inspired him. He loved Blake with a wonderful, unsexual love, and he yearned to lay himself at his feet, to offer him of his best—gifts of the gods, given with free hands from a free heart.

Something of the sweet foolishness must have shown upon his face, for when he reached his destination, Blake's *concierge*, usually a taciturn individual, offered him a welcome as he stepped from the brilliant sunshine into the dim cool hallway, and gave him the information he needed with a good grace.

So far, well! But happy assurance emanated from him, and success is compounded of such assurance. He knocked upon Blake's door, certain that Blake himself and not his servant would answer to his summons; and as though the gods smiled at the childish confidence, his certainty was rewarded. The sound of a familiar step set his pulses racing, a hand was laid upon the door, and desire became accomplished.

"What! Max?"

"Yes, Max! Is he welcome?" All the hoarded strength of the night was audible in the words. Max threw up his head, met Blake's eyes, held out his hand—the boy in every particular.

"Welcome? As welcome as the flowers in May! Come in! Come along in!" Blake had accepted the masquerade; all was as before.

Together they passed into the *salon*, and instantly Blake became host— the *rôle* of *rôles* for him.

"Now, boy, don't tell me you have breakfasted! But even if you have, you must breakfast again. Come, sit down! Sit down! My fellow makes most excellent coffee—good as Madame Gustav's of the rue Fabert! Remember the rue Fabert?"

So he rattled on, placing a second chair, seeking an additional cup, and ever Max listened, happy with an acute happiness that almost touched the verge of tears.

But though emotion choked him he played his part gallantly. He was the boy of old days to the very life, swaggering a little in a youthful forgivable conceit, playing the lord of creation to an amused, sympathetic audience.

"Ned," he cried at last, flinging his words from him with all the old frank ease, "tell me to apologize!"

Blake looked up, and the affection, the tolerance in the look quivered through Max's senses.

"Now, boy! Now!" he warned. "Be careful what you're saying! It's only very ordinary friends talk about apologies. And I don't think we have ever been very ordinary friends."

"No! No! But still—"

"Well, say your say!"

The tone was full of indulgence, but, also, it was touched with subtler things. This unexpected invasion had pleased and flattered Blake; it spoke an influence used on his behalf that he dared not have claimed—dared not have expected.

Max walked to the window, looked down an instant into the brilliant, sunlit street, came back to Blake's side, all with a swift impulsiveness.

"Ned, I am the same friend—the same comrade?"

"Indeed, yes!"

"But you do not think I possess a soul?"

Blake, taken unawares, colored like any boy.

"Oh, come!"

"But it is true. I know, for I have been told. And you are wrong—quite wrong."

Blake was about to laugh, but he looked at the young face, suddenly grown grave, and his own words came back to him guiltily. 'Max's lips were made for laughter—his eyes are too bright for tears!'

"Poor little faun!" he said, with jesting tenderness. "Have I misjudged you?"

Max nodded seriously. "You have. She has made me realize."

"Ah! That was like her!" It was Blake's turn to walk to the window; and the boy, watching him eagerly, was unable to place the constraint that suddenly tinged his voice, suddenly veiled his manner.

"Ned," he was urged to say, "tell me! Has she brought us nearer together—my sister Maxine?"

Blake hesitated; for even your Irishman, brimming to confide, is reticent when he stands before his holy of holies.

"Ned, tell me!"

The tone was enticing. Blake turned from the window, strode back across the room, cast an affectionate arm about the boy's shoulder.

"She is a worker of miracles—your sister Maxine!"

The words were warm, the clasp was warm; Max's inspiration gushed up, a fountain of faith.

"She understands you? She shows you 'the higher things'?"

"By God, she does!"

"Then you shall see her once more!" The ideal was predominant; zeal and youth, the white-hot gifts, were lavished at Blake's feet. "Come to the studio to-night, and I shall leave you in her company willingly, gladly, with all my heart. Ned! Say you will come!"

And Blake, dreaming his own dream, pressed the boy's shoulder and laughed, and answered with the jest that covers so many things.

"Will I come? Will a man turn back from the gate of heaven when Saint Peter uses his key?"

CHAPTER XXXII

PERFECT self-deception can be a rare, almost a precious thing, ranking with all absurd, delightful faiths from the child's sweet certainty of fairydom to the enthusiast's belief in the potency of his own star.

Maxine, in her little white bedroom, arraying herself for Blake, was wrapped in a cloud of illusion, translated to a sphere above the common earth by this magic blindness. Never again while life lasted was she to stand as she stood to-night, eyes searching her mirror with perfect steadfast sincerity, lips parted in breathless joy of confidence. Never again! But for the moment the illusion was complete. She saw the triumphing soul of Max glimmer through her own fair body, saw the boy's faith carried like a banner in her woman's hands.

Her dressing was a tremulous affair, tinged with a fine excitement. Again she clothed herself in the soft white dress, the long gray cloak of former meetings; but, banishing the willing Jacqueline, she coiled her hair with her own hands and last, most significant touch, pinned a white rose at her breast.

It was the night of nights! No need to assure herself of the fact; the knowledge sang in her blood, burned in her cheeks. The night of nights! When Maxine would receive the soul of Blake and place it, mystic and sacramental, in the keeping of Max!

The folly of the affair, the naivety of it, made for tears as well as smiles; and Maxine, glowing to the eternal, aspiring flame, looked her last into the little mirror that had so carefully preserved its secrets, and passed across the hall to the *salon*, where the night stretched beckoning, velvet fingers through the open window.

Young, luxurious summer palpitated through the dusk, fanning the ardor in her heart. She ran forward, drawn by its allurement; then, all at once, she stopped, her hand flying to her heart, her breath suspended in a little cry of surprise. Blake had slipped unheard into the *appartement*, and was awaiting her on the balcony.

At her cry, he turned—wheeled round toward her—and his eyes scanned her surprised, betraying face.

"You are glad!" he cried, in sudden self-expression. "You are glad to see me!" The words were hot as they were abrupt, they seared her with their swiftness and their conviction, they were as a raiding army before which all ramparts fell. Mentally, morally, she felt herself sway until preconceived ideas drifted to and fro, weeds upon a tide.

"Yes," she answered, scarcely aware of her own voice. "I am glad."

Where now were the subtle ways, the divers interlacing paths wherein Maxine was to pursue her chase, delivering her quarry into the hands of Max? Where were the barbed and potent shafts whereby that capture was to be achieved? All had vanished into the night; she stood before her intended victim unarmed, ungirt, and—miracle of miracles—undismayed!

She and Blake confronted each other. Their lips were dumb, but their looks embraced. Fate—life—was in the air, in the myriad voices of the night, the myriad pulses of their bodies, the myriad thoughts that wheeled and flashed within their brains.

This knowledge rushed in upon her swimming senses, upon eyes suddenly opened, ears suddenly made free of the music of the spheres; and her hand—the hand that had first girded on her boy's attire—went out to Blake like that of any girl.

It was nature's signal, stronger in its frailty than any attained art of woman; and he answered to it as man has ever answered—ever will answer.

"Oh, my love!" he cried. "My love!" And his arms went round her.

It is sacrilege to attempt analysis of birth or love or death. Death and birth, the mysteries! Love, the revelation! Man, as he has existed through all time, had being in Blake's embrace; woman, as she has been from the first, lived in Maxine's leap of the heart, her leap of the spirit as the ecstasy of his touch thrilled her. Here was no coldness; here was no sensuality. Divinity manifested itself, no longer above, but within them. The lights in the sky were divine, but so were the lights of the town. Divinity fired their souls, merging each in each; but as truly it fired their clasping hands, their lips trembling to kiss.

Maxine—removed by fabulous distances from Max, from the studio, from all accepted things—breathed her wonderment in an unconscious appeal.

"Speak to me!"

And Blake, awed and enraptured, whispered his answer.

"There is nothing to say that you do not know. I worship you. I bent my knee and kissed the hem of your garment the first moment it brushed my path. There is nothing to say that you do not know. I have waited all my life for this."

"All your life?"

"All my life. But love is not reckoned by time. One dreams—and one wakes."

"You dreamed—" She closed her eyes, her ears drank in the cadences of his voice.

"Always! As a child, I dreamed over my play; as a boy, I dreamed over my books—and as a man, over my loves. I was never in love with woman—always in love with love."

"And now?"

"I am awake—I have come into my inheritance! My love! My love!" It was an instant of intense sensation. She could feel the beating of his heart; his fingers and hers were interlaced. "Maxine! Open your eyes! Look at me!"

Obediently—any woman to any man—she opened them and met his gaze.

"You know? You understand?"

She stood rigid, her eyes wide, her nostrils dilated—a creature swaying upon the verge of an abyss, contemplating a plunge into space.

"Maxine!" he said again. "Maxine!"

It was the primitive human cry. She heard and acknowledged it in every fibre of her being; she drew a swift, sharp breath, then, with a free gesture, cast her arms about his neck.

"Ned! Ned! Say again that you love me! Say it a thousand, say it a million times and for every time you say it, I will tell you twice that I love you."

Passion, intoxication sped the words, and Blake's mouth, closing upon hers, broke the ecstasy of speech.

"I love you! I worship you! You are my life. You are myself."

Reality vibrated through his speech; and Maxine, hearing, lost herself. With arms still clasped about him, she leaned her body backward, gazing into his face.

"Again! Say it again!"

"You are my life! We are one! Maxine! Maxine!" His glance burned her, his arms were close about her. With a sudden ardent movement, she caught his face between her hands, drew it down, and kissed it full upon the mouth, not once but many times, fiercely, closely; then, with a little cry, inarticulate as the cry of an animal, she freed herself and fled through the *salon*, through the hall and out upon the landing, the door of the *appartement* closing behind her.

CHAPTER XXXIII

THE door of her *appartement* closed behind Maxine, and she turned, swift as a coursed hare, to the door of M. Cartel.

No hesitation touched her; she needed sanctuary; sanctuary she must have. She opened her neighbor's door, careless of what might lie behind, bringing with her into the quiet rooms a breath of fierce disorder.

The living-room, with its piano and its homely chairs and table, was lighted by a common lamp; and the little Jacqueline, the only occupant, sat in the radius of the light, peacefully sewing at a blue muslin gown that was to adorn a Sunday excursion into the country.

At the sound of the stormy entry she merely raised her head; but at sight of her visitor, she was on her feet in an instant, the heap of muslin flowing in a blue cascade from her lap to the floor.

"Madame!"

"Hide me!" cried Maxine.

"Madame!"

"Lock the outer door! And if M. Blake should knock—"

Jacqueline made no further comment. When a visitor's face is blanched and her limbs tremble as did those of Maxine, the Jacquelines of this world neither question nor hesitate. She went across the room without a word, and the key clicked in the lock.

Maxine was standing in the middle of the room when Jacqueline returned; her body was still quivering, her nostrils fluttering, her fingers twisting and intertwisting in an excess of emotion; and at sight of the familiar little figure, words broke from her with the fierceness of a freed torrent.

"Jacqueline! You see before you a mad woman! A mad woman—and one filled with the fear of her madness! They say the insane are mercifully oblivious. It is untrue!" She almost cried the last words and, turning, began a swift pacing of the room.

"Madame!" Jacqueline caught her breath at her own daring. "Madame, you know at last, then, that he loves you?"

Maxine stopped and her burning eyes fixed themselves upon the girl. This speech of Jacqueline's was a breach of all their former relations, but her brain had no room for pride. She was grappling with vital facts.

"I know at last that he loves me?" she repeated, confusedly.

"That he loves you, madame; that, unknowingly, he has always loved you. How else could he have treated Monsieur Max so sacredly—almost as he might have treated his own child?"

But Maxine was not dealing in psychological subtleties.

"Love!" she cried out. "Love! All the world is in a conspiracy over this love!"

"Because love is the only real thing, madame."

"Perhaps! But not the love of which you speak. The love of the soul, but not the love of the body!"

"Madame, can one truly give the soul and refuse the body? Is not the instinct of love to give all?"

The little Jacqueline spoke her truth with a frail confidence very touching to behold. She was a child of the people, her sole weapons against the world were a certain blonde beauty, a certain engaging youthfulness; but she looked Maxine steadfastly in the eyes, meeting the anger, the scorn, the fear compassed in her glance.

"I know the world, madame; it is not a pretty place. When I was sixteen years old, I left my parents because it called to me—and in the distance its voice was pleasant. I left my home; I had lovers." She shrugged her shoulders with an extreme philosophy. "I tried everything—except love. Then—I met Lucien!" Her philosophy merged curiously to innocence, almost to the soft innocence of a child. "I ran away again, madame; I fled to Lize." She paused. "Poor Lize! She has a good heart! That was the night at the Bal Tabarin. That night Lucien opened his arms, and I flung myself into them."

She spoke with perfect artlessness, ignorant of a world other than her own, innocent of a moral code other than that which she followed.

Once again, as on the day she had first visited the *appartement* and made acquaintance with the old painter and his wife, dread of some mysterious force filled Maxine. What marvellous power was this that could smile secure at poverty and oblivion—that could cast a halo of true emotion over a Bal Tabarin?

"It is not true!" she cried out, in answer to herself.

"Not true, madame? Why did I choose Lucien, who is nothing to look upon—who is an artist and penniless?"

She ran across to Maxine; she caught her by the shoulders.

"Oh, madame! How beautiful you are—and how blind! You bandage your eyes, and you tighten the knot. Oh, my God, if I could but open it for you!"

"And reduce me to kisses and folly and tears?"

"One may drift into heaven on a kiss!" Jacqueline's voice was like some precious metal, molten and warm.

"Or one may slip into hell! Do you think I have not known what it is to kiss? It was from a kiss I fled to-night."

Her tone was fervent as it was reckless, and Jacqueline stood aghast. The entire denial of love was comprehensible to her, if inexplicable; but her mind refused this problem of realization and rejection.

"Madame—" she began, quickly, but she paused on the word, listening; the sound of Max's door opening and closing came distinctly to the ear, followed by a footstep descending the stairs. "Monsieur Édouard!" she whispered, finger on lip.

Maxine, also, had heard, and a look of relief broke the tension of her expression.

"He is gone. That is well!"

Something in her look, in her voice startled Jacqueline anew.

"Why do you speak like that, madame? Why do you look so cold?"

"I am sane again, Jacqueline."

"And Monsieur Édouard? Is he sane, I wonder? Is he cold? Oh, madame, he loves you!"

"I am going to prove his love."

"But, madame! Oh, madame, love isn't a matter of proving; it is an affair of giving—giving—giving with all the heart."

"Trust me, Jacqueline! I understand. Good-night!"

Jacqueline framed no word, but her eyes spoke many things.

"Say good-night, Jacqueline! Forget that you have entertained a mad woman!"

"Good-night, madame!"

But the little Jacqueline, left alone, shook her head many times, leaving her heap of blue muslin neglected upon the floor.

"Poor child!" she said softly to herself. "Poor child! Poor child!"

CHAPTER XXXIV

IT was midway between the hours of nine and ten on the morning following. Max was standing in the studio; the easel, still bearing the portrait, had been pushed into a corner, its face to the wall; everywhere the warm sun fell upon a rigid severity of aspect, as though the room had instinctively been bared for the enacting of some scene.

Max himself, in a subtle manner, struck the same note. The old painting blouse he usually wore had been discarded for the blue serge suit, severely masculine in aspect; his hair had been reduced to an usual order, his whole appearance was rigid, active, braced for the coming moment.

And this moment arrived sooner even than anticipation had suggested. The clocks of Paris had barely clashed the half hour, when his strained ears caught a step upon the landing, a sharp knock upon the door, and before his brain could leap to fear or joy, Blake was in the *appartement*—in the room.

There was no mistaking Blake's attitude as he swung into the boy's presence; it was patent in every movement, every glance, even had his white, strained face not testified to it. Coming into the studio, he affected nothing—neither apology, greeting, nor explanation; without preamble he came straight to the matter that possessed his mind.

"You know of this?" He held out a square white envelope, bearing bold feminine handwriting—writing over which time and thought and labor had been expended in this same room ten hours earlier. "You know this?"

"Yes." Max's tongue clicked dryly against the roof of his mouth, but his eyes bore the fire of Blake's scrutiny.

"You know the contents?"

"Yes."

"'Yes!' And you can stand there like a graven image. Do you realize it, at all? Do you grasp it?"

"I—think I understand."

"You think you understand?" Blake laughed in a manner that was not agreeable. "Understand, forsooth! You, who have never seen anything human or divine that you rate above your own little finger! Understand!"

He laughed again, then suddenly his attitude changed. "But I haven't come here to waste words! You know that, your sister has left Paris?"

Max nodded, finding no words.

"She tells me here that she has gone—gone out of my life—that I am to forget her."

"Well?"

"Well, that has only one meaning, when it comes from the one woman. I must know where she is."

Max set his lips and studiously averted his face.

"Come! Tell me where she is! Time counts."

"I do not know."

"I expected that! You're lying, of course; but when you're up against a man in my frame of mind, lies are poor ammunition. I don't ask you why she has gone—that's between her and me, that's my affair. But I must know where she is."

"I cannot tell you."

"You cannot refuse to tell me! Look here, boy, you've always seen my soft side, you don't believe there is a hard one. But we Irish can surprise you."

Max had no physical fear, but he backed involuntarily before the menace in Blake's eyes.

"I'm not lying to you, Ned. I cannot tell you, because I do not know. My sister Maxine has ceased to exist—for me, as much as for you."

"Stop!" Blake stepped close to him and for an instant his hand was raised, but it fell at once to his side, and he laughed once more, harshly and self-consciously. "Don't play with me, boy! I've had a hard knock."

"I'm not playing. It's true! It's true!" Dark eyes, with dark lines beneath them, stared at Blake, carrying conviction. "It's true! It's true! I do not know."

"God, boy!" Blake faltered in his vehemence.

"It's true!" said Max again.

"True that she's gone—vanished? That I can't find her? That you can't find her? It isn't!"

"It is."

The blood rushed into Blake's face. For a moment he stood rigid and speechless, drinking in the fact; then his feelings broke bounds.

"It's true? And you stand there, gaping! God, boy, rouse yourself!" He caught him by the shoulder and shook him. "Don't you know what this is? Have you never seen a man dealt a mortal blow?"

"Love is not everything!" cried Max.

"Not everything? Oh, you poor, damned little fool, how bitterly you'll retract that prating! Not everything? Isn't water everything in a parched desert? Isn't the sun everything to a frozen world?" He stopped, suddenly loosing the boy, casting him from him, a thing of no significance.

Max, faint and pale, caught at his arm.

"Ned! Ned! I am here. I am your friend. I love you."

Blake, in all his whirl of passion, paused.

"You!" he said, and no long eloquence could have accentuated the blank amazement, the searing irony of the word.

But Max closed all his senses.

"Ned! Ned! Look at the truth of life! There is in me everything but one thing."

"Then, by God, that one thing is everything! It's the woman and the man that rule this world. The woman and the man—the soul and the body! All other things are dust and chaff."

"You feel that now. But time—time balances. We will be happy yet. We will relive the old days—"

Blake turned, wrenching away his arm. "The old days? Do you imagine Paris can hold me now she is gone?"

"Ned!"

"Do you imagine I can live in this town—climb these steps—stand on that balcony, that breathes of her?"

Max was leaning back against the window-frame. His brain seemed empty of blood, his heart seemed to pulse in a strange, unfamiliar fashion, while somewhere within his consciousness a tiny voice commanded him urgently to preserve his strength—not to betray himself.

"You will go away?" he heard himself say. "Where will you go? To Ireland?"

"To Ireland—or hell!" Blake walked to the door.

"Then you are leaving me?"

"You shall know where I am."

"And if I should need you?"

Blake made no answer; he did not even look back.

"If—if she should need you?"

He turned.

"I will come to her at any moment—from anywhere."

The door closed. He was gone, and Max stood leaning against the window. His blood still circulated oddly, and now the inner voice with its reiterated commands was rising, rising until it became the thunder of a sea that filled his ears, annihilating all other sounds. A swift, sharp terror smote him; he sought desperately to maintain his consciousness, but, breaking across the effort an icy breath crept up from nowhere, fanning his cheek, suspending all struggle, and a palpable darkness, like the darkness of brooding wings, closed in upon him, bringing oblivion.

CHAPTER XXXV

WHO shall depict the soul of woman? As well essay to number the silk hairs on the moth's wing, or paint truly the hues in the blown bubble! The soul of woman dwells apart, subject to no laws, trammelled by no precedent; mysterious in its essence, strong in its very frailty, it passes through many phases to its ultimate end, working as all great agents work, silently and in the dark.

With the passing of Blake, the spiritual Maxine entered upon a new phase—was arbitrarily forced into a new phase of existence. The passing of Blake was sudden, tremendous, devastating in its effect, leaving as consequences a moral blackness, a moral chaos.

It was a new Maxine who wakened to the realization of facts; rather, it was a new Max, for it was the masculine, not the feminine ego that turned a set face to circumstance in the moment of desertion—that sedulously wrapped itself in the garment of pride spun and fashioned in happier hours.

'Now is the test! Now is the time!' Max insisted, drowning by insistence the poignant cry of the heart; and to this watchword he marched against fate.

With set purpose he faced life and its vexed questions in that bitter, precipitate moment. Again it was the beginning of things; but it was the rue Müller and not the Gare du Nord that was the scene of action; the May sun fell burning on the Parisian pavements, while the blood of the adventurer ran slow and cold. The illusions bred of the winter dawn had been dispersed by the light of day; life was no glad enterprise—no climbing of golden heights, but the barren crossing of a trackless region where no hand proffered guidance and false signs misled the weary eyes. One weapon alone was necessary in the pursuance of the gray journey—a sure command—a sure possession of one's self!

This thought alone made harmony with the music of the past, and toward its thin sound his ears were strained. Comradeship had come and gone—love had come and gone—the fundamental idea that had lured him to Paris alone remained, stark, colorless, but recognizable!

One must possess one's self! And to achieve this supreme good, one must close the senses and seal up the heart, and be as a creature already dead!

To this profound end, Max locked himself in his studio and sat alone while the May morning waxed; to this profound end, moving as in a dream, he at last rose at midday and left the *appartement* in quest of his customary meal. What that meal was to consist of—whether stones or bread—did not touch his brain, for his mind was solely exercised with wonder at the fact that his will could command the search for food—could compel his dry lips to the savorless duty of eating.

As he left the little *café*, paying his score, he half expected to see his wonder reflected on the good face of madame the proprietress, and was curiously shocked to receive the usual cheerful smile, the usual cheerful 'good-day!' that took no heed of his heavy plight.

It was that cheerful superficiality of Paris that can so delightfully mirror one's mood when the heart is light—that can ring so sadly hollow when the soul is sick. It cut Max with a bitter sharpness; and, like a man fleeing from his own shadow, he fled the shop.

Outside in the dazzling glitter of the streets, the sun blinded him, accentuating the scorching pain of unshed tears; the very pavements seemed to rise up and sear him with their memories. Here in this very street Blake and he had strolled and smoked on many a night, wending homeward from the play or the opera, laughing, jesting, arguing as they paced arm-in-arm up and down before the sleeping shops. The thought stung him with an amazing sharpness, and he fled from it, as he had fled from the *café* and its smiling proprietress.

His descent upon Paris was a descent upon a region of beauty. The sense of summer lay like a bloom upon the flowers for sale at the street corners, and shimmered—a ribbon of silver sunlight—across the pale-blue sky. The trees in the grand boulevards shone in their green trappings; rainbow colors glinted in the shop windows; everywhere, save in the heart of Max, was fairness and youth and joy.

Supremely conscious of himself, adrift and wretched, he passed through the crowds of people—passed from sun to shade, from shade to sun—with a hopeless eager haste that possessed no object save to outstrip his thoughts.

It is a curious fact that, to the desponding, water has a magnetic call; without knowledge, almost without volition, his footsteps turned toward the river—that river which has so closely girdled Paris through all her varied life. Smooth and pale, it slipped secretly past its quays as Max approached, indifferent to the tragedies it concealed, as it was indifferent to the ardent life that ebbed and flowed across its many bridges. On its breast, the small, dark craft of the city nestled lazily; to right and left along its banks, the sun struck glints of gold and bronze from spire and monument; while, close against its sides, on the very parapet of its quays, there was in progress that quaint book traffic that strikes so intimate a note in the life of the quarter.

It is a charming thought that in the heart of Paris—Paris, the pleasure city—there is time and space for the vender of old books to set out his wares, to lay them open to the kindly sky, to tempt the studious and idle alike to pause and dally and lose themselves in that most fascinating of all pursuits—- the search for the treasure that is never found. Max paused beside this row of tattered bookstalls, and quivered to the stab of a new pain. Scores of happy mornings he had wandered with Blake in this vicarious garden of delight, flitting from the books to the curio shops across the roadway, from the curios back again to the books, while Blake talked with his easy friendliness to the odd beings who bartered in this open market.

It was pain inexpressible—it was loneliness made palpable—to stand by the tressel stalls and allow his eyes to rest upon the familiar merchandise; and for the third time in that black morning he fled from his own shadow— fled onward into the darker, older Paris—the Paris of tradition, where the church of Notre Dame frowns, silently scornful of those who disturb its peace.

As he approached the great building, its sombre impressiveness fell upon his troubled spirit mercifully as its shadow fell across the blinding sunlight. He paused in the wide space that fronts the heavy doors, and caught his breath as the fugitive of old might have caught breath at sight of sanctuary.

Here was a place of shade and magnitude—- a place untouched by memory!

Blindly he moved toward the door, entered the church, walked up the aisle. Few sight-seers disturbed the sense of peace, for outside it was high noon and Paris was engrossed in the serious business of *déjeuner*; no service was in progress; all was still, all dim save where a taper of a lamp glowed before a shrine or the sun struck sharp through the splendor of stained glass.

There are few churches—to some minds there is no other church— where the idea of the profound broods as it does in Notre Dame. The sense of dignity, the curious ancient scent compounded by time, the mystic colors of the great windows breathe of the infinite.

Max, walking up the aisle, looked at the dark walls; Max—modern, critical—looked up at the wondrous rose window, and felt the overshadowing power of superhuman things. The modern world crumbled before the impassive silence, criticism found no challenge in its brooding spirit, for the mind cannot analyze what it cannot measure.

Max subscribed to no creed; but, by a strange impulsion, born of dead ages, his eyes fell from the glowing window and turned to the high altar. He did not want to pray; he rebelled against the idea of supplication; but the circling thoughts within him concentrated suddenly, he clasped his hands with a clasp so fierce that it was pain.

"Oh, God!" he said, under his breath. "God! God, let me possess myself!" And as if some chord had snapped, relieving the tension in his brain, he dropped upon his knees, as he had once done at the foot of his own staircase and, crouching against a pillar, wept like a lost child.

PART IV

CHAPTER XXXVI

THE last days of August in Paris! A deadly oppression of heat; a brooding inertia that lay upon the city like a cloak!

In the little *appartement* every window stood gaping, thirsting for a draught of air; but no stir lightened the haze that weighed upon the atmosphere, no faintest hint of breeze ruffled the plantation shrubs, dark in their fulness of summer foliage. Stillness lay upon Montmartre—upon the rue Müller—most heavily of all, upon the home of Max.

It was an obvious, weighty stillness unconnected with repose. It seemed as though the spirit of the place were fled, and that in its stead the vacant quiet of death reigned. In the *salon* the empty hearth hurt the observer with its poignant suggestion of past comradeship, dead fires, long hours when the spring gales had whistled through the plantation and stories had been told and dreams woven to the spurt of blue and copper flames. The place had an aspect of desertion; no book lay thrown, face downward, upon chair or table; no flowers glowed against the white walls, though flowers were to be had for the asking in a land that teemed with summer fruitfulness.

This was the *salon*; but in the studio the note of loss was still more sharply struck. Not because the easel, drawn into the full light, offered to the gaze a crude, unfinished study, nor yet because a laden palette was cast upon the floor to consort with tubes and brushes, but because the presiding genius of the place Max—Max the debonair, Max the adventurous—was seated on a chair before his canvas, a prey to black despair.

Max was thinner. The great heat of August—or some more potent cause—had smoothed the curves from his youthful face, drawn the curled lips into an unfamiliar hardness and painted purple shadows beneath the eyes. Max had fought a long fight in the three months that had dwindled since the morning of Blake's going, and a long moral fight has full as many scars to leave behind as a battle of physical issues. The saddest human experience is to view alone the scenes one has viewed through other eyes— to walk solitary where one has walked in company—to have its particular barbed shaft aimed at one from every stick and stone that mark familiar ways. All this Max had known, wrapping himself in his pride, keeping long silence, fighting his absurd, brave fight.

'The first days will be the worst!' he had assured himself, walking back from Notre Dame in the searching sun, heedless of who might notice his red eyes. 'The first days will be the worst!' And this formula he had repeated in the morning, standing uninspired and wretched before a blank canvas. Then had come Blake's first message—a note written from Sweden without care or comfort, importing nothing, indicating nothing beyond the place at which the writer might be found, and tears—torrents of tears—had testified to the fierce anticipation, the crushing disappointment for which it was responsible.

He had sent no answer to the cold communication—no answer had been desired, and calling himself by every name contempt could coin, he had pushed forward along the lonely road, companioned by his work. But he himself had once said: 'One must come naked and whole to art, as one must come naked and whole to nature,' and he had spoken a truth. Art is no anodyne for a soul wounded in other fields, and Art closed arms to him when most he wooed her. He threw himself into work with pitiable vehemence in those first black weeks. By day, he haunted the galleries and attended classes like any art student; by night, he ranged the streets and *cafés*, seeking inspiration, returning to his lonely room to lie wakeful, fighting his ghosts, or else to sob himself to sleep.

His theory of life had been amply proved. Blake had prated of the soul, but it had been the body he had desired! Again and again that thought had struck home, a savage spur goading him in daytime to a wild plying of his brushes, gripping him in the lonely darkness of the night-time until his sobs were suspended by their very poignancy and the scalding tears dried before they could fall.

He saw darkly, he saw untruly, but the world is according to the beholder's vision, and in those sultry days, when summer waxed and Paris emptied, opening its gates to the foreigner, all the colors had receded from existence and he had tasted the lees of life.

And now to-day it seemed that the climax had been reached. Seated idly before his canvas, the whole procession of his Paris life unwound before him—from the first tumultuous hour, when he had entered the Hôtel Railleux on fire for freedom, to this moment when, with dull resentful eyes, he confronted the sum of his labors—an unfinished, sorry study devoid of inspiration.

He stared at the flat canvas—the rough outline of his picture—the reckless splashing on of color; and, abruptly, as if a hand had touched him, he sprang to his feet, making havoc among the paint tubes that strewed the floor, and turned summarily to the open window.

It was after eight o'clock, but the hazy, unreal daylight of a summer evening made all things visible. He scanned the plantation, viewing it as if in some travesty of morning; he looked down upon the city, sleeping uneasily in preparation for the inevitable night of pleasure, and a sudden loathing of Paris shook him. It seemed as if some gauzy illusive garment had been lifted from a fair body and that his eyes, made free of the white limbs, had discerned a corpse.

By a natural flight of ideas, the loathing of the city turned to loathing of himself—to an unsatiable desire for self-forgetfulness, for self-effacement. Solitude was no longer tenable, the walls of the *appartement* seemed to close in about him, stifling—suffocating him. With a feverish movement, he turned from the window, picked up his hat and fled the room.

On the landing he paused for a moment before the door of M. Cartel. He had paid many visits to M. Cartel under stress of circumstances similar to this, and invariably M. Cartel—and, moving in his shadow, the demure Jacqueline—had proffered a generous hospitality—talking to him of work, of politics, of Paris, but with a Frenchman's inimitable tact.

For all this unobtrusive attention he had been silently grateful, but to-night he stood by the door hesitating; for long he hesitated, honestly fighting with his mood, but at last the desperation of the mood prevailed. Who could talk of work, when work was as an evil smell in the nostrils? Who could talk of politics, when the overthrow of nations would not stimulate the mind? He turned on his heel with a little exclamation, hopeless as it was cynical, and ran down the stairs with the gait of one whose destination concerns neither the world nor himself.

CHAPTER XXXVII

MAX swung down the Escalier de Sainte-Marie in as reckless a mood as ever possessed being of either sex. Nothing of the sweet Maxine was discernible in face or carriage; the boy predominated, but a boy possessed of a callousness that was pathetic seen hand-in-hand with youth.

For the first time he was viewing Paris bereft of the glamour of romance; for the first time the Masque of Folly passed before him, licentious and unashamed. Many an hour, in days gone by, he had discussed with Blake this lighter side of many-sided Paris, and with Blake's wise and penetrating gaze he had seen it in true perspective; but to-night there was no sane interpreter to temper vision, to-night he was bitterly alone, and his mind, from long austerity, long concentration upon work, had swung with grievous suddenness to the opposing pole of thought. He had no purpose in his descent from the rue Müller, he had no desire of vice as an antidote to pain, but his loathing of Paris was drawing him to her with that morbid craving to hurt and rehurt his bruised soul that assails the artist in times of misery.

The streets were quiet, for it was scarcely nine o'clock, and as yet the lethargy of the day lay heavy on the air. The heat and the accompanying laxity breathed an atmosphere of its own; every window of every house gaped, and behind the casements one caught visions of men and women negligent of attire and heedless of observation.

Romance was dead! Of that supreme fact Max was very sure. A hard smile touched his lips, and hugging his cynicism, he went forward—crossing the Boulevard de Clichy, plunging downward into the darker regions of the rue des Martyrs and the rue Montmartre, where the lights of the boulevards are left behind, and the sight-seer is apt to look askance at the crude facts that the street lamps divulge to his curious eyes. To the boy, these corners had no terrors, for in his untarnished friendship with Blake all sides of life had been viewed in turn, as all topics had been discussed as component parts of a fascinatingly interesting world. To-night he went forward, mingling with the inhabitants of the district, revelling with morbid realism in the forbidding dinginess of their appearance. He was not of that quarter—that was patent to every rough who lounged outside a *café* door, as it was patent to every slovenly woman who gave him a glance in passing. He was not of the quarter, but he was an artist—and a shabby one at that—so the men accorded him an indifferent shrug and the women a second glance.

Forward he went, possessed by his morbidity—forward into the growing murkiness of environment until, association of ideas suddenly curbing impulse, he stopped before the door of a shabby *café* bearing the fanciful appellation of the Café des Cerises-jumelles. Once, when bound upon a night exploration in this same region, he and Blake had stopped to smile at this odd name and wonder at its origin, and finally they had passed through the portal to find that the twin cherries smiled upon doubtful patrons. The vivid memory of that night smote him now as, drawn by some unquestioned influence, he again entered the *café*, passing through a species of bar to a long, low-ceiled eating-room set with small tables. How Blake had talked that night! How thoughtfully, how humanely and tolerantly he had judged their fellow-guests, as they sat at one of these tables, rubbing shoulders with the worst—or, as he had laughingly insisted, the best—of an odd fraternity!

The recollection was keen as a knife when Max entered the eating-room, sat down and ordered a drink with the supreme indifference of disillusion. Six months ago he would have trembled to find himself alone in such a place; to-night he was beyond such a commonplace as fear.

He smiled again cynically, emptied his glass and looked about him. His first experience of the place had been in the hours succeeding midnight, when the quarter hummed with its unsavory life; but now it was early, the lights were not yet at their fullest, the waiters had not as yet taken on their nocturnal air of briskness. In one corner three men were engrossed in a game of cards, in another a thin girl of fifteen sat with her arm round the neck of a boy scarce older than herself, whispering jests into his ear, at which they both laughed in coarse low murmurs, while in the middle of the room, with her back turned to him, a woman in a tight black dress and feathered hat was eating a meal of poached eggs.

In a vague way, absorbed in his own thoughts, Max fell to studying this solitary woman, until something in her impassivity, something in the sphinx-like calm with which she went through the business of her meal, blent with his imaginings, and he suddenly found her placed beside Blake in the possession of his thoughts—an integral part of their joint lives. In a flash of memory the large black hat, the opulent figure took place within his consciousness and, answering to a new instinct, he rose and took an involuntary step in the woman's direction.

She changed her position at sound of his approach, her large hat described new angles, and she looked back over her shoulder.

"What!" she said aloud. "The little friend of Blake! But how droll!"

She showed no surprise, she merely waved her hand to a chair facing her own.

Max sat down; a hot and dirty waiter came forward languidly, and wine was ordered.

Lize pushed aside the glass of green-tinted liquid that she had been consuming through a straw, and waited for what was to come. Max, looking at her in the crude light of a gas-jet, saw that her face was whiter, her eyes more hollow than when her wrath had fallen on him at the Bal Tabarin; also, he noted that a little dew of heat showed through the mask of powder on her face.

Silence was maintained until the wine was brought; then she drank thirstily, laid down her empty glass and turned her eyes upon him.

"You have parted with your friend, eh?"

The surprise of the question was so sharp that it killed speculation. He did not ask how she had probed his secret—whether by mere intuition or through some feminine confidence of Jacqueline's. The fact of her knowledge swept him beyond the region of lucid thought; he accepted the situation as it was offered.

"Yes," he said. "I have parted with my friend."

"And why? He is a good boy—Blake!" She looked at him with her inscrutable eyes, and after many days he was conscious of the touch of human compassion. He did not analyze the woman's feelings—he did not even conjecture whether she knew him for boy or girl. All he comprehended was that out of this sordid atmosphere—out of the lethargy of the sultry night—some force had touched him, some force was drawing him back into the circle of human things. Strange indeed are the workings of the mind. He, who had shrunk with an agonized sensitiveness from the sympathy of M. Cartel—from the tender comprehension of the little Jacqueline—suddenly felt his reserve melt and break in presence of this woman of the boulevards with her air of impassive *ennui*. Theoretically, he knew life in all its harder aspects, and it called for no vivid imagination to trace the descent of the fresh *grisette* of the *Quartier Latin* to the creature who sought her meals in the Café des Cerises-jumelles, yet hers was the accepted compassion.

"Madame!" he said, suddenly. "Madame, tell me! You knew him once?"

Lize wiped the dew of heat from her forehead; emptied a second glass of wine. "A thousand years ago, *mon petit*, when the world was as young as you!"

"In the *Quartier*?"

"In the *Quartier*—on the Boul' Mich'—at Bulliers—" She stopped, falling into a dream; then, suddenly, from the farthest corner of the room, came the sound of a loud kiss, and the boy and girl at the distant table began to sing in unison—a ribald song, but instinct with the zest of life. Lize started, as though she had been struck.

"They have it—youth!" she cried, with a jerk of her head toward the distant corner. "The world is for them!" Then her voice and her expression altered. She leaned across the table, until her face was close to Max.

"What a little fool you are!" she said. "It is written in those eyes of yours—that see too little and see too much. Go home! Think of what I have said! He is a good boy—this Blake!"

Max mechanically replenished her glass, and mechanically she drank; then she produced a little mirror and made good the ravages of the heat upon her face with the nonchalance of her kind; finally, she looked at the clock.

"Come!" she said. "We go the same way."

He rose obediently. He made no question as to her destination. He had come to drown himself in the sordidness of Paris and, behold, his heart was beating with a human quickness it had not known since the moment he held Blake's first letter unopened in his hand; his throat was dry, his eyes were smarting with the old, half-forgotten smart of unshed tears.

He followed her with a strange docility as she passed out of the unsavory Cerises-jumelles into the close, ill-smelling street. In complete silence they walked through what seemed a nightmare world of unpleasant sights, unpleasant sounds, until across his dazed thoughts the familiar sense of Paris—the sense of the pleasure-chase—swept from the Boulevard de Clichy.

Lize paused; he saw her fully in the brave illumination—the large black hat, the close-clad figure, the pallid face—and as he looked, she smiled unexpectedly and, putting out her hand, patted him on the shoulder.

"Good-bye, *mon enfant*! Go home! Youth comes but once; and this Blake—he is a good boy!"

Before he could answer, before he could return smile or touch, she was gone—absorbed into the maze of lights, and he was alone, to turn which way he would.

CHAPTER XXXVIII

THE fifth floor was dim and silent, the door of M. Cartel's *appartement* was closed; but Max, mounting the stairs two steps at a time, was not daunted by silence or lack of light. Max was once again a prey to impulse, and under the familiar tyranny, his blood burned—raced in his veins, sang in his ears.

Without an instant's pause, he knocked on M. Cartel's door, and when his knock was answered by Jacqueline—fair and cool-looking, oven in the great heat—words rushed from him as they had been wont to rush when life was a gay affair.

"You are alone, Jacqueline?"

Jacqueline nodded quickly, comprehending a crisis.

"Ah, I thank God!" He caught both her hands; he gave a little laugh that ended in a sob; he passed into the *appartement*, drawing her with him.

"Oh, *la, la*!" she cried, hiding her emotion in flippancy, "you take my breath away."

Max laughed again. "You see I've lost my own!"

She gave a scornful, familiar toss of the head. "Do not be foolish! What has happened?"

"I have made a discovery, Jacqueline. Youth comes but once!"

"Indeed! You need not have left the rue Müller to learn that."

"It comes but once, and while it is with me I am going to look it in the face." His words tumbled forth, pell-mell, and as he spoke he pulled her forcibly into the living-room.

"Jacqueline, I am serious. I have been down in hell; I must see heaven, or my faith is lost."

Jacqueline stood very still, making no effort to loose the hot clasp of his hands, but all at once her gaze concentrated piercingly.

"You have sent for him!" she exclaimed.

"I have! Oh, I may be weak, but listen! listen! In the old days when the world was religious and people observed Lent, there was always *Mi-Carême*, was there not? Well, I have fasted, and now I must feast."

They gazed at each other; the one aglow with anticipation, the other with curiosity.

"You have sent for him—at last?"

"I have sent a telegram with these words: 'Meet me at midday on Tuesday in the Place de la Concorde.—MAXINE.'"

"And this is Friday," said Jacqueline. "In four days' time you will see him again!"

"Again!" Max spoke the word inaudibly.

"And—when you meet?" Jacqueline's blue eyes were sharp as needle-points.

Max colored to the temples. "*Ma chérie*, I have not even thought! All I know is that youth comes but once, and that youth is courage. I have been a coward—I am going to be brave."

"You are going—to confess?"

Max said nothing, but with her woman's instinct for such things, Jacqueline read assent in the silence.

"Then the end is assured! He will take you—with your will, or without! Monsieur Max, or the princess!"

Max shook his head. "I do not think so. But that is outside the moment—that is the afterward. First there must be midday and the Place de la Concorde! First there must be my *Mi-Carême*—my hour!"

"Ah!" whispered the little Jacqueline, "your hour!" And who shall say what memories glinted through her quick brain—what conjurings of the first waltz with M. Cartel at the Moulin de la Galette, and the last waltz at the Bal Tabarin, when she stepped through the tawdry doorway into her paradise? "Your hour! And where will it be spent—madame?"

"Ah!" Max's eyes sought heaven or, in lieu of heaven, M. Cartel's ceiling; Max's hands freed Jacqueline's and flew out in ecstatic gesture. "Ah, that is for the gods to say, *chérie*! And the gods know best."

CHAPTER XXXIX

RAPTURE gilded the world; rapture trembled on the air like the vibrations of a chord struck from some celestial harp. Coming as a divine gift, the first autumnal frost had lighted upon Paris; during the night fainting August had died, and with the dawn, golden September had been born to the city.

Blake, waiting at the foot of the Cours la Reine, consumed with anticipation, drank in the freshness of the morning as though it were a draught of wine; Maxine, crossing the Place de la Concorde, lifted her face to the sky, striving to quiet her pulses, to cool her hot cheeks in the wash of gentle air.

Her hour had arrived; none could hinder its approach, as none could mar its beauty. She scarcely recognized the earth upon which she trod; the fierce excitement, the melting tenderness of her moods warred until emotion ran riot and the sifting of her feelings became a task impossible.

She passed the spot where, eight months earlier, Max had saluted the flag of France. Her heart leaped, her glance, flying before her, discovered Blake waiting at his appointed place, and all her wild sensations were suspended.

The violently beating heart seemed to stop, the blood moved with a sick slowness in her veins, it seemed impossible that she should go forward, and yet, by the curious mechanism of the human machine, her feet carried her on until Blake's presence was tangible to all her senses—until suspense was engulfed in actuality, and joy was singing about her in the air, a song so triumphant, so penetrating that it drowned all whispering of doubt—all murmurs of to-morrow or of yesterday. Tears welled into her eyes, her hands went out to him.

Standing in the full light, she was a tall, slight girl, fastidiously, if simply dressed—veiled, gloved, shod as befitted a woman of the world; and as he gazed on her, one thought possessed Blake. She, who typified all beauty—whose presence was a fragrance—had called to him, chosen him. All the romance stored up through generations welled within him; he would have died for her at that moment as enthusiastically as his ancestors had died for their faith. Catching her hands, he kissed them without a thought for passing glances.

"Princess!"

The sound of his voice went through her, she laughed to break the sob that caught her throat, she looked up, unashamed of the tears trembling on her lushes.

"Monsieur Ned!"

"Oh, why the 'monsieur'?"

"Why the 'princess'?"

They both smiled.

"Maxine!"

"*Mon ami! Mon cher ami!*" It thrilled her to the heart to say the words; she glanced at him half fearfully, then broke forth afresh, lest he should have time to think. "Ned, tell me! It is true—all this? I am not asleep? It is not a dream?"

He pressed her hands. "Look round you! It is morning."

Her lips trembled; she obeyed him, looking slowly from the cool sky to the tree-tops, where the heavy leaves were still damp with the night's frost.

"Yes, it is morning!" she said. "We have all the day!"

Watching her intently, he did not add, as would the common lover, "we have many days"; she seemed to him so beautiful, so naïve that her words must compass perfection.

"We have all the day," he echoed. "How shall it be spent?"

Then she turned to him, all graciousness, her young face lifted to the light. "Ah, you must decide! I do not wish even to think; the world is so—how do you say—enchanted?"

He laughed in delight at her charming, pleading smile, her charming, pleading hesitation; he caught her mood with swift intuition.

"That's it! The world is enchanted! Away behind us, is the Dreaming Wood. What do you say? Shall we go and seek the Sleeping Beauty?"

She nodded silently. He was so perfectly the Blake of old—the Blake who understood.

"Then the first thing is to find the magic coach! We must have nothing so mundane as a carriage drawn by horses. A magic coach that travels by itself!" He signalled to a passing automobile.

"Drive to the Pré Catelan—and drive slowly!" he directed; he handed her to her seat with all the courtliness proper to the occasion, and they were off, wheeling up the long incline toward the Arc de Triomphe.

They were silent while the chauffeur made a way through the many vehicles, past the crowds of pedestrians that infest the entrance to the Bois; but as the way grew clearer—as the spell of the trees, of the green vistas and glimpsed water began to weave itself—Maxine turned and laid her hand gently upon Blake's.

"*Mon cher*! How good you are!"

He started, thrilling at her touch.

"My dearest! Good?"

"In coming to me like this—"

He caught her hand quickly. "Don't!" he said. "Don't! It isn't right—- from you to me. You never doubted that I'd come? You knew I'd come?"

"Yes; I knew."

"Then that's all right!" He pressed her hand, he smiled, he reassured her by all the subtle, intangible ways known to lovers, and it was borne in upon her that he had altered, had grown mentally in his months of exile—that he was steadier, more certain of life or of himself, than when he had rushed tempestuously out of Max's studio. She pondered the change, without attempting to analyze it; a deep sense of rest possessed her, and she allowed her hand to lie passive in his until, all too soon, their cab swept round to the left, sped past a bank of greenery and drew up, with a creaking of brakes, before the restaurant of the Pré Catelan.

Everywhere was light, silence and, best boon of all, an unexpected solitude—a solitude that invested the white building with a glamour of unreality and converted the slight-stemmed, moss-grown trees into spellbound sentinels.

"Here is the Castle!" said Blake. "Look! Even the waiters doze, until we come to wake them!" He handed her to the ground, gave his orders to the chauffeur, and as the cab disappeared into some unseen region, they mounted the wide steps.

"Monsieur desires *déjeuner*?" A sleek waiter disengaged himself from his brethren and came persuasively forward. At this early hour everything at the Pré Catelan was soft and soothing; later in the day things would alter, the service would be swift and unrestful, the swish of motor-cars and the hum of voices would break the spell, but at this hour of noon Paris, for some obscure reason, ignored the fruitful oasis of the Bois, and peace lay upon it like balm.

"How charming! Oh, but how charming!" The exclamation was won from Maxine as her glance skimmed the palms, the glittering glasses and the white table-linen, and rested upon the spacious windows that convey the fascinating impression that one whole wall of the room has been removed, and that the ranged trees outside with their satiny green stems actually commune with the *gourmet* as he eats his meal.

"It's what you wanted, isn't it?" Blake's pleasure in her pleasure was patent. Every look, every gesture manifested it.

"It is wonderful!" she said, gently.

"Good! And now, what is the meal to be? Dragon's wings *en casserole*? Or Moonbeams *surprise*?"

She laughed, and a flash of mischief stole through the glance she gave him.

"What do you say, *mon ami*, to *poulet bonne femme*?"

She watched for a gleam of remembrance, but he was too engrossed in the present to recall the trivialities of the past. He gave the order without a thought save to do her will.

Delay was inevitable, and while the meal was in preparation they wandered into the open and visited the farm at the rear of the restaurant, conjuring the farm-like traditions of the place after the accepted custom—entering the sweet-smelling, shadowy cow-shed, stroking the sleek, soft-breathing cows, amusing themselves over the antics of the monkey chained beside the door.

It was all very pleasant, the illusion of Arcadia was charmingly rendered, and they returned, happy and hungry, in search of their meal. That meal from its first morsel was raised above common things, for was it not the first time Blake had broken bread with Maxine? And what true lover ever forgets the rare moment when all the joys of intimacy are foreshadowed in the first serving of his lady with no matter what triviality of meat or bread, or water or wine? The points of the affair are so slight and yet so tremendous; for are they not sacramental—a typifying of things unspeakable?

No intimate word was spoken, but at such times looks speak—more poignantly still, hearts speak; and their gay voices, as they laughed and talked and laughed again, held notes that the ear of the waiter never caught, and their silences vibrated with meaning.

At last the meal was over; they rose and by one consent looked toward the spacious world outside.

"Shall we go into the gardens?"

Blake put the question; Maxine silently bent her head.

Softly and assiduously their sleek waiter bowed them to the door, and they passed down the shallow steps into the slim shadows of the trees as they might have passed into some paradise fashioned for their special pleasure.

It was a place—an hour—removed from the mundane world; passing out of the region of the trees, they came upon a shrubbery—a shrubbery that enclosed a lawn and flower-beds, and here, by grace of the gods, was a seat where they sat down side by side and gave their eyes to the beauty that encompassed them.

It was an exotic beauty, yet a beauty of intense suggestion. Summer lay lavishly displayed in the shaven lawn, the burdened shrubs, the glory of flowers, but over her redundant loveliness autumn had spun an ethereal garment. No words could paint the subtlety of this sheath; it was neither mist nor shadow, it was a golden transparency spun from nature's loom— the bridal veil of the young season.

"How exquisite!" whispered Maxine, as if a breath might break the spell. "Look at those yellow butterflies above the flowers! They are the only moving things."

"It is the place of the Sleeping Beauty, sweet! It is the place of love." Blake took her hands again and kissed them; then, with a gentle, enveloping tenderness, he drew her to him, looking into her face, but not attempting to touch it.

"My sweet, I have come back. What are you going to do with me?"

She did not answer; she lay quite still within his arms, her half-closed eyes lingering on the garden—on the white roses, the clustering mignonette, the hovering yellow butterflies.

"What are you going to do with me?"

She lifted her eyes, dewy with the beauty of the world.

"Wait!" she whispered. "Oh, wait!"

"I have waited."

"Ah, but a little longer!"

"But my love, my dear one—"

She stirred in his embrace; she turned with a swift passion of entreaty, putting her fingers across his mouth.

"Ned! Ned! I know. But do this great thing for me! Shut your eyes and your ears. Forget yesterday, think there will be no to-morrow. Hold this one moment! Give me my one hour!"

She pleaded as if for life, her body vibrating, her eyes beseeching him; and his answer was to press her hand harder against his lips, and to kiss it fervently. He gave no sign of the struggle within him—the doubt that encompassed him. Something had been demanded of him, and he gave it loyally.

"There was no yesterday, there will be no to-morrow!" he said. "But to-day is ours!"

It was the perfect word, spoken perfectly; Maxine's eyes drooped in supreme content, her lips curled like a pleased child's.

"Ah, but God is good!" she said, and with a child's supreme sweetness, she lifted her face for his kiss.

CHAPTER XL

THE hour was sped, the day past; night, with its dark wings, covered the eastern sky and, one by one, the stars came forth—stars that gleamed like new silver in the light sharpness of the September air.

Having closed eyes to the world at the Pré Catelan, Maxine and Blake had lengthened the coil of their dream as the day waxed. Three o'clock had seen them driving into the heart of the Bois, and late afternoon had found them wandering under the formal, interlaced trees in the gardens of the Petit Trianon. At Versailles they dined, falling a little silent over their meal, for neither could longer hold at bay the sense that events impended—that all paths, however devious, however touched by the enchanter's wand, lead back by an unalterable law to the world of realities.

With an unspoken anxiety they clung to the last moment of their meal; and when coffee had been partaken of, Maxine demanded yet another cup and, resting her elbows on the table, took her face between her hands.

"Ned! Will you not offer me a cigarette?"

He was all confusion at seeming remiss.

"My dear one! A thousand pardons! I did not think—"

"—That I smoked? Are you disappointed?"

He smiled. "It is one charm the more—if there is room for one."

He handed her a cigarette and lighted a match, his eyes resting upon her as she drew in the first breath of smoke with a quaint seriousness that smote him with a thought of the boy.

"Dearest," he said, suddenly, "I have been so happy to-day that I have thought of no one but ourselves, and now, all at once—"

Her eyes flashed up to his; she divined his thought, and it was as though she put forth all her strength to ward off a physical danger.

"Oh, *mon cher*, and was it not your day—our day? Would you have marred it with other thoughts?"

"No; but yet—"

"No! No!" She put out her hand, she pleaded with eyes and lips and voice. "Look! Until this little cigarette is burned out!" She held up the glowing tip. "When that is over, our day is over; then we return to the world—but not until then. Is it—what do you say—a bargain?" Her white teeth flashed, her glance flashed with the brightness of tears, her fingers rested for a second upon his.

The restaurant was practically empty; a few summer tourists were dining at tables close to the door, but Blake had chosen the farthest, dimmest corner and there they sat in semi-isolation, living the last moments of their day with an intensity that neither dared to express and that each was conscious of with every beat of the heart.

Maxine laughed as she drew her second puff of smoke, but her laugh had a nervous thinness. Blake filled their liqueur-glasses, but his gesture was uneven and a little of the brandy spilled upon the cloth.

"A libation to the gods!" he said. "May they smile upon us!" He lifted his glass and emptied it.

Maxine forced a smile. "The gods know best!" she said, but as she raised her glass, her hand, also, trembled.

But Blake ignored her perturbation, as she ignored his. The coming ordeal lay stark across their path, but neither would look upon it, neither would see beyond the tip of Maxine's cigarette—the tiny beacon, consuming even as it gave light!

A silence fell—a silence of full five minutes—then Blake, yielding once more to the craving for the solace of contact, put his hand over hers.

"Dear one, I know nothing of what is coming, but that I am utterly in your hands. But let me say one thing. To-day has been heaven—the golden, the seventh heaven!"

She said nothing, she did not meet his eyes, but her cold fingers clasped his convulsively, and two tears fell hot upon their hands.

That was all; that was the sum of their expression. No other word was spoken. They sat silent, watching the cigarette burn itself out between Maxine's fingers.

She held it to the very last, then dropped it into her finger-bowl and rose.

"Now, *mon cher*!" In the dim light she looked very tall and slight and seemed possessed of a curious dignity. All the animation had left her face, beneath the eyes were shadows, and in the eyes a tragic sadness—the sadness that the soul creates for itself.

Blake rose also and, side by side, very quietly, they left the restaurant. In the street outside, the cab that had assisted in the day's adventures still waited their pleasure.

He handed her to her place and paused, his foot upon the step.

"And now, liege lady—where?"

She looked at him gravely and answered without a tremor, "To Max's studio."

Surprise—if surprise touched him—showed not at all upon his face. He gave the order quietly and explicitly, and took his place beside her.

Down the broad street of Versailles they wheeled, but both were too preoccupied to see the lurking ghosts of a past *régime* that lie so palpably in the shadows, and presently Blake's hand found hers once more.

"You are cold?"

She shook her head.

Through the cool night they drove, under the jewelled cloak of the sky, rushing forward toward Paris as Max had once rushed in the mysterious north express.

Blake did not speak or move again until the city was close about them; then, with a gesture that startled her by its unexpectedness, he drew from his hand the signet ring he always wore—a ring familiar to Max as the stones of the rue Müller—and slipped it over her third finger.

"Oh, Ned!" She started as the ring slipped into place, and her voice trembled with fear and superstition.

He pressed her hand. "Don't refuse it! The ring is the emblem of the eternal, and all my thoughts for you belong to eternity."

No more was said; they skimmed through the familiar ways until Maxine could have cried aloud for grace, and at last they stopped at the corner of the rue André de Sarte.

She stood aside as Blake dismissed the cab, she knew that had speech been demanded of her then she could not have brought forth a word, so parched were her lips, so impotent her tongue.

Her ordeal confronted her; no human power could eliminate it now. To her was the disentangling of knotted threads, the sorting of the colors in the scheme of things. She averted her face from Blake as they mounted the Escalier de Sainte-Marie, and her hand clung for support to the iron railing.

Familiar to the point of agony was the open doorway, the dark hall of the house in the rue Müller. Side by side they entered; side by side, and in complete silence, they made the ascent of the stairs, each step of which was heavy with memories.

On the fifth floor she went forward and opened the door of Max's *appartement*. Within, all was dark and quiet, and Blake, loyally following her, passed without comment through the tiny hall, on into the little *salon* where the light from the brilliant sky made visible the pathetically familiar objects—the old copper vessels, the dower chest, the leathern arm-chair.

This leather chair stood like a faithful sentinel close to the open window, and as his eyes rested on it he was conscious of a pained contraction of the heart, for it stood exactly where it had stood when last he watched the stars and rambled through his dreams and ideals, with the boy for listener. The thought came quick and sharp, goading him as many a puzzled thought had goaded him in his months of solitude, and as at Versailles, he turned to Maxine, a question on his lips.

But again she checked that question. Stepping through the shadows, she drew him across the room toward the window. Reaching the old chair, she touched his shoulder, gently compelling him to sit down.

"Ned," she said, and to her own ears the word sounded infinitely far away. "I seem to you very mad. But you have a great patience. Will you be patient a little longer?"

She had withdrawn behind the chair, laying both her hands upon his shoulders, and as she spoke her voice shook in an unconquerable nervousness, her whole body shook.

"My sweet!" He turned quickly and looked up at her. "What is all this? Why are you torturing yourself? For God's sake, let us be frank with each other—"

But she pressed his shoulders convulsively. "Wait! wait! It is only a little moment now. I implore you to wait!"

He sank back, and as in a dream felt her fingers release their hold and heard her move gently back across the room; then, overwhelmed by the burden of dread that oppressed him, he leaned forward, bowing his face upon his hands.

Minutes passed—how few, how many, he made no attempt to reckon—then again the hushed steps sounded behind him, the sense of a gracious presence made itself felt.

Instinctively he attempted to rise, but, as before, Maxine's hands were laid upon his shoulders, pressing him back into his seat. He saw her hands in the starlight—saw the glint of his own ring.

"Ned!"

"Dear one?"

"It is dim, here in this room, but you know me? Your soul sees me?" Her voice was shaking, her words sobbed like notes upon an instrument strung to breaking pitch.

"My dear one! My dear one!" His voice, too, was sharp and pained; he strove to turn in his chair, but she restrained him.

"No! No! Say it without looking. You know me? I am Maxine?"

"Of course you are Maxine!"

"Ah!"

It was a short, swift sound like the sobbing breath of a spent runner. It spoke a thousand things, and with its vibrations trembling upon her lips, Maxine came round the chair and Blake, looking up, saw Max—Max of old, Max of the careless clothes, the clipped waving locks.

It is in moments grotesque or supreme that men show themselves. He sprang to his feet; he stared at the apparition until his eyes grew wide, but all he said was 'God!' very softly to himself. 'God!' And then again, 'God!'

It was Maxine who opened the flood-gates of emotion; Maxine who, with wild gesture and broken voice, dressed the situation in words.

"Now it is over! Now it is finished—the whole foolish play! Now you have your sight—and your liberty to hate me! Hate me! Hate me! I am waiting."

"God!" whispered Blake again, not hearing her, piecing his thoughts together as a waking man tries to piece a dream. 'God!'

The reiteration tortured her. She suddenly caught his arm, forcing him into contact with her. "Do not speak to yourself!" she cried. "Speak to me! Say all you think! Hate me! Hate me!"

Then at last he broke through the confusion of his mind, startling her as such men will always startle women by their innate singleness of thought.

"Hate you?" he said. "Why, in God's name, should I hate you?"

"Because it is right and just."

"That I should hate you, because I have been a fool? I do not see that."

"But, Ned!" she cried; then, suddenly, at its sharpest, her voice broke; she threw herself upon her knees beside the chair and sobbed.

And then it was that Blake showed himself. Kneeling down beside her, he put both arms about the boyish figure and, holding it close, poured forth—not questions, not reproaches, not protestations—but a stream of compassion.

"Poor child! Poor child! Poor child! What a fool I've been! What a brute I've been!"

But Maxine sobbed passionately, shrinking away from him, as though his touch were pain.

"My child! My child! How foolish I have been! But how foolish you have been, too—how sweetly foolish! You gave with one hand and took away with the other. But now it is all over. Now you are going to give with both hands—- I am to have my friend and my love as well. It is very wonderful. Oh, sweet, don't fret! Don't fret! See how simple it all is!"

But Maxine's bitter crying went on, until at last it frightened him.

"Maxine, don't! Don't, for God's sake! Why should you cry like this? What is it, when all's said and done, but a point of view? And a point of view is adjusted much more quickly than you think. At first I thought the earth was reeling round me, but now I know that 'twas only my own brain that reeled; and I know, too, that subconsciously I must always have recognized you in Max—for I never treated Max as a common boy, did I? Did I, now? I always had a queer—a queer respect for him. Dear one, see it with me! Try to see it with me?"

His appeal was pathetic; it was he who was the culprit—he who extenuated and pleaded. The position struck Maxine, wounding her like a knife.

"Oh, don't!" she cried in her own turn. "Don't, for the sake of God!"

"But why? Why? My sweet! My love! My little friend! Max—Maxine!"

It was not to be borne. She wrenched herself free and sprang to her feet, confronting him with a pale face down which the tears streamed.

"Because I am not your love! I am not your friend! I am not your Max—or your Maxine!"

Swift as she, he was on his feet, his bearing changed, his manhood recognizing the challenge in her voice, his instinct of possession alive to combat it.

"Not mine?" he said; and to Maxine, standing white and frail before him, the words seemed to have all the significance of life itself. Now at last they confronted each other—man and woman; now at last the issue in the war of sex was to be put to the test.

She had always known that this moment would arrive—always known that she would meet it in some such manner as she was meeting it now.

"Not mine?" Blake said again.

She shook her head, throwing back her shoulders, clasping her hands behind her, unconsciously taking on the attitude of defiance.

"And why not?"

It was curt, this question, as man's vital questions ever are; it was an onslaught that clove to the heart of things.

She trembled for an instant, then met his eyes.

"Because I will belong to no one. I must possess myself."

He stared at her.

"But it is not given to any one to possess himself! How can you separate an atom from the universal mass?"

"An atom may detach itself—"

"And fall into space! Is that self-possession? But, my God, are we going to split hairs? Maxine! Maxine!" He came close to her and put out his arms, but with a fierce gesture she evaded him; then, as swiftly, caught his hand.

"Oh, Ned! Oh, Ned! Can't you see?"

"No!" said Blake, simply. "I cannot."

"Listen! Then listen! I know myself for an individual—for a definite entity; I know that here—here, within me"—she struck her breast—"I have power—power to think—power to achieve. And how do you think that power is to be developed?" She paused, looking at him with burning eyes. "Not by the giving of my soul into bondage—not by the submerging of myself in another being. That night in Petersburg I saw my way—the hard way, the lonely way! Oh, Ned!" She stopped again, searching his face, but his face was pale and immobile—curiously, unnaturally immobile.

With a passionate gesture, she flung his hand from her. "Oh, it is so cruel! Can't you see? Can't you understand? I left Russia to make a new life; I made myself a man, not for a whim, but as a symbol. Sex is only an accident, but the world has made man the independent creature—and

I desired independence. Sex is only an accident. Mentally, I am as good a man as you are."

"Ten times a better man," said Blake, startingly. "But not near so good a woman. For I know the highest thing—and you do not."

"The highest thing?"

"Love."

"Ah!" She threw up her hands in despair and walked to the window, looking up blankly at the stars. Then, suddenly, she spoke again, tossing her words back into the room.

"I suppose you think I am happy in all this?"

He was silent.

"I suppose you think I find this heaven?"

At last he answered. He came across to her; he stood looking at her with his strange new expression of inscrutability.

"Oh, Maxine!" he said, "why must you misjudge me? Little Maxine, who could be taken in my arms this minute and carried away to my castle, like a princess of long ago—but who would break her heart over the bondage! I haven't much, dear one, to justify my existence—but the gods have given me intuition. I do not think you are in heaven."

He waited a moment, while in the sky above them the stars looked down impartially upon the white domes of the church and the beacons of pleasure in the city below.

"Maxine! Shall I say the things for you that you want to say?"

She bent her head.

"Well, first of all, God help us, the world is a terrible tangle; and then you have a strange soul that has never yet half revealed itself. You sent me away from you because you feared love; you called me back because you feared your fear—"

"No! No! You are reasoning now, not justifying! You are entrapping me!"

"Am I?"

"Yes, and I refuse to be entrapped! I know love—I know all the specious things that love can say; the talk of independence, the talk of equality! But I know the reality, too. The reality is the absolute annihilation of the woman—the absolute merging of her identity."

"So that is love?"

"That is love."

He stood looking at her with a long profound look of deep restraint, of great sadness.

"Maxine," he said, at last, "you have many gifts—a high intelligence, a young body, a strong soul, but in the matter of love you are a little child. To you, love is barter and exchange; but love is not that. Love is nothing but a giving—an exhaustless giving of one's very best."

She tried to laugh. "I understand! I should give!"

"No, sweet, you should not. You cannot know the privileges of love, for you do not know love."

"Oh, Ned! How cruel! How cruel!"

"You do not know love," he spoke, very gently, without any bitterness, "and I do know it; for it has grown in me, day by day, in these long months away from you. I am not to be praised, any more than you are to be blamed. But I do love you—with my heart and my soul—with my life and my strength. I would die for you, if dying would help you; and as it won't, I will do the harder thing—live for you."

Her lips were parted, but they uttered no sound; her eyes, dark with thought, searched his face.

"Oh, Maxine!" He caught her hand. "How low you have rated me—to think I would wrest you from yourself! Is it my place to make life harder for you?"

Still she gazed at him. "I do not understand," she said, in a frightened whisper.

"Never mind, sweet! It doesn't matter if you never understand. Just give me credit for one saving grace."

He spoke lightly, as men speak when they are bankrupt of hope, then with a sudden breaking of his stoicism, he caught her in his arms, straining her close, kissing her mouth, talking incoherently to himself.

"Oh, Maxine! Little faun of the green groves! If you could know! But what am I that I should possess the kingdom of heaven?"

His ecstasy frightened her; she struggled to free herself.

"What is it?" she asked. "What is it?"

"Just love—no more, no less! Good-bye! Take your life—make it what you will; but know always that one man at least has seen heaven in your eyes." Again he held her to him, his whole life seeming to flow out upon his thoughts and to envelop her, then his arms relaxed and very soberly he took, first one of her hands, and then the other, kissing each in turn.

"Maxine!"

"Ned!" The word faltered on her lips.

"That's right!" he whispered. "I only wanted you to say my name. Good-bye now! Don't fret for me! After all, everything is as it should be."

She stood before him, the conqueror. All preconceptions had been scattered; she had not even won her laurels, they had been placed at her feet; and all the pomp and circumstance she could summon to her triumphing was a white face, a drooping head, and speechless lips.

"Good-bye, Maxine!" The words cried for response, and by a supreme effort she summoned her voice from some far region.

"Good-bye!"

He did not kiss her hand again, but bending his head, he solemnly kissed his own ring, lying cold upon her finger.

CHAPTER XLI

ALL was finished. Mystery was at an end. The pilgrim's staff had been placed in Maxine's hand, her feet set toward the great white road. She leaned back against the window of the *salon* and her mental eyes scanned that road—the coveted road of freedom, the way of splendid isolation—and in a vague, dumb fashion she wondered why the whiteness that had gleamed like snow in the distance should take on the hue of dust seen at close quarters. She wondered why she should feel so absolutely numbed—why life, with its exuberances of joy and sorrow, should suddenly have receded from her as a tide recedes.

There had been no battle; hers was a bloodless victory. Fate had been exquisitely kind, as is Fate's way when she would be ironical. Maxine could call up no cause for grief or for resentment, no cause even for remorse. She had confessed herself; she had been shriven and blessed, and bade to go her way!

Passing in review these phantom speculations, her eyes suddenly refused the vision of the mythical white road, stretching away in brain-sickening length, and her physical sight caught at the familiar picture revealed by the balcony—the thrice-known, thrice-loved shrubbery, where already the glossy holly leaves were stirring under September's fingers, whispering one to the other of fine cold autumn hours when gales would sweep the heights, bringing death to their frailer brethren, while they themselves nestled snug and strong, laughing at the elements. She traced the familiar outline of these sturdy bushes, and her perfect triumph seemed like a winding sheet about her limbs. She was above the world, removed from care, and all she knew was that she would have given her heart for one moment of the hot human grief that had seared her not four months ago.

She turned from the trees, turned from the stars and moved back into the unlighted room. All was quiet and dim; she stumbled against the arm-chair and recoiled as though a friend had touched her inopportunely; then she passed blindly onward, finding the little hall, finding the outer door with groping hands.

Outside was a deeper darkness, for here no starlight penetrated; but M. Cartel's door was ajar, and through the opening came a streak of lamplight and the hum of voices.

Pausing, Maxine caught the deep, humorous tones of M. Cartel himself, broken first by an unknown voice, quick, tense, typically Parisian, then by the light laugh of Jacqueline.

In her cruel perfection of triumph, she had no need to fear these voices—these little evidences of sociability. They could not hurt her, for was she not impervious to pain?

Another laugh, full and contented, came to her ear, then the opening of the piano and the masterful striking of a chord.

A murmur of pleasure gave evidence of an audience, and instinctively she moved forward, as a wanderer on a dark night draws near to a lighted dwelling. Gaining the door, she softly pushed it open, as M. Cartel executed a *roulade*, which melted into a brilliant piece of improvization.

A bright lamp shone in the hall; but beyond, the open door of the living-room displayed a half-lighted interior, with a handful of people grouped about it. Foremost figure was M. Cartel seated at his music within a radius of yellow light shed by four candles, while, beside him, a tall thin boy, and, behind him, Jacqueline seemed enclosed in a secondary, fainter circle of luminance. The rest of the room was in shadow, and as Maxine entered, she scarcely noticed the three other occupants—two men and a woman—who sat in a row close to the door, their backs to the wall.

No one commented upon her entry. The little Jacqueline glanced round once, smiling a quick welcome, but returned immediately to her contemplation of M. Cartel; the younger of the two men by the door—an Italian—paused in the lighting of a cigarette, but his companion—an old Polish Jew with a classic head and long, gray beard—retained his attitude of rapt attention, while the woman, who sat a little apart, and whose large black hat hid her face, made no sign.

Treading softly, Maxine entered and crept into a seat opposite the trio, realizing, with an indifference that surprised her, that the woman was Lize of the Bal Tabarin and the Café des Cerises-jumelles.

The music poured forth, a glittering stream of sound. The young Italian lighted cigarette after cigarette, smoking furiously and beating soundless time upon the floor with his foot, the old Pole sat lost in an emotional dream, tears gathering slowly in his eyes and trickling unheeded down his cheeks, while Lize, in her moveless isolation, gazed with fixed intensity at the wall above Maxine's head.

Time passed; time seemed of small account in that atmosphere—as the outside world was of small account. Not one of the little audience questioned how the other lived. It mattered nothing that in other hours the artistic fingers of the young Italian were employed in the manufacture of fraudulent antiques—that the enthusiast by the piano wrote humorous songs at a starvation wage for an unsuccessful *comique*—that Lize, finding humanity foolish, made profit of its folly! 'What would you?' they would have asked with a shrug. 'One must live!' For the rest, there were moments such as this—moments when the artist was paramount in each of them—when pure enthusiasm made them children again!

M. Cartel played on. He had forsaken improvization now, and was interpreting magnificently; occasionally the boy by the piano threw up his hands ecstatically, muttering incoherently to himself; occasionally the young Italian broke silence by a sharp, irresistible '*Brava*'; but for the most part respectful silence spoke the intensity of the spell.

Then at last Maxine, sitting in her corner, saw Jacqueline bend over the shoulder of M. Cartel, her hair shining like sun-rays in the candlelight—saw her whisper in his ear—saw him look up and nod in abrupt acquiescence, and saw his square-tipped fingers lift for an instant from the keys and descend again to a series of new chords.

A little murmur of interest passed over the listeners. The Italian threw away his half-smoked cigarette and lighted another, the Pole smiled tolerantly with half-closed eyes, as the old smile at the vagaries of the young, and Maxine in her shadowed seat felt her heart leap tumultuously as the little Jacqueline, her arm naïvely round the shoulder of M. Cartel, her head thrown back, began to sing the first lines of the duet in *Louise*:

'Depuis le jour où je me suis donnée, toute fleurie semble ma destinée.
Je crois rêver sous un ciel de féerie, l'âme encore grisée de ton premier baiser!'

And M. Cartel, lifting his head, broke in with the single electric cry of Julian the lover:

'Louise!'

Then, as if answering to the personal note, Jacqueline melted into Louise's sweet admission of absolute surrender:

'Quelle belle vie!
Ah, je suis heureuse! trop heureuse ... et je tremble délicieusement,
Au souvenir charmant du premier jour d'amour!'

The effect was instant. The youth by the piano smiled radiantly and nodded in vehement approval; the young Italian puffed fiercely at his cigarette; a flash of light crossed Lize's gaze, causing it to concentrate.

Jacqueline had no extraordinary voice, but music was native to her, and she sang as birds sing, with a true light sweetness exquisite to the ear:

'Souvenir charmant du premier jour d'amour!'

The declaration came to the listeners with a pure sincerity, it abounded in simplicity, in youthfulness, in conviction. A quiver ran through Maxine, her numbed senses vibrated. By an acute intuition she realized the composer's meaning; more, she appreciated the thrill called up in the soul of M. Cartel. Her ears were strained to catch each note, each phrase, with an intentness that astonished her; it suddenly appeared that out of all the world, one thing alone was of significance—the close following of this song, the apprehending of its purpose.

'Souvenir charmant du premier jour d'amour!'

The first night with Blake upon the balcony sprang back to memory, and with it the wonder, the delight, the illimitable sense of kinship with the universe. Again the spiritual sense lived in her, not warring with the physical, but justifying, completing it. She sat upright against the wall, suddenly fearful of this overwhelming mental disturbance—fighting the cloud of memory almost as one fights a bodily faintness.

The music grew in meaning; she heard Julian's ardent question:

'Tu ne regrette rien?'

and Louise's triumphant answer:

'Rien!'

The words, simply human, divinely just, assailed her ears, and by light of the intuition—the superconsciousness that was dominating her—the whole truth of this confessed love poured in upon her soul. She saw the halo about the head of the little singer, she appreciated the sublime giving of herself that cried in the music of the song. It was no mere sentiment on the lips of this fair child, it was the proclamation of a tremendous fact.

She leaned back against the wall, lips set, hands clasped. She clung to the rock of her theories like a drowning man, and like the drowning man she realized the imminence of the inundation that threatened her.

The music swelled, and now it was not Jacqueline alone who sang; M. Cartel's voice rose, completing, perfecting the higher feminine notes, blending with them as the music of wind or running water might harmonize with the singing of a bird. It was not art but nature that was at work in the words:

'Nous sommes tous les amants, fidèles a leur serment! Ah, le divin roman!

Nous sommes toutes les âmes que brûle le sainte flamme du désire!
Ah, la parole idéale dont s'enivre mon corps tout entier!
Dis encore ta chanson de délice! Ta chanson victorieuse, ta chanson de printemps!'

The duet wore on, enthralling in its closeness to common human life, with its touches of tears, its touches of laughter, its hints of tenderness and bursts of passion. Not one face but had softened in comprehension as Louise painted the picture of her home—of the gentle father, the scolding mother, the little daily frictions that wear patience thin; not one heart but had leaped when passion broke a way through the song, mounting, mounting as upon wings, until Louise in her ecstasy of love and joy and incredulity exclaims:

'C'est le paradis! C'est une féerie!'

And Julian answers:

'Non! C'est la vie! l'Eternelle, la toute puissante vie!'

It was the supreme, the psychological moment! The duet continued, but Maxine heard no further words. They echoed and re-echoed in her brain, they obsessed her, lifting her to a sublimal state.

Across the room she saw the Italian throw away his cigarette and forget to replace it; she saw Lize lean forward breathlessly, and she knew that in fancy she was back in the Quartier Latin when life was young—when love laughed, and her hair was wreathed with vine leaves. She saw her at last as a living woman—felt the grape-juice run down her neck—felt the kisses of the Jacque Aujet who was ten years dead!

This, then, was the sum of life! Not the holding of fair things, but the giving of them!

She rose up; her limbs shook, but she paid no heed to physical strength or weakness; she was on a plane where the soul moved free, regardless of mortal needs. Neither Max nor Maxine had any place in her conceptions. She saw Lize, broken but justified, because she had given when life asked of her; she saw the little Jacqueline, with the halo of candle-light turning her blonde hair to gold; in a distant dream she saw the frail, steadfast Madame Salas, and in a near, poignant vision she saw Blake, and her soul melted within her.

She conceived the world as one immense censer into which men and women poured their all, and from which a wondrous white smoke, a scent incredibly lovely, rose continually, enveloping the universe.

To give! To give without hope of recompense, without question, without fear! That was the message of life.

She looked round the little room; she yearned to put out her arms, to clasp each hand, to touch each forehead with the kiss of living fellowship. Love consumed her, humility rilled her, she was a child again, with all things to learn.

The music was reaching its climax, it was filling every corner of the room, and as she glanced toward the piano in a last long look, the two voices rose in unison.

Silently—none knowing the revolution within her soul—none seeing the heights upon which she walked—Maxine moved to the door and slipped out into the hall, the picture of the lovers before her eyes, in her ears the symbolic cry:

'C'est la vie! l'Eternelle, la toute puissante vie!'

Like a being inspired, she passed back into her own *appartement*, and there, with a strange high excitement that was yet mystically calm, entered her little bedroom and lighted candles until not a shadow was left in all the white circumscribed space; then, standing in the illumination, like an acolyte who ministers to some secret rite, she slowly unburdened herself of her boy's garments.

The task was brief; they fell from her lightly, leaving her fair and virginal and untrammelled in body, as she was virginal and untrammelled in mind; and with a sweet gravity she clothed herself, garment by garment, in the dress of the morning.

Ardent and eager—yet restrained, as befitted a woman aware of her high place—she left the room and passed down the Escalier de Sainte-Marie. A rush of cool air came to her across the plantation, kissing her hot cheeks, the holly bushes whispered their secrets—which were her secrets as well, the eyes of the stars looked down, smiling into her eyes. She observed no face in the thronging faces that passed her; she made her steadfast way to the one point in the universe that was her goal by right divine. Even in the hallway of Blake's house she did not stop to question, but mounted the stairs and knocked upon his door, regardless of the stormy beating of her heart, the faintness of anticipation that encompassed her.

A moment passed—a moment or a century; then he was before her, appealing to the innermost recesses of her being.

He stared at her, as one might stare upon a ghost.

"Maxine!"

Her lips parted, trembling with a pleading tenderness.

"Maxine!" he said again; and now his voice shook, as hers had shaken in Max's little starlit studio.

It was the cry she had waited for—the confirmation of her faith. Her hands went out to him; her soul suddenly poured forth allegiance in look and voice.

"Ned! Ned! Take me! Take me and teach me! Take me away to your castle, like the princess of old. Show me the white sky and the opal sea, and the seaweed that smells like violets!"

His hands clasped hers, his incredulous eyes besought her. "Maxine, this is some dream?"

"No; it is no dream. We are awake. It is life!"